***"Have you ever read one of Stephen Larsen's books?"***

"Yeah," Darci said. "I'm reading one right now. He takes on some tough subjects. This one deals with the mob. Think about it! The subjects he's covered—I bet he has more enemies than you do, Ophelia."

"Thanks a lot."

"He's been writing a long time. He's had more opportunity to tick people off. You just started a couple of years ago," she said brightly.

Rolling my eyes, I finally connected her dots. "And one of those enemies followed him to Iowa and shot him?"

She nodded her head emphatically. "Right."

"So now I have a hit man after me?"

"Yeah."

"That's comforting," I muttered. "Why would the hit man be after me?"

"Hmm, well." Her pretty face puckered in a frown. "I haven't figured that out yet."

# the witch's grave

## AN OPHELIA AND ABBY MYSTERY

# SHIRLEY
# DAMSGAARD

**A V O N**

*An Imprint of HarperCollinsPublishers*

AVON BOOKS
*An Imprint of* HarperCollins*Publishers*
10 East 53rd Street
New York, New York 10022-5299

First Avon Books paperback printing: January 2009

Avon Trademark Reg. U.S. Pat. Off. and in Other Countries, Marca Registrada, Hecho en U.S.A.
HarperCollins® is a registered trademark of HarperCollins Publishers.

Printed in the U.S.A.

10  9  8  7  6  5  4  3  2  1

*For the Innocents*

# Acknowledgments

Serendipity is the effect by which one accidentally discovers something fortunate, especially while looking for something else entirely.

With every book, I've been fortunate to experiene a certain amount of serendipity, but this one has had more than its share! And I would be remiss not to thank those who took the time to ferret out information for me, answered my endless questions, and basically held my hand through the whole process!

Sarah Durand—it's been a real pleasure working with you on this series, and you've had a tremendous impact on who Ophelia and Abby have become. You truly have the patience of Job when it comes to working with your authors! Best of luck always!

Stacey Glick—you're the greatest! Your support has meant so much to me, and I thank my lucky stars that I have you in my corner!

Joanna Campbell Slan—your friendship means the world to me, J.! Your words of wisdom and no nonsense advice always pull me through. Thanks for helping me keep things in perspective, and, yes, I'll remember to "quit worrying about it and just write the dang story!"

The Grasset family—Luc-Olivier, Barbara, and Fiona.

Many, many thanks for being my "eyes" on Paris! Barbara, I still can't believe you went to the town archives and researched garbage collection circa 1941 for me! And Fiona and Luc-Olivier, the information you provided for me on the Catacombs, points of interest, and places where the characters might have lived in Paris were invaluable.

Armando Villareal, Administrator for the Division of Latino Affairs—thanks, Armando, for taking the time out of your busy schedule to give e a perspective on what it's like for undocumented workers in this country.

Ron and Linda Mark—thanks for letting me use your name, Ron! And thanks to both of you for all the background into the Iowa wine industry! I'll look forward to opening a bottle of your wine when this book is released!

My friends—Cheryl, Cindy, June, and Theresa. I know murder and mayhem isn't always your favorite topic of discussion, but thanks for listening to me anyway!

And as always, my family—Eric, Christine, Scott, and Sara. It isn't easy having a writer for a mom, but thanks for respecting my work and understanding how important it is to me.

Oh, and one last thing—any mistakes in this book are strictly mine!

All the best,
Shirley

# *Prologue*

*Do you ache?*
*Do you burn*
*With the half remembered dream*
*Of a lifetime long ago*
*Where your soul touched mine?*
*Do you wait?*
*Do you long*
*To find the forgotten feelings*
*Of a moment gone in time*
*Where your soul touched mine?*
*Do you mourn?*
*Do you cry*
*Over the once lost love*
*Of a past life ended*
*Where your soul touched mine?*
*Do you pray?*
*Do you hope*
*For the grace and redemption*
*Of a promised tomorrow*
*Where your soul touches mine?*

# One

"Isn't this great?" I exclaimed as my eyes swept down the path winding between the tidy rows. Woody vines grew straight out of the Iowa soil as their branches reached out like open arms to embrace the hot, August sunshine. Dark green leaves draped those branches, and peaking out from beneath them, clusters of deep, red grapes hung heavy in the sun. The scene looked like something out of a Grant Wood painting.

Darci lowered her sunglasses, and her blue eyes rimmed with black mascara studied me with skepticism. "Who are you and what have you done with the grumpy Ophelia Jensen we all know and love?"

"Ha ha," I shot back, giving her a playful shove. A bubble of excitement tickled through me. "I'm just having a good time, that's all. This is a great party," I said with a sweep of my arm.

"Exactly my point—you don't *like* parties. You hate socializing—"

"Since I'm the librarian in Summerset and this *is* a fund-raiser for the library," I interjected, "I couldn't very well not attend."

"True—Claire did a terrific job organizing the event—but you always try and wiggle out of stuff like this."

I shrugged one shoulder. "Maybe I'm trying to change."

Darci crossed her arms. She didn't look convinced.

Ignoring her, I turned away from the railing and watched the crowd assembled on the deck of the winery.

Men and women gathered in small groups and large groups, some sitting in lawn chairs and some standing. Their laughter rode on the breeze and mingled with the sound of the live band that played in the arbor located on the lawn below. Everyone held long-stemmed wine-glasses, while plastic buckets with dark bottles of wine nestled in clear cubes of ice were within easy reach. A couple of men were casting surreptitious glances our way—Darci's way.

I understood the attention. With her big, blond hair and her curvy figure, in black cigarette pants and a hot pink halter top, she was gorgeous. Add a blinding smile that could charm almost anyone, and you had a pretty potent package. But there was more to the package than just Darci's appearance—intelligence hid behind those big, blue eyes. And any guy not smart enough to recognize it usually lived to regret it.

*Me? Did men notice me?* Dressed in my navy sun dress, I looked okay, but not outstanding. Just your everyday small-town librarian. In my thirties, five-four, brown eyes, brown shoulder-length hair, with no noticeable scars or impediments. Someone passing me in the street wouldn't give me a second glance. I smiled to myself. I looked normal—and normal's good. It's something I've wanted to be all my life. Unfortunately, I didn't fall into anyone's definition of "normal." Not with the witch-psychic thing that ran strong in the women of my family.

My eyes traveled to my grandmother, Abby, someone else who always drew attention, deep in conversation with her elderly boyfriend, Arthur. Her voice still carried the soft cadence of the mountain in Appalachia where she'd been raised. I didn't know if it was her voice or the air of gentleness that always seemed to surround her, but people were drawn to her like moths.

Today, her silver hair was coiled in an elegant knot on the top of her head, and her flowing skirt, stirred by the soft breeze, floated around her ankles. A very classy woman, my grandmother, and I felt a stirring of pride as I observed her. She didn't consider herself, or me, peculiar at all. She might not broadcast her talents, but still reveled in her ability to see things and cast spells.

Not far from Abby, Claire Canyon, our library board president, talked with a blond man I didn't recognize.

I poked Darci. "Hey, who's the guy talking to Claire?"

"I don't know . . . some politician. The place is crawling with them, all stumping for votes in the upcoming election." She smirked. "But whoever he is, Claire isn't happy with him."

With her glasses lowered, Claire was peering at him over the rims. It was "the look." The look that made a person feel like they were something to be scraped off the bottom of a shoe. She raised her other hand and pointed a finger at his chest as she made her point.

*Glad it was him and not me.* I avoided such confrontations with Claire at all costs. *Wonder what he'd done to irritate her?*

Darci interrupted my thoughts with a nudge. "Let's get back to the 'new' Ophelia." She leaned against the railing, her back to the vineyard, and studied me closely. "What's brought on this big change?"

Tracing the beads of moisture trickling down my glass, I tried to think of a way to explain.

A feeling best described as part anticipation, part anxiety, seemed to chase after me wherever I went these days. A sense that something waited right around the next corner. Okay, so I'm a witch and a psychic, and that might have *something* to do with what I was experiencing. But the dreams . . .

My skin grew suddenly warm. Fanning myself with my hand, I let a long breath escape from my lips.

Darci pushed away from the railing in concern. "What is it? You're flushed," she said, laying her palm on my arm.

Touching my cheek, I gave a nervous laugh. "Seems to be happening to me a lot lately."

She grabbed the bottle of wine we were sharing from our bucket and filled my glass with the pale pink liquid.

I took a drink and let the sweet cool wine trickle slowly down my throat. When I lowered my glass, I felt her eyes still on me.

"Okay, spill it—what's going on?" she demanded. "Are you worried about Tink?"

"No, not really." I gave my head a little shake. "It was hard to watch her walk out the door today—the kidnapping wasn't that long ago, but I know she's safe with Nell and her mom."

Her lips tightened when I mentioned the kidnapping of my soon-to-be adopted daughter. "I hope those two crazies, Winnie and Gert," she said grimly, referring to Tink's kidnappers, "are locked up for years and years."

"Oh, they will be." I took another sip of wine. "The district attorney has refused their plea bargain, so they're looking at a long stretch in prison. Tink will be grown, with children of her own, by the time those two get out."

"Good, serves them right," she replied emphatically. "So if it's not Tink that's bothering you, what is it?"

"I can't shake the feeling something's about to happen—"

"Oooh," she said, cutting me off. Her face glowed with excitement. "Mur—"

"Stop right there," I said, holding up my hand. "It's not that kind of feeling." I made quotations marks in the air with my fingers.

"Shoot," she said in a voice tinged with disappointment. "No psychic premonition?"

"Shh, your voice will carry," I hissed as I glanced over her shoulder at the nearest group of revelers. Taking her arm, I guided her down the deck's steps to the shade of a big maple tree.

Stopping under the tree, Darci watched me expectantly as I tugged at my bottom lip and tried to frame my words.

"It's weird . . . I've been having strange dreams almost every night. Then I wake up with this feeling . . . like there's something I'm supposed to do, but I can't remember what it is."

She tapped her chin with a long red fingernail. "Have you mentioned this to Abby?"

I gave a snort. "Are you kidding?" I pictured my seventy-plus grandmother's bags of potions, herbs, and magick spells. "You know how she'd react. She'd look at the moon signs, whip out her crystals, and want to do a little hocus-pocus." I shook my head. "No, I'm handling this one on my own."

"Why?" Darci asked, sounding perplexed.

"I, well, hmm," I stalled. "See these dreams are . . . ah . . . well—"

"Are what?" she asked with a flounce. "If they're not prophetic?"

I felt hot blood rush to my face again. "Ah, you see . . . " My voice faltered. "I don't think they're visions of future events. I play a starring role and I never have premonitions about myself. My talent doesn't work that way. The dreams are . . . well, *really* personal." I inhaled sharply. "And they're, um . . . erotic," I finished in a whisper.

She ripped her sunglasses off and scooted toward me. "And you don't want Abby to pick up on them?" she asked, her eyebrow arching.

"My God, no!" I said with passion. "Would you want *your* grandmother to know that you're dreaming about some hot guy in a field of wildflowers?"

She giggled. "No. Hot guy, huh? Who? Rick, Ned, Henry?" She rattled off a list of men who'd drifted in and out—mostly out—of my life over the past couple of years. Darci snapped her fingers. "I've got it, Ethan!"

Ah yes, Ethan, slash, Cobra, the elusive DEA agent who kept popping up when I least expected it.

"No, it's not Ethan—that's the strange part—it's someone I've never met, but it's like I've known him all my life."

"Maybe you're dreaming of your own true love."

I took a step back. "My own 'true love'?"

"Yeah." Her face took on a dreamy expression and her voice seemed to trill. "Your soul mate, the man you've been waiting for all your life. Two hearts calling to one another through—"

"Don't go flying off into some romantic rapture," I scoffed. "It's not like that."

She fisted her hand on her hip. "So what *is* it like?"

"I don't know." I shoved my hands into the deep pockets of my dress. "I've never experienced anything like this before. I've had plenty of dreams involving murder or mayhem, but these . . . " Staring off into the distance, I recalled one of the dreams. "We're in this field of wildflowers, and I'm dressed in a long, loose dress. Bees are flitting from flower to flower, and the sky's scattered with white, puffy clouds. He's waiting for me at the top of a rise, and it's like I can't wait to be with him." Another blush began to creep up my neck and into my face, and I stopped.

"Go on," she prodded with anticipation, "what happens next?"

"Never mind," I said, waving the images away. "Let's just say for a witch and a psychic, these are pretty *good* dreams."

She tapped a foot on the hard, cracked ground in annoyance. "Okay, if you're not going to give me the details, at least tell me what this guy looks like."

"He's dressed in a white shirt, with billowing sleeves . . . " I paused. "You know, like the ones pirates wear?"

Darci rolled her eyes. "Maybe you've checked in one too

many romance novels and the cover art seeped into your subconscious."

"Listen," I said in a curt voice. "Do you want to know what he looks like or not?"

"Okay, okay," she mumbled. "Sorry."

"He's blond, tall with wide shoulders, and his eyes are blue—an incredibly deep blue. As dark as sapphires. Eyes that just pull you in . . . " A softness stole over me as I imagined the man in my dreams. The way he made me feel, the way his arms . . . I shook myself out of my revelry, banishing the gooiness I felt inside. "That's about it," I commented, trying to put a hard edge back in my voice.

"Does he say anything?"

"No, he just smiles a lot."

"Humph, I bet," she said with a knowing glance.

I felt my cheeks bloom bright red.

"Okay," she said, her eyes scanning the crowd. "Tall, blond—"

"Yes, but," I interjected swiftly before she jumped to conclusions, "he wasn't the man arguing with Clair."

"Okay, so blue eyes, wide shoulders." Her eyes stopped. "How about the guy surrounded by all the women? He's tall, has wide shoulders and blond hair, but I can't tell if his eyes are blue. He's wearing sunglasses."

I spun around and followed her gaze to where it rested on a stranger.

The man Darci referred to wore dark navy jeans and a bright white sport shirt. From the side view, he fit Darci's description—built exactly like the stranger from my dreams, but I couldn't know at that distance without seeing his eyes.

Feeling my stare, his head moved in my direction and he removed his sunglasses.

A slow smile spread across his face, and, as our eyes locked, my heart almost stopped.

It was him—literally the man of my dreams.

# TWO

"Ophelia, Ophelia."

Darci's voice sounded very far away, and the chatter of the crowd dimmed until all I could hear was the thump of my heart pounding in my ears. My fingers, holding the stem of my wineglass, felt numb as I watched the man make his way with an easy stride to where Darci and I still stood by the maple tree.

He looked down at me. "Hi, I'm Stephen Larsen."

Images of my dreams flickered through my mind, and I prayed I wasn't blushing again. My tongue felt thick in my mouth, making it difficult to talk.

"Ophelia Jensen," I managed to mumble.

"Have we met?" he asked, giving me a quizzical grin.

"Ah, no, ah, I don't think so," I stammered.

Stephen's eyes shifted toward Darci.

"Hi, I'm Darci West," she said, shaking his hand.

"My pleasure," he replied quickly before turning his deep blue eyes back to me.

"Well . . . " Darci paused. "If you'll excuse me," she continued with a tinge of amusement in her voice. "It appears we need a new bottle."

My attention remained riveted on the stranger, but I heard her three-inch mules slap across the hard ground as she walked away. A moment of panic hit me.

I wasn't good at making small talk with strangers, especially a stranger who'd haunted my dreams for the last couple of weeks. The silence between us grew while Stephen continued to stare at me.

"Are you sure we haven't met?" he asked in a puzzled voice.

"Have you ever been to the library in Summerset?"

Stephen's laugh rang out. "I've been in lots of libraries, but not that one."

I cocked my head. "You visit libraries?"

"Yeah," he said with a crooked grin. "I'm an author."

My mind scrambled while I tried to run through our list of authors. *Stephen Larsen, Stephen Larsen—nope, the name didn't mean anything to me.*

"Are you famous?" I blurted.

A smile quivered at the corner of his mouth. "I don't know if you'd call it 'famous.' I write nonfiction under my real name, but horror under the pen name of M. J. LaSalle."

"Oh, my gosh." My eyes widened in shock. "You're M. J. LaSalle?"

He nodded shyly.

"I'm sorry . . . I didn't recognize you," I exclaimed.

"That's okay. Most people don't," he said good-naturedly. "After all, who really pays attention to a picture on a dust jacket?"

I thought of all the books I'd entered into our system over the years and their authors—John Grisham, Barry Eisler, J. A. Konrath, Charlaine Harris, Debbie Macomber—all had works very popular with our patrons. However, most readers had problems remembering the titles, let alone what the author looked like.

"You're right, not many, but your books fly off our shelves."

His eyebrows shot up. "You own a bookstore?"

"No, I'm the librarian in Summerset," I explained with pride.

"Ahh," he said slowly, "that's why you asked me if I visited libraries."

I gave my head a quick dip. "So what's a *New York Times* best-selling author doing here in our little corner of Iowa?"

Stephen's eyes drifted over to a group of men standing by the arbor and talking to one of vineyard's employees. His gaze held for an instant, and a shadow of a frown crossed his face. "Mind if we take a walk?" he asked without answering my question.

Although confused by the sudden change in his expression, I fell into step next to him. "Umm, no, that would be great."

Just as long as we stay away from any field of wildflowers, I thought. What happens when I'm dreaming is one thing, but I didn't intend to make those dreams a reality . . . not yet.

We walked down the gravel drive away from the winery, away from the noise of the crowd and the sound of the music. As we strolled by past several residents of my small Iowa town, I noticed a couple of eyebrows lift in surprise.

Peachy. By tomorrow morning it would be all over town that I was spotted at the fund-raiser with a strange man. I'd be fielding questions all day. Edna Simpson, with her false teeth sliding precariously around in her mouth, would want to know who Stephen was, where he lived, and what his lineage was, dating back to the *Mayflower*. I didn't think anyone would recognize his picture from the back of his book cover. I certainly hadn't.

As we strolled, silence hung in the air, but it wasn't strained. It felt comfortable, and there was a sense that if I did talk, Stephen would find what I said interesting.

The feeling of having known him all my life settled around me.

"I—"

"You—"

We both spoke at the same time.

"Go ahead," I said, laughing.

"I'm trying to think of a way to say this." He stopped, shoving both hands in his front pockets. "I have the strongest feeling that I know you." A chagrined expression crossed his face. "Flaky, isn't it?"

"No," I said with a slight shake of my head. "I was just thinking the same thing—that I feel like I've known you a long time."

"Wow, maybe I can read your mind," he said with a chuckle.

Oh God, I hope not, I thought, not meeting his eyes. In my experience, reading minds wasn't all that much fun.

He tilted his head and gave me a funny look. "Has this ever happened to you before?"

"No." I paused, thinking about all the strange things, due to my so-called gift, that I'd encountered. "No," I repeated firmly.

"Good, then we're in this together," he said, removing his hand from his pocket and taking mine.

At his touch, a tingle shot up my arm, catching me off guard. *Did he feel it, too?* I gave him a slanted glance. *No, no reaction at all.*

Stephen led me near the trees marking the boundary of the vineyard.

Clearing my throat, I tried to make small talk. "You didn't say why you're in Iowa," I said. "Why you're here at the winery."

A shuttered expression flashed in his eyes. "I've been in eastern Iowa doing research, and I heard that someone I wanted to meet would be here."

"Research, huh?" I asked, trying to ignore how it felt to have his fingers wrapped around mine. "For a Stephen Larsen book, or an M. J. LaSalle?"

"A Stephen Larsen." He squeezed my hand and chuckled again. "It's confusing—there are mornings I wake up and don't know which persona I'll be for the day."

"I never thought about that—I suppose it is. I've met authors before. When I lived in Iowa City, I attended events at Prairie Lights Bookstore, but I've never had a conversation with a writer."

"I hope I don't disappoint you," he replied with a wink. "Haven't you had authors visit your library?"

"No. Summerset's not exactly on the book tour circuit."

"Personally, I enjoy libraries and meeting librarians." His hand tightened. "Especially this librarian."

My hand in his, twitched. *Is he flirting with me?* Nervous, I changed the subject. "How long will you be in Iowa?"

"I don't know. It depends on how the research goes; how much background information I dig up. From here, I'm headed to Texas."

I couldn't make the connection between Iowa and Texas in my head. "You must be writing some story. What's it about?"

Stephen's lips tightened, and I worried that I'd offended him.

"I'm sorry, I didn't mean to pry—" I tensed and gave my hand a little tug.

"It's okay," he broke in without releasing my hand. "I'm a little superstitious. I always think if I talk about a book too soon, it will somehow jinx it."

Relaxing, I smiled. "I wouldn't want to do that. May I ask this . . . Where do you live?'

Stephen laughed. "That's a question I can answer. St. Louis. A condo near Laclede's Landing."

"Laclede's Landing?"

"Yeah, it was named for the founder of St. Louis, Pierre Laclede, and it was where the fur trappers rendezvoused. Now the old warehouses are converted to businesses."

I heard the fondness in his voice as he talked of his home.

"Sounds like you enjoy living there."

"I do. I love the energy at Laclede's. There's always some-

thing to do, blues festivals, live music, fine restaurants, bars."
He smiled. "For a writer, it's a great place to people watch. And
my assistant, Karen Burns, lives nearby, so that's handy."

A weird little spark of jealousy ran through me at the
mention of another woman in Stephen's life.

*Jeez, Jensen, get a grip.*

"Do you discuss your writing with her?" My question
came out on the snippy side, and Stephen gave me a funny
look.

"A little, mainly just the M. J. LaSalle manuscripts. Like I
said, I don't talk much about my work while I'm writing."

"It sounds like you have a very interesting life."

"It is . . . to me anyway," he said with satisfaction. "What
about you?"

Hmm, good question. Was my life interesting? I was raising a teenage daughter, I had my job at the library, I had
this psychic/witch thing going on. *And* there was my little
habit of tripping over bodies. Yeah, I guess I could say my
life was interesting, but I had no intention of explaining it to
Stephen.

"No, not really," I lied, glancing up to the sky. "Just your
typical small-town life."

Looking back at Stephen, the grin on his face told me he
didn't believe me.

"No, honest, it's really pretty boring," I protested.

"It's okay, Ophelia. Part of the fun of getting to know
someone is learning their secrets," he said, rubbing my bare
arm with his other hand.

*Oh, buddy, you have no idea.*

Stephen took a step closer, and I felt pinned to the ground
as I stared into his blue eyes. He placed a hand on my shoulder and drew me near. My mouth went dry and my eyelids
drifted shut as his cool, soft lips brushed mine in the sweet-
est kiss I'd ever had in my life.

Gentleness filled the kiss, and I felt my heart expand with
a longing so sharp, it hurt.

In an instant the kiss was over, and I found myself staring into his grinning face.

"I think I might have to stay in Iowa longer than I planned."

I lowered my eyes and smiled. A smile that's lit every woman's face since the beginning of time. A smile that said she knows she's wanted.

From behind me a flock of crows suddenly filled the sky, their caws marring the moment. Turning, I frowned at their bad timing, as Stephen stepped around me, his eyes scanning the woods.

Facing the trees, he called over his shoulder, "Something must have disturbed them."

"Probably a deer." I made a move toward him. "The woods are full of them right now—"

I jumped as a sharp crack echoed through the woods. It happened so quickly, only later would I recall that it was followed by the faint smell of sulfur.

Stephen staggered, then pivoted toward me. A look of surprise mingled with horror registered on his face. He glanced down at his chest.

My eyes followed his.

Blood spread across his white shirt in a growing stain. He took one step and crumpled to the ground.

I think I screamed—I know I screamed—as I rushed to where he lay faceup on the ground. Panic, fear, and disbelief fought inside of me. I knelt and laid my hand over his chest to stop the slow seep of blood. It leaked from between my fingers while I watched his face grow pasty white.

"In my pocket . . . book . . . give to Karen." He struggled to say the words.

With one hand I reached in the pocket of his pants and withdrew a small book.

I felt hot tears run down my cheeks and sobs clog my throat as hands lifted me up and away from Stephen's still body.

Shoving my bloody hands in my pockets, I watched while two men worked on Stephen—one tried to stanch the blood and the other performed mouth-to-mouth. I don't know how long they labored over Stephen, seconds, minutes? Time had stopped.

People appeared from nowhere, and I felt myself being crowded to the back of the group as everyone jockeyed for a view of the men fighting to save Stephen. In the distance the whirl of helicopter blades and the sound of sirens came closer and closer. The company parted suddenly.

An ambulance, followed by a patrol car, pulled down the lane, the dust rolling in thick clouds behind them. Both vehicles skidded to a halt, and three EMTs in their blue jumpsuits flew out of the doors of the ambulance. A deputy exited the patrol car and motioned the crowd back. To my numb brain, he reminded me of someone trying to herd reluctant cattle.

Craning my neck, I saw one of the EMTs rush over to Stephen, while the other two pulled equipment out of the back. Without delay, they joined their partner kneeling over Stephen. In fast, precise movements they cut the front of his shirt and pulled it to the side, revealing a small round hole to the left of his sternum. One EMT pressed down hard on the wound, while the other two inserted IVs in his arms and a tube down his throat.

A hand on my arm spun me around.

Abby.

"Ophelia, are you all right?" Her words came out fast, and heavy with the sound of the South. A sure sign of how upset she was. "What happened?"

Before I could answer, she threw her arms around me and embraced me tightly.

"I'm not hurt," I mumbled into her shoulder. "Someone shot Stephen, a man I just met."

She released her death grip on me and stepped back, her eyes scouring my face. Satisfied, she nodded once and turned her attention to the EMTs.

We watched while they carefully placed a board under Stephen's still body and, lifting slowly, moved him onto the gurney. Then, moving rapidly, they wheeled him toward the waiting ambulance. The EMT with his hand on the wound kept it in place as they moved him. Once the gurney was secured in the back, the doors were slammed shut and the ambulance peeled away, sirens blaring and lights flashing.

# Three

I sat huddled on a chair in the dining room of the winery. Darci knelt in front of me with a wineglass in her hand, trying to get me to drink. From behind me, Abby stood making soft clucking sounds while she stroked my head.

With a grimace, I turned my head away. "Water," I croaked, my mouth dry and sour.

Magically, the water appeared in her hand, and she pressed the rim to my lips.

I drank eagerly in big gulps, but when the cold water hit my stomach, I felt it lurch. Shaking my head, I pushed the glass away.

People gathered in tight little groups around the room, and their hushed voices penetrated my mind at some level, but I couldn't comprehend their words. The sound was only a buzz in my brain as I stared off into nothingness.

I shivered.

"Would someone please get us a blanket?" Darci commanded.

Feet scurried across the polished wood floor, and soon I felt soft wool being draped around me. On each side of me, Abby and Darci swiftly tucked the blanket about my shoulders and legs. My eyes felt gunky and swollen, my face gritty with dried tears.

"When you meet your true love, he's not supposed to be shot, is he?" I asked Darci in a bleak voice.

Abby threw a glance Darci's way. "What's she talking about?"

"Nothing," Darci replied, running a trembling hand through her blond hair. "I'll explain later."

The sound of boot heels crossing the floor drew our attention as a big man strode into the room, his hat pulled low on his forehead. Pausing, he removed it and wiped his shiny bald head with a large hand. He spotted me and his lips thinned. With a shake of his head, he continued toward us.

Sheriff Bill Wilson—I should've known he'd be there. I struggled to stand up. "Stephen?" I asked him.

"Sit down, Ophelia," Bill's booming voice called out as he marched up to me. He grabbed a chair and moved it close to mine. "He's hanging in there," he said quietly. "He survived the chopper ride to Regional Medical Center and he's in surgery now." Bill stopped and studied me intently. "What happened?"

"I don't know . . . we were walking down the path . . . we stopped . . . I heard a sharp crack . . . Stephen staggered." I clutched my hands in my lap. "I couldn't stop the blood, Bill . . . I—"

He patted my shoulder, and I clamped my jaw shut. "Right before you heard the shot, did you see anything, hear anything?"

"Crows . . . " I hesitated. "A flock of crows from behind me . . . in the woods . . . suddenly took flight. Stephen stepped around me, toward the trees. That's when I heard the shot."

"Hmm, so Larsen was standing in front of you, looking at the woods?"

"Yes."

"I see." Bill scratched his chin while he chewed on his lip. "How long have you known Mr. Larsen?"

"I just met him today."

"Did he appear scared, nervous, worried?"

"No."

"What did you talk about?"

"Nothing. He told me he was an author, lived in St. Louis, there were wildflowers—no wait—no wildflowers." Lifting a hand, I rubbed my temples. Everything was jumbled in my mind and I couldn't seem to separate dreams from reality.

"She doesn't know what she's saying, Bill," Abby said from behind me. "She's in shock. We need to get her home."

"Just a couple more questions. Ophelia, do you—"

"Those questions can wait until tomorrow," Abby broke in, her voice stern. "We're leaving now."

She reached down and grasped my upper arm, gently pulling me to my feet. Bill rose at the same time.

No, I needed answers—I tugged my arm from Abby's grasp. "Do you know what happened, Bill?"

"No, it's too early in the investigation," he said, twirling his hat in his hands. "We don't even know if the shooting was intentional. There's a chance some hunter's shot went wild."

"Either way, Stephen's fighting for his life, isn't he?" I scanned his face, hoping to find some reassurance that Stephen would live.

Bill bowed his head and stared at a spot on the floor without answering.

"I should've seen this coming," I said, stricken. "I should've been able to stop this."

Raising his eyes, he squirmed uncomfortably and rubbed his bald head. "I'm only concerned with the facts right now, Ophelia," he replied in a low voice. "We'll talk about your 'impressions' later."

Once home, Darci hustled me upstairs while Abby made her remedy for all crises—tea. Darci led me to the bathroom and gently shoved me down onto the vanity chair. With care, she wiped Stephen's blood from my hands with a warm washcloth. Doesn't she know the stain will never go away? I thought numbly.

" 'Out, out damn spot,' " I mumbled in a low voice.

"What?" Darci eyed me with concern.

"Lady Macbeth." I paused. "Never mind, I'm talking crazy."

"I agree with Abby. You're in shock." She tossed the washcloth in the trash and helped me to my feet. "Do you need help changing?" she asked, handing me a T-shirt and pair of sweatpants.

"No," I answered in a small voice.

She left the room, and I quickly stripped off the navy dress. I rolled it into a tight ball and it followed the washcloth into the trash. I never wanted to see it again. Shivering in spite of the heat, I threw on the clothes Darci had given me and tottered into the hallway where she stood waiting.

With a hand on my elbow, she steered me into my bedroom, toward the bed. Flipping back the covers, she settled me onto the bed and piled the blankets on top of me.

I felt like a friggin' invalid.

"Better?" she asked.

"Yeah." I heard the weary note in my voice. "Darci, why—"

"All tucked in?" Abby bustled into the room, carrying a steaming mug. "Here, drink this," she said as she handed the cup to me.

I sniffed the rising steam suspiciously. "What is it?"

With Abby, one never knew what kind of concoction she'd made. She wasn't above slipping "a little something extra" into the tea if she thought it might help me sleep. And I wasn't so sure I wanted to sleep. With sleep came dreams.

She waved away my concerns with a toss of her hand. "Don't worry about it. It's chamomile. It will help you relax."

I took a cautious sip and felt the hot, sweet tea warm the cold spot that lay deep inside my heart. My vision blurred as the tears gathered in my eyes. With trembling hands, I raised the cup to my lips again and choked down the rest of the tea, almost scalding my tongue. I didn't care. I needed the heat to break through the numbness wrapped around me like a chain.

Darci stepped away from the bed as Abby sat next to me. Seeing the tears, she took my hand in hers and rubbed it softly. "There, there," she murmured. "It's all right, Ophelia."

"No, it's not, Abby. I saw a man shot down; I saw the blood seep out of his chest." A tremor ran up my spine. "I've seen violence in my dreams, but it's different seeing it in real life. In dreams, I can't change anything—it's already happened, but this . . . " I pushed my head back against the pillow and shut my eyes.

Sudden weariness fogged my brain, and I couldn't seem to string my thoughts together. "I don't get it." Opening my eyes, I looked at her. "I knew something was about to happen, but I thought it was going to be something good . . . not bad." I clenched my jaw and exhaled slowly. "Did you sense anything?"

Abby shook her head. "No, but then I wasn't trying to pick up any vibes. We don't see everything, Ophelia."

"I did—I *did* see, but I read the signs wrong," I argued, more with myself than her. "If the vision had given me more of a warning, I could have stopped this from happening. I failed again. What if Stephen dies? I—"

"Don't go there." She squeezed my hand . . . hard. "Don't resurrect the past. You know you weren't responsible for Brian's death, and you're not responsible for that young man today. There are things we can't change, nor are we supposed to."

"That's what you always say," I mumbled, fighting to stay awake.

"I say it because it's true. And I'll keep saying it until you believe it." Abby's face swam in front of me as I tried to focus. Losing the battle, my eyelids slowly drifted down.

*Damn, she did put something in the tea.*

I woke up to a bedroom dark except for moonlight. A warm body curled next to mine. Stretching out my hand, my fingers found soft, thick fur. A low purr greeted me. The bed moved, and my cat, Queenie, shifted her body closer to mine.

Combing her fur with my fingers, my eyes traveled around the room, spotting familiar shapes and shadows: my nightstand with an antique lamp sitting on its marble top; my dresser along the east wall; my comfy reading chair, placed just right by the window located on the west wall.

The chair's shadow suddenly altered. A form came out of the depths of the chair, and, in the faint light, I caught the glimmer of blond hair.

Tink.

"Are you awake?" she whispered in the darkness.

"Yeah." Slowly scooting up, I flicked on the antique lamp, filling the room with warm, mellow light. "How long have you been sitting there?"

"Not long." Tink rose and crossed the room. With a sigh, she plopped down on the bed next to me. "Are you okay?" she said while her violet eyes roamed my face.

"Umm-hmm," I replied with a smile.

She gave me a skeptical look. "You sure? You seemed really out of it."

"Ah, well, I think there was more than just tea in that cup." I rubbed my forehead with my fingers as if trying to scrub away the residual lethargy. "Abby 'medicated' me."

"Valerian drops, I bet," Tink said with a nod. "Calms you down and helps you sleep."

My mouth twisted in a wry grin. "Whatever it was, it worked."

"Did you dream?"

"Nope."

*Thank goodness.* I'd have to deal with dreams eventually. As a psychic, I knew I couldn't experience something as traumatic as the shooting without some kind of mental fallout. But for now, I was safe.

"Is Abby still here?"

"Yeah, she's downstairs on the phone with Arthur. He was worried about you, too." Tink paused. "Abby told me what happened. She said someone was shot."

I hesitated. Tink, like Abby, had a habit of rushing into situations best left alone. If it had been attempted murder, I wanted her as far away from the investigation as possible. The less she knew, the better. But before I could answer, she spoke again.

"Who tried to kill him?"

So much for keeping her in the dark.

I held up my hand. "Wait a second. We don't know that it was attempted murder. Bill said it might have been an accident. A hunter whose shot went wild."

"Right, and it's just a coincidence that you were standing there."

"Yes." My voice didn't sound convincing even to me.

"This was just something that 'happened'?"

I didn't like the direction this conversation was going. "What do you mean?"

Tink lifted a thin shoulder in a careless shrug. "Abby says there's no such thing as coincidence."

*Brother, how many times have I heard that one? And if they learned about my dreams . . . ?* I needed to nip this in the bud right now.

"Tink," I said, my voice serious, "what happened was awful enough without making more of it than it is. Bill will discover the truth."

Tink ignored me. "Maybe you're supposed to discover the truth. Maybe the Universe put you there for a reason."

I snorted. "You sound more like Abby every day."

She smiled proudly. "Thanks."

I wasn't sure I meant my remark as a compliment.

"Tink—"

Abruptly, she leaned forward and gave me a hug. "I've got to get to bed." Standing, she smiled again. "Don't worry, Ophelia, you'll figure out what the Universe wants you to do." Pivoting, she headed for the door.

I sat forward. "Wait a second . . . I'm not—"

I spoke to an empty room.

# *Four*

I tossed around in bed trying to find a comfortable place.

*Was Tink right? Was Abby right?*

I glanced at the clock. Eleven.

*Did Stephen survive his surgery? If I called the hospital would they tell me?*

Probably not—I wasn't a relative, and I doubted the nurses would release information to a stranger. I'd have to wait until morning to learn of Stephen's condition.

Suddenly hot, I kicked off the covers and jumped out of bed. Queenie, routed from her cozy position, rose, stretched, and with an indignant look at me, jumped off the bed and sauntered out of the room. Crossing to the window, I pulled back the curtain and stared out into the backyard of my little Victorian cottage. A full moon lit the night. Long shadows cast by the trees ringing my property dappled the ground, and a hazy mist floated just above my freshly mowed grass. The scene was peaceful, yet eerie.

The air in my bedroom felt stifling, and I took a deep breath as if I couldn't get enough oxygen into my lungs. All of a sudden I felt caged—the room seemed to grow smaller and smaller. Shoving my feet into a pair of clogs, I fled.

Quietly, I moved swiftly down the hall to the stairs.

I didn't want to rouse Tink or Abby. I needed to think before we had any more discussions about the shooting. Creeping down the stairs, I heard Abby's voice coming from the main floor guest room. The way her voice carried, it seemed she was still on the phone with Arthur, who often took out his hearing aids at night. Good, she'd be concentrating on making herself heard, and not paying attention. The irony hit me. This was just like high school, trying to sneak out from under the watchful eye of my mother.

As I rounded the corner at the bottom of the stairs, from over my shoulder I spied my dog, Lady, curled up in the living room by the fireplace. She lifted her head and one blue eye, one brown eye, watched me in speculation while her tail thumped the floor.

Turning, I placed a finger on my lips. "Shh," I whispered, and patted my leg softly. "You want to go outside?"

She scrambled to her feet, and together we slipped out the back door onto the patio. I chose the chaise lounge, while Lady ran toward the trees, her nose close to the ground, sniffing for the trail of some elusive squirrel. Leaning my head back, I took another deep breath and let the night calm me.

The sounds of crickets chirping, and Lady rustling through the underbrush as she searched for her squirrel, filled the night. The air, though heavy with humidity, felt good against my bare arms. Stars, scattered across the sky above me, winked and sparkled like glitter.

In my mind, I returned to my original question: Were Tink and Abby right? Was I supposed to be there? Did the Universe have some task for me?

*Yes.* And it scared the crap out of me. It had only been a couple of months since Tink's kidnapping, one of the worst experiences in my life. We'd all struggled so hard to find her. It had been a battle of a lifetime, and I didn't know if I was up to facing another ordeal so soon. What if my psychic gift had been depleted? What if my "batteries" needed to be re-charged? It might account for why I hadn't sensed the danger before it struck Stephen down.

Abby always said to trust myself, to have faith. *Right.* At times, that's easier said than done. Facing challenge after challenge can beat you down until all you want is a little peace in your life. Some respite.

A long sigh escaped while I stared at the night sky. One thing I'd learned over the past couple of years—it didn't make a difference if I was ready or not. Another fight was on the horizon, and I'd better be prepared.

Reclining on the chaise, tiredness slithered up my body and my limbs felt too heavy to lift. *Damn Abby's potions— how long were they going to linger in my system?*

A comet shot across the heavens above as sleep once again claimed me.

I walked through fields of wildflowers as before, only this time the world wasn't sunny and bright. Storm clouds roiled across the sky and, from miles away, the low sound of thunder rumbled. Wind whipped the tall grass, bending it low to the ground. Each step was a struggle against the force of the wind.

Stephen stood on the crest of a hill, as he had in the other dreams, but he faced away from me. I shouted his name, but the shrieking wind blew the words back in my face. Yelling his name again, I lowered my head and fought to move forward. I had to reach him—somehow I knew my life, his life, depended on it. I lifted one foot, but it felt as if it were encased in mud. Struggling, I tried to hurry through the weeds, but the more I tried, the heavier my steps became. Vines wrapped around my ankles and I fell facedown. Thistles scratched my face. Arms trembling with exertion, I pushed myself to my knees.

Lifting my head, I called out, "Stephen, help me!"

Stephen's body slowly rotated until he faced me.

Bleak blue eyes stared at me from across the meadow, and I stretched a hand toward him.

"Stephen . . . " I ripped away the vines and shoved myself to my feet. If I could only reach him, everything would be okay.

With my eyes focused on him, I watched him raise his hands in a helpless gesture as a small circle of bright red appeared in the center of his white shirt. The dot grew bigger and bigger, spreading beyond Stephen to color the meadow in a crimson haze.

Wind roared in my ears, and I shut my eyes to block the sound and the sight of the once beautiful field now stained scarlet. Dizziness swept over me. Shaking my head, I fought against it.

The world suddenly righted, and the wind stopped. A shove in the middle of my back had my eyes flying open.

"Hurry."

Racks and racks of clothing surrounded me, and the small room seemed clogged with people. Tall, rangy women stood in a line and were being poked and prodded by a small man with a thin mustache. A tape measure dangling from around his neck swayed as he flitted down the line from woman to woman. Each one stood patiently while he yanked at their clothes and fluffed their hair. Then with a push, he sent them out between curtains hung across the doorway. Each time the curtains parted, the cloying smell of perfume wafted through the room.

What was he doing?

"Madeleine, get in line. You're next."

As I looked around to spot Madeleine, a rotund woman grabbed my arm and began to pull me toward the little man.

*Me? I'm Madeleine?* I tried to take a step, but something was wrapped around my knees. I stumbled.

"What is wrong with you today?" she asked with a yank, righting me.

*This is so weird.* I minced along beside the woman until I was in front of the little man.

"Tsk tsk," he hissed while pinching at my waist. "No more croissants for you. You're lucky this still fits."

Wait a second, this might be a dream, but I didn't need some strange little man telling me what I could or couldn't eat. I tried to take a deep breath in order to deliver a scathing reply, but the bodice was so tight, my ribs barely moved. My eyes traveled down.

No jeans, no long flowing dress—instead I wore a tight-fitting jacket that flared over my hips. It had shoulder pads that made my silhouette look like a linebacker's. Its material was black with tiny white polka dots. A body-hugging skirt of the same material completed the ensemble and seemed to swaddle my legs to mid-calf. No wonder I couldn't walk.

"Look at me," the man commanded. He lifted my chin and turned my head from side to side. "More powder," he said with a snap of his fingers.

A woman in a white smock scurried over and dusted my nose and cheeks with a soft puff full of fine, light powder.

I sneezed.

"Zzt, none of that," he scolded. "Do you want them to think you're sick?" Reaching up, he drew a net veil down over my face.

It felt scratchy on my nose, and I lifted a hand to brush it away, but the man stopped me.

"Leave it alone. I know you don't like hats, but the customers do."

With a shove, he sent me out through the curtains.

My startled eyes flew around the room.

The entire room was decorated in white and gold. The walls were white satin and the floor was covered with gold carpet. Large vases of creamy white lilies on gold pedestals littered the room. Elegantly dressed women, with hair so blond it was almost white, stood in clusters, sipping pale liquid from fluted, crystal glasses. The tall women I'd seen in the little room strolled from group to group, pausing in front of each and doing a little pirouette. The blond women studied them with arctic blue eyes, and a couple of the blondes lifted thin, penciled eyebrows as they sized up the clothes the tall women wore.

*I'm at some kind of a fashion show and I'm one of the models.*

The thought ricocheted through my brain and I stifled a laugh.

*Me? Ophelia Jensen? The fashion challenged Ophelia Jensen? A model?*

It was ridiculous even for a dream. Had to be the stuff Abby put in the tea to make me dream something as crazy as this.

I took one halting step forward then stopped when I noticed the blondes' companions—a group of men in the corner sitting rigidly on white chairs trimmed in gold. They were dressed in gray uniforms, with epaulets on the shoulders and collars trimmed in silver braid. Their posture was stiff and they all looked bored. One man, with close-cropped hair, drummed his fingers impatiently on his thigh as he spun a peaked hat with a visor in his other hand. He stopped and shifted uncomfortably in his chair. As he did, the gold medal on his jacket pocket caught the light. An iron cross with some kind of insignia stamped in its center.

The veil covering my face made it difficult to see, and I squinted for a better look.

My god—a swastika.

Where the hell was I?

# Five

A cold, wet nose nudging my arm had my eyes flying open while my heart still raced. I shot straight up in the chair and took a long, deep breath of the moist night air. With a groan, Lady nuzzled her head in my lap as if trying to comfort me. The pounding of my heart slowed, and I reached down to scratch her ears.

"It's okay, girl," I said softly.

She cocked her head to the side, and I could see the doubt in her eyes.

Stroking her ears, I forced a smile in the darkness. "No, really, I'm okay, but that was one heck of a dream. Remind me not to drink any more of Abby's tea."

Was it the tea? It had to be. All my life I've had dreams, but never one that strange. Never had I dreamt of events that had happened long ago. Chewing my lip, I tried to recall the images. It didn't take a rocket scientist to figure out the men in my dream were Nazis. The swastika on the medal was a big clue.

Okay, the dream was taking place during World War II, or there about. I've never been a fan of military history, so why would I dream of that time period? I searched my memory for anything that might have triggered the dream. Had I read any articles about the war? Had we received any books on the subject in the recent past? Nope—not that I could recall.

And what about the model thing? What possibly could've caused me to imagine that? As Darci frequently pointed out, I had no sense of fashion, and she'd made it a life mission to clear out all of the polyester in my closet. I wore linen in the fall and tweed in the spring—according to Darci—a big "no-no." She'd even made me throw away my favorite hair accessory—scrunchies. Had Darci's constant efforts to give me some style filtered into my subconscious, causing me to dream of being a model?

I snickered at the thought.

With a sigh, I tried to put the images out of my mind. I had enough to think about in this time period, instead of worrying about a silly dream of a time long dead. As the pictures in my head faded, I felt a band of anxiety squeeze my chest, and with it came the same feeling that I'd described to Darci earlier. The sense that there was something I needed to do, but couldn't remember what it was.

Could the runes Abby had given me help? The glyphs acted as my guideposts and brought clarity to my thoughts, giving me some sense of what my visions might mean. But the dream hadn't been a vision, and my mind was too jumbled to attempt using the runes tonight. Shaking my head in frustration, I thrust the dream away. I needed to focus on reality. To think about that day and the events leading up to the shooting.

Bill had asked me if anything in Stephen's demeanor seemed odd. No. We'd walked down the lane talking. The conversation was normal for two people meeting for the first time. We stopped, then Stephen kissed me. I was facing away from the woods, so I couldn't see if there'd been any movement in the trees. Stephen stepped around me when we heard the crows.

My face twisted at my next memory—the crack of gun-

fire and the smell of sulfur, the expression on Stephen's face,
how he had staggered and fallen, his last words.

I slapped my forehead and sprang to my feet startling
Lady. *Jensen, you're an idiot. The book.*

I rushed to the back door, opened it softly and crept into
my now dark and quiet house. Not wanting to alert Abby,
I snuck upstairs and into the bathroom with Lady at my
heels. Seeing the dress lying on top of the trash, I reached
down and with two fingers lifted it out of the trash. Dark
streaks, almost black, where I'd swiped my bloody hands,
marred the navy material. My stomach clenched at the
sight.

At my side, Lady sniffed the air, took two steps back and
gave a low whimper.

"I know . . . you don't like the dress either," I whispered.

At the sound of my voice, she plunked down on the floor
and stared up at me.

With hesitation, I stuck my hand in the deep pocket and
rummaged around until my fingers found the smooth leather
cover. Grasping the book, I pulled it out. Bloody fingerprints
etched the cover.

Dropping the dress back into the trash, I stared at the
book in my hand. My common sense told me that I should
turn it over to Bill, but a little voice inside my head asked a
question.

*What's in this book?*

I forced myself to open it.

It was a date book with appointments scrawled in large,
loopy letters.

I flipped through the pages and saw the phone numbers
and addresses of his agent, editor, and Karen Burns, his assistant. Examining the dates, I noticed Stephen had been on
a book tour for the last few weeks. He'd had signings at Cor-
nerstone Books in Salem, Massachusetts; Mystery Lovers
Bookshop in Oakmont, Pennsylvania, last month; Booked
for Murder in Madison, Wisconsin, and Once Upon a Crime

in Minneapolis, last week; and The Bookworm in Bellevue, Iowa, just prior to coming to Summerset.

He hadn't said anything about a book tour. He said he was conducting research for the next Stephen Larsen book and that his next stop was Texas.

I read his entries for the month of September. He had signings listed for I Love a Mystery in Mission, Kansas; Main Street Books in St. Charles, Missouri; Big Sleep Books in St. Louis, and Mysterious Galaxy in San Diego, California. I flipped forward to October, but only found an entry for an appearance at The Women's Expo in Kingsport, Tennessee. Nothing about a stop in Texas. Turning back, I looked at the date listing The Bookworm. Next to it was a phone number with a 515 area code. I knew that was for central not eastern Iowa, where The Bookworm was located.

Turning the page, I noticed that last Friday, just two days ago, Stephen had written *Vargas* and a phone number next to the date. He'd circled it twice.

Vargas? Vargas? We had a Vargas family living in Summerset, and the phone number was a local one. A coincidence? No, it had to be the same family. I'd seen Mr. Vargas on the street with his wife and daughter, and knew that he worked at the winery, along with many other Latinos in the area. Stephen said he'd heard there was someone at the fundraiser whom he wanted to meet. His entry indicated that the meeting must have been with Vargas.

It didn't make sense. Stephen had been in eastern Iowa. How would he have known of the Vargas family? And why did he want to talk with them? As far as I knew, they were a quiet family, staying mostly to themselves. I knew their little girl, Evita. She came to the library a couple of days a week, after school, but the only time I ever ran into her mother, Deloris, was when she picked up Evita.

A smile played at the corner of my mouth. Evita was a real sweetheart. About ten years old, with black ringlets floating around her shoulders, she was bright, inquisitive, an avid reader, and for some reason, attached herself to me whenever she came to the library. The reason could've been the candy jar we kept at the counter to encourage children to return books. Every time they returned their books, they received a piece. But Evita? I always slipped her two pieces. For whatever reason, her brown eyes sparkled as she followed me around, asking questions and munching her candy. Already she was reading way above her age level.

Her mother didn't share Evita's friendliness. She seemed very shy and never engaged in conversation when she picked up Evita. She did adore her daughter, though. Her face lit up at the sight of her bopping around the library. The greeting was always the same. Evita would fly into her mother's arms, rattling off words in rapid Spanish, Deloris would laugh and enfold her in a big hug, and then with a nod and a small smile at me, the two would leave the library hand in hand.

They appeared to be a happy family, and I couldn't imagine why Stephen would be interested in them.

I glanced at Lady still lying on the floor watching me. "Well, girl. One way to find out—I'll call Mrs. Vargas, then Karen Burns. Maybe she knows why Stephen wanted to talk with the Vargases. Never hurts to ask questions, right?"

"What are you doing?"

I jumped at the sound of Abby's voice coming from the door way of my home office. With a hand to my chest, I glanced over my shoulder. "Jeez, Abby, you shouldn't sneak up on people like that."

"That doesn't answer my question," she replied, crossing to where I sat at my desk.

I tugged my linen jacket on with one hand fiddling with the clip holding back my hair with the other hand. "I thought I'd catch up on a few things before work," I said, my eyes darting to the scanner holding Stephen's date book. I knew I had to turn the book over to Bill, but it didn't mean I couldn't copy it first.

Abby leaned against the corner of the desk, crossed her arms and cocked an eyebrow. "Do you think going to the library is wise?"

"Yes," I answered, trying to sound confident. "Work is the best thing for me now. I don't need to be there until noon, so I'm going to the hospital first."

Her expression softened as she placed a hand on my shoulder. "Of course you want to see him." She lifted her hand and smoothed my hair. "I'm worried about you—yesterday was a shock."

"Yeah, but I'm not the one who was shot. Stephen is the one hurt."

Abby released a long sigh. "I'm concerned about him, too, but you're my granddaughter—you're my primary concern. You might've been hurt."

Standing, I gave her a quick squeeze. "But I wasn't, and now I need to know why him."

A look of surprise flickered on Abby's face. "This isn't like you. I've never seen you willing to get involved in a situation like this."

A wry smile played at my lips as I thought of my words to Darci. "Maybe I'm trying to change."

Returning my smile, Abby patted the side of my face. "Not too much, I hope," she said. "I rather like you just the way you are."

## Six

I slipped my car into a parking space at Regional Medical Center and quickly opened the door. The hot morning air poured into the cool interior, and the sudden brightness had me shading my eyes. Only 10:00 A.M. and already heat shimmered in waves off the concrete lot. Grabbing my purse, I settled my sunglasses on my face and exited the car. I walked with purposeful steps past the heliport where the helicopter that had transported Stephen sat waiting for the next emergency. A couple of women dressed in navy scrubs milled around the emergency room entrance, while at the main entrance a car waited for a man who was being wheeled out the doors by a nurse.

I slowed my steps and tightened my grip on my purse as an unpleasant thought crossed my mind. *What would Bill say when I told him about Stephen's date book? Could he arrest me for withholding evidence?*

Entering the revolving doors, I shook my head to chase the thought away—Bill always threatened to arrest me. As I entered the hospital lobby, the smell of carnations, roses, and lilies from the gift shop near the information desk assaulted me.

Behind the desk sat a woman manning the phones. A wide gold bracelet winked in the artificial light as she picked up the receiver and lifted it to her ear. I heard her answer the caller in a crisp, polite tone. Walking up to the desk, I waited while the woman efficiently pressed buttons, transferring the call to the correct room.

"May I help you?" she asked, looking up at me.

"I'm here to see Stephen Larsen, please," I replied.

She ran a finger down the patient list and stopped. A frown wrinkled her brow. "Are you a family member?"

"Ah . . . " I hesitated for an instant while I debated about telling a lie, but since I've always been a rotten liar, I said, "No."

"Mr. Larsen is in the Cardiac Surgery Intensive Care Unit and only family members are allowed."

"I'm Ophelia Jensen and Stephen is a friend. May I speak with his doctors, then?" I pleaded.

Her face softened with sympathy. "I'm sorry, but that's not allowed either." She gave a quick glance over her shoulder and continued in a hushed voice. "We've had a lot of reporters asking questions."

"I understand, but could you at least tell me how he's doing?" I asked, giving it one more shot.

"All I can say is, at this time he's in critical but stable condition." She sounded as if she were delivering a canned statement.

My forehead wrinkled. "That's it?"

"I'm sorry," she answered with a nod.

Defeated, I spun on my heel and walked out the doors into the bright sunshine. Hoisting my shoulder strap higher, I paused and shoved my hands in my pocket. *Dang, dang, dang!* I'd really wanted to see Stephen for myself, but the guardians at the gate weren't going to let me. With the toe of my loafer, I nudged a small piece of gravel and pondered my next move. *You don't have one, Jensen.* Pursing my lips, I blew out a long breath and took a half step forward.

"Wait," someone called from behind me.

Turning, I saw a man dressed in a tan suit, with navy shirt and striped tie, running down the sidewalk toward me.

"Did you say you're a friend of Stephen Larsen's?" he asked.

Caught off-guard, I stuttered, "Yes."

The man came closer. "Did I hear you say you're Ophelia Jensen?"

Suspicious now, I eyed him cautiously. "Yes."

"Weren't you with him during the shooting?"

I shaded my eyes against the bright sun and looked over the man's shoulder. Right behind him stood a technician holding a video camera.

*Crap, a reporter!*

I stepped to the side in an effort to go around him. "No comment."

His steps mirrored mine and he blocked me. "What do you think happened? Was it an accident or attempted murder?"

"No comment," I replied, trying again to dodge him.

"Did Larsen say anything at the time of the shooting?"

His question stopped me, and I clutched my purse containing Stephen's date book tightly to my side as a light from the camera hit me in the eyes.

"Ah, ah, no," I stammered.

The reporter moved in and stuck a mike in my face. "How long have you known Larsen? What was he doing in Iowa?" he asked, firing off the questions.

"That's enough," a rough voice boomed from next to me as a hand grabbed my arm and began hustling me back toward the hospital.

"She said 'no comment,'" Bill called back to the reporter.

Once inside the building, he marched me past the woman at the desk. With a surprised look on her face, she watched Bill escort me down a hallway.

"I figured you'd show up this morning," he muttered as we made a left at the end of the hall.

"They won't let me see Stephen," I said, rushing to keep my steps even with Bill's. "The lady at the desk said he's critical but stable."

I felt Bill's hand on my arm tense.

"The bullet hit Larsen in the heart—"

My steps faltered. "The heart? How did he—"

"Live?" Bill finished the sentence for me. "The bullet didn't rip the heart, but acted like a plug and prevented him from bleeding to death." With a tug, we continued down the hallway.

"The surgeon repaired the hole, but during the surgery, Larsen aspirated fluid into his lungs, so now they're worried about pneumonia."

"Are you going to let me see him?" I asked.

His eyes darted my way. "You got two minutes, then you're going to answer some questions."

Oh, goody.

With a punch of his meaty hand, Bill hit the large button next to a double door and it whished open. Feelings of pain and suffering rushed out at me. I pulled back.

Dang—I'd been so focused on seeing Stephen that I hadn't thought about what it would be like visiting an intensive care unit. I hadn't taken the time to guard my senses, and they were now on full alert.

Bill gave me a puzzled look, but I ignored him and shut my eyes. Lowering my head, I envisioned a white shield surrounding me, a bubble of light that nothing could penetrate. When I felt it strengthen and hold, I opened my eyes and joined him.

Industrial carpeting led to a circular nurse's station complete with monitors and computers. The individual rooms all had double glass doors, and were positioned in a horseshoe shape around the station, so while sitting there one could observe all the patients.

I waited nervously while Bill approached a woman near the nurses' station, wearing a white coat and holding a clipboard. Jerking his head in my direction, they spoke softly for a couple of minutes. With a nod, he pivoted and came back to me.

"This way," he said, taking my arm and leading me to Stephen's cubicle.

Although I trusted my shield to block the sensations eddying through the unit, I still kept my head down as we walked past the rooms. I didn't want to risk it wavering. We stopped in front of a glass door. I raised my head.

Stephen lay like a marble statue atop a bed surrounded by medical equipment. Numerous wires and tubes led from the equipment to his still form. Standing in the doorway, I heard the soft whoosh of a pneumatic machine.

I approached the bed and pointed to the machine with a tube leading to Stephen's mouth. "What's that?" I asked

"A respirator. And the doctors have him highly medicated. They want him to stay as still as possible. No thrashing around."

As I asked my next question, I wasn't sure I wanted to hear the answer. "Will he make it?"

Bill shifted uncomfortably. "You know how doctors are . . . noncommittal. He's made it this far."

Stephen looked so alone and defenseless—his only company the machines, the only sound the whoosh of the respirator and the rhythmic beep of the monitors. Laying my hand on his arm, the tears gathered in my eyes and slid down my cheeks. With trembling fingers I flicked them away.

"Does he have any family?" I asked in a thick voice.

"We managed to track down his agent today. He said Larsen's mother is in France right now on a tour. He's trying to reach her. He also gave us the name of an assistant, Karen—"

"Burns." I finished his sentence. "Stephen mentioned her."

"Did he mention how to reach her? His agent gave us a number, but there's no answer."

Thinking of the book in my purse with Karen's number listed, I put a protective hand on the strap resting on my shoulder. "No," I replied honestly. It was the truth—Stephen hadn't given me her number or address—I'd found it. And no need to tell him I'd already tried the number and had the same result.

"Come on," Bill said, taking my arm again. "We have to leave now."

With a last glance over my shoulder, I allowed him to lead me from the room and down the hall to a door that said FAMILY. He motioned me inside.

My legs suddenly weary, I sank gratefully down onto one of the love seats. Bill seated himself on a chair at a right angle to mine.

"You seem calmer today, so I want to hear everything that happened from the moment you met Larsen," he said without preamble as he removed a notebook from his pocket.

With a sigh, I told the story again, more coherently this time, but leaving out the kiss. It had no bearing on Stephen's shooting.

" . . . I was trying to stop the blood seeping from the wound when Stephen asked me to take the book from his pocket—"

"What book?" Bill exclaimed, jumping to his feet.

"Ah, this one," I replied as I removed the Baggie from my purse and handed it to him.

He towered over me and his eyes drilled into mine. "Why didn't you tell me about this yesterday?"

"Um, I forgot all about it." I squirmed against the back of the love seat. "With all the excitement . . . "

Bill watched me with skepticism.

"Honest . . . I was in shock . . . I stuck the book in my pocket when they pulled me away from Stephen and didn't remember it until last night."

"Why didn't you call me then?" he asked, settling down on the love seat.

My teeth gripped my bottom lip for a second. "It was late?"

"That sounds like more of a question than an answer." He held up a hand when I opened my mouth to reply. "Never mind." Bill paused and rubbed his bald head absentmindedly. "I'm sure I already know the answer. Did you read it?"

Lowering my head, I stared at a spot on the floor. "Yes."

Based on his reaction when he learned I had the book, I wondered what he'd say if he knew I not only read it, but copied it. The thought gave me a chill.

Seconds ticked by in silence. Raising my head, I turned toward him. "There's not much in there. Just Stephen's schedule and some phone numbers." I stopped. "One thing I noticed—I think he either did, or planned to, talk to Antonio Vargas."

"Vargas? The family that lives on the old Murphy place?"

Since Bill's handcuffs still hung on his belt after my confession, I felt more at ease.

"Yes." I crossed my legs and laid an arm across the back of the love seat. "Isn't that odd? I mean . . . why would Stephen want to talk to Mr. Vargas? How did Stephen even learn of the Vargas family in the first place? Why—"

Bill shook a finger, stopping me. "That's enough, Ophelia," he said in a stern voice. "We've been through this before. Stay out of it."

Dropping my arm, I leaned forward. "But Bill, I could help," I argued. "Haven't my talents—"

He cut me off before I could finish. "Stop right there. I haven't decided what's up with this 'talent' of yours." He rubbed his head again. "I don't know if you really do have some kind of gift, or if it's just blind luck. You do seem to have the uncanny ability to—"

"But—" I tried interrupting him.

"I mean it, Ophelia. I won't have you blundering around in *this* investigation like you have in the past." He shoved his handkerchief in his pocket. "You're only going to put yourself in more danger."

More danger? I didn't like the sound of that.

"Stephen's the one in danger," I said. "Unless you think the shooting was an accident, someone tried to kill him," I pointed out reasonably.

"Maybe."

"What do you mean, 'maybe'? Stephen and I were alone— no one else was in the area when the shooting occurred."

"If this was attempted murder, some forethought had to go into it. If it was premeditated, the victim was selected and a plan set in motion." Bill sat forward, his book clutched in his hand. "You follow me so far?"

"Yes."

Looking down, he trailed a finger over the pages of his notebook. "You were facing away from the woods with your back toward the shooter. Larsen stepped around you right before you heard the shot."

"But—"

He snapped his notebook shut and stood. "I checked with Claire. Larsen was a surprise guest." Bill watched me with concern written on his face. "You weren't. Everyone expected you to be there."

# *Seven*

Driving back to Summerset, I stewed over Bill's words. Me? Did I have enemies? Well . . . yeah. Over the last couple of years I'd been pulled into several police investigations, but as far as I knew, all guilty parties were now safely locked away as guests of the prison system. Enough time hadn't elapsed for anyone to be paroled.

My mind flew back to Tink's kidnapping. It had been perpetrated by a woman who was a follower of Tink's crazy, and homicidal, Aunt Juliet. Winnie had totally bought into Juliet's fractured view of the world and of magick. Her plan had been to nab Tink, spring Juliet from the mental facility holding her, and resume their happy cult. Not very realistic on her part.

Were there any other former cult members carrying a grudge against me? I didn't know. They'd all seemed to fade into the shadows prior to the night Juliet tried to raise a demon. And the truth was, except for Winnie, I hadn't met any of them. If they were lurking about, I wouldn't have recognized them.

Anyone else? I ticked off the names of people I'd helped put in jail. Did they have families or friends looking for revenge? Maybe . . . anything's possible.

My thoughts brought me no comfort. In fact, if I didn't watch it, paranoia would become my new best friend.

The ringing of my cell phone broke into my unpleasant thoughts, and grateful for the distraction, I flipped it open.

"Hello."

"Jensen, sounds like you came close to losing your grip on that broom yesterday."

I almost dropped the phone in surprise. "Ethan . . . how did you—"

His low chuckle sounded in my ear. "I heard a news report about the shooting of some author near Summerset, Iowa. Knowing you, I figured you'd be involved, so I called Bill and he filled me in."

"Where are you? Are you going to be popping up in Summerset again?" I crossed my fingers as I asked the question. In spite of all our disagreements, Ethan believed in my talent—he'd help me figure out what was happening.

"The answer to your first question is, 'I can't tell you.' "

"Right. The undercover thing. My second question?"

"No." I heard the regret in his voice. "Not this time. I'm right in the middle of something."

A surprising pang of anxiety hit me. "Something dangerous?"

"Hey, Jensen, you almost sound like you care."

"Ah, well, I owe you. You helped me find Tink—"

Ethan laughed. "And almost received a reprimand as a result of our less than 'by the book' tactics."

"See what I mean . . . I owe you."

His voice grew serious. "No, I'm safe. This assignment is more tedious than dangerous, but that's all I can say about it. How about you? Are you going to stay out of trouble?"

His question hit too close to home. "I suppose Bill told you his crazy theory?"

"Yup. You don't agree?"

"No, it's nuts," I blustered. "I'm just a librarian. Who'd want to shoot me?"

"You mean other than Bill every now and again?" he asked with a laugh.

"Very funny." I frowned and gave a long sigh. "This is serious. Stephen might die." My words sounded bleak.

Silence at the other end lengthened, and for a moment I thought I'd lost our connection. When Ethan spoke, the teasing tone had disappeared from his voice. "I know you don't want to think someone took a bullet meant for you, but you need to consider the possibility."

"I have, and everyone who might hold a grudge is still in jail."

"Look, Ophelia, Bill's a good cop. If he thinks you might have been the target, you should listen to him—"

"It doesn't feel right," I said, cutting him off. "There's more to this. I sense Stephen was the shooter's quarry, and I was there for a reason . . . " I paused. " . . . but I haven't figured that part out yet."

Ethan's voice took on a hard edge. "Don't be stupid, Jensen. Don't rely on your talent to keep you safe."

"If I can't count on myself, who can I count on?" I shot back.

"I told you—Bill," he replied curtly.

My eyes narrowed and I felt my mouth settle into a stubborn line. It was pointless to argue. Regardless of Ethan's teasing, he was still a cop, and cops stick together.

"Is delivering a lecture the only reason you called?" I asked finally.

"I wanted to make sure you didn't do anything dumb."

"Well, thank you so much for your faith in my ability to take care of myself," I said sarcastically, and snapped the phone shut, disconnecting us.

I was still fuming when I reached the library twenty minutes later. Marching up the steps, I flung the door open.

The library was empty except for Darci. She took one look at my face and stepped away from the counter. "Forget that question. I was going to ask how you were, but I can see."

I slung my purse on the shelf under the counter and gave her a scathing look. "How am I? I'm tired of everyone treating me like I'm some kind of idiot. I'm tired of everyone hovering over me as if I can't take care of myself. I'm tired of no one listening to me."

"All righty then," she said with a bright smile, and scooped up a pile of books. "I think I'll just return these to the shelves now."

"I'm sorry," I said with a shake of my head. "It's been a frustrating morning."

"No sweat," she replied, placing the books back on the counter. "Do I dare ask *who's* not listening to you?"

With a deep breath, I tried to compose myself as my eyes traveled around the room that had been my home away from home for the last several years. A mobile that local students had made during National Library Week spun gently, while the new air conditioner hummed quietly in the background. Rows and rows of neatly arranged books filled the old building, and I felt a sense of pride at what I'd accomplished since moving to Summerset.

The place had been falling apart. The roof leaked. The beautiful wood plank floors were covered with ugly rust carpeting. It was drafty in the wintertime and roasting in the summer.

I'd worked hard, and so had the community, to restore the character of the old building. We now had a library everyone could be proud of, and every year we had more and more books checked out.

*Contrary to what Bill and Ethan might think—I wasn't an idiot. I'm good at a lot of things, and being a psychic was one of them,* I told myself.

Feeling better, I turned to Darci and quickly related the morning's events.

"Wow," she said thoughtfully when I was finished. "You don't think there's a chance—"

"No," I interrupted, "Bill and Ethan are both wrong. I

*know* it. Whoever pulled that trigger wanted Stephen dead. I just don't know why or who yet."

Darci didn't answer, and I saw the doubt in her eyes. Disheartened, my short-lived confidence faded and my shoulders sagged. "You don't believe me either."

"It's not that," she replied kindly, "but let's be honest . . . your visions haven't always been on target."

"I read the signs wrong."

"Are you sure you're reading them right this time?"

"Yes, and I'll prove it." I clenched my hands at my sides. "There's some kind of connection between Stephen and me. And whatever that connection is, it's going to lead me to who shot him and why."

Darci leaned against the counter. "How do you intend to do that? Use the runes? They won't convince Bill and Ethan."

"I know. I'm going back to the vineyard after work. After school, Tink's helping Abby at the greenhouse. I'll have time to run out there then." I snapped my fingers. "I'll call Claire and ask her for a copy of the guest list. See if someone had a connection to Stephen."

"She'll tell Bill."

I flounced away from behind the counter and headed for the stairs leading to my office. "So? I don't care. He can't arrest me for asking for a list."

"Humph," Darci snorted. "Bill said last time he had a jail cell with your name on it. What if he decides to put you in protective custody?"

I turned at the top of the stairs and faced her. "He can't without just cause."

Darci rolled her eyes and glanced up at the ceiling. "You need to be careful."

I laughed. Darci telling me to be careful? What a switch. Thanks to some of her brilliant ideas, we'd rifled files, snooped through offices, been chased by killers, and been locked in a magician's box at gunpoint.

Her cheeks turned a faint pink as if she read my mind. "You know what I mean," she defended herself. "You've had a rough time of it lately. What if your abilities are a little off-track as a result?"

My eyes widened in surprise. Her words mirrored the same thoughts I'd had last night.

Sensing an advantage, Darci took a step toward me. "I want you to think about something before you rush off to prove that you're right. You're willing to risk your own safety, but are you willing to risk Tink's and Abby's?"

Darci stayed at the counter while I caught up on paperwork in my basement office. Alone with my thoughts, I tried to concentrate on ordering books. The words and cover pictures swam before my eyes, and a task I normally enjoyed failed to hold my attention.

My gaze caught the photo of Abby and Tink, smiling at me from the corner of my desk, and my mind wandered to Darci's question. My answer was no. I'd do whatever necessary to protect them. If I pursued my "hunch," would my actions place them in danger? Possibly. But if Bill's theory was correct, and someone wanted me dead, they might be at risk under those circumstances, too. *What was it called? Oh yeah, collateral damage. Inadvertent casualties.* The thought was unacceptable to me.

Pushing myself back in my chair, I gave up reading the catalogs. Maybe it would be better if I took a vacation and left town. Could Abby hunt me down using her psychic talents? Nope. Remote tracking hadn't worked that well when we were trying to find Tink, but knowing Abby, she'd give it her best shot. I'd already mentioned to Abby that I wanted to know why Stephen.

What if I changed my tactics? Went back to acting like the "old" Ophelia—the one who had to be dragged into a mess like this kicking and screaming. I'd pretend that I had no intention of being involved, keep them in the dark about any potential danger to me. Say nothing about any dreams, premonitions, rune warnings, etc. Neither one of them knew I felt a strong connection with Stephen. It might work.

I slapped my forehead. Darci—I'd already shot my mouth off to her about what I intended to do, and she knew about my dreams. If she thought I was up to something, she'd go straight to Abby with her concerns. I'd have to fix that. I'd use the same approach with her as I planned with Abby. I'd tell her she was right, that I'd reacted out of stress.

*Come on, Jensen, Darci's no dummy.* I scratched my head. *Okay, so I'd wing it when the time came.*

I leaned forward, picked up a pen and doodled on my order form. Exactly what were my options? I felt deep inside that staying out of the investigation wasn't one of them. If my instincts were correct, I was being led down some preordained path to, at this time, a murky conclusion. One choice would be to pursue what few leads I had and *get* in trouble. I wrote the word *trouble* and underlined it.

Or, if Bill was right and I was the intended victim, unless he put me in protective custody, he couldn't watch me 24/7. I'd be waiting for the killer to come after me and *be* in trouble. I wrote *trouble* again.

I stared down at the order form. *Hmm, trouble versus trouble.* Either way I was screwed. So which approach did I take? Offensive or defensive? The answer hinged on how much faith I had in my ability to find a solution. Bill blew off my ideas, Ethan doubted me, and even Darci was skeptical. I wouldn't be getting any support from them, and I couldn't risk asking Abby or Tink for help. I'd be on my own.

*Did I have enough strength to see me through?*

*Yes.*

I picked up the phone and dialed Claire.

# Eight

Claire picked up on the second ring. "Hi, Claire—Ophelia."

"Ophelia." She sounded pleased. "I've been meaning to call you today. How are you?"

"I'm fine." I picked up my pen and began to draw little stars around the first *trouble* written on the order form.

"Have you heard anything about Stephen Larsen's condition?" Claire asked.

"I drove to the hospital this morning before work—" I hesitated, remembering the pat line the receptionist had given me. "He's in critical but stable condition."

Claire sighed deeply. "I feel terrible about what happened, and I'm worried about how this will affect our fund-raising efforts."

"Claire," I replied in a shocked voice. "A man's lying in the hospital, and you're worried about *bad press*?"

"Yes, I'm concerned about bad press. Recently, a new employee kidnapped your daughter, now an author is shot at our fund-raiser," she chided. "Let's be honest . . . that's not the kind of attention we want for our library."

"No, of course not, but the two incidents were unrelated," I argued as I moved to the second *trouble* and continued making stars. "The shooting could have been an accident. And with Tink's kidnapping, it was a case of something out of the past coming back to haunt us. No one had control over either situation."

"True," she replied cautiously.

"I really wouldn't worry about it, Claire. You know how small towns are," I said, my pen flying over the paper as I scribbled more and more stars. "People will forget about what happened as soon as the next scandal comes along."

*Here's hoping I'm right.*

I could almost hear Claire turning my words over in her mind.

"That's a valid statement. No sense in anticipating trouble," she finally replied.

I looked down at the words *trouble,* with stars circling around them, and stifled a snort.

*Nope . . . no sense looking for it when it seems to come looking for you.* I cleared my throat. *Time to cut to the chase, Jensen.*

Shoving out of my chair, I stood and walked around the corner of my desk. "The reason I called—may I have a copy of the guest list?"

Claire hesitated. "Why?"

"Um, well . . . " My voice trailed away as I began to pace the floor. *Dang, I hadn't thought this through. Why did I want the guest list?* Inspiration flashed and I froze. "Thank-you notes," I blurted out as I crossed my fingers.

"Thank-you notes?"

"Yes," I answered, and resumed my pacing. "Even though the day ended badly, shouldn't we still thank everyone who attended?"

"Well, yes . . . " She paused. "But how are you going to address the shooting?"

"I won't. Everyone knows what happened. I'll simply say something like. 'Thank you so much for your support.'" I talked faster. "It will be a good project for me. Help distract me."

"Okay," she said reluctantly. "A handwritten note is always a nice touch . . . but I'll take care of the note to Chuck Krause. He came at my specific invitation. Hmm, good idea," she murmured more to herself than me. "A personal note from me will show there are no hard feelings."

"Hard feelings?"

"You didn't meet him, did you?" she mused. "In all the excitement, I didn't have a chance to introduce you to Chuck. He's running for state representative in the next election, and we had a very heated discussion concerning his politics."

"A tall man with blond hair?" I asked, remembering the man I'd seen Claire give "the look."

"That's him. Chuck was born and raised in California, but he moved here when he married Jolene. Did you meet him?"

"No, but I noticed you talking with him. I take it his views are conservative?"

"In some ways. You'd think someone from California would be more liberal. He's taking a hard line on crime prevention, but I mainly disagree with his views concerning undocumented immigrants."

I didn't get it. "Undocumented immigrants?"

"Illegal aliens," she explained, "but that's not a politically correct term."

"I see."

"I like Chuck," she said, warming up to the subject, "but he doesn't see the big picture. He thinks it can be addressed at a state level. He wants a deportation crackdown, to cut state spending on educational programs"—she continued to rattle off a list of Krause's policies—"to penalize employers who knowingly hire undocumented workers, make it harder for low income—which these people are—to receive public services."

"Well, those programs do spend tax dollars," I answered, crossing back to my desk and sitting. "And if he grew up in California, that state—"

"These people pay taxes, too—sales tax, for one," she interjected, cutting me off. "And if they have a false Social Security number and work for an employer, they pay not only federal and state taxes, but Medicare and Social Security." Claire caught her breath. "There are billions that they've paid in, but that will never be claimed because of their legal status."

Picking up my pen, I tapped it on the edge of my desk. "That's interesting, but you know how nonpolitical I am. I don't keep up on these things."

"Ophelia," she said in a frosty voice, as I imagined her peering at the phone over the top of her glasses, "how can you make an informed decision at the polls if you don't keep abreast of the issues?"

She had me on that one.

"Well, ah, I . . . " I stuttered.

Claire ignored my mumbling. "The status of undocumented workers needs to be addressed on both a national and international level." Her voice rose in excitement. "And between the countries engaged in the fair trade agreements . . . "

My eyes glazed over listening to her as I tried to think of a graceful way to end the conversation. Claire would keep me on the phone for hours expounding her political views.

" . . . then there are the corporations that actually lure immigrant workers to this country with flyers promising jobs. Once here, without documents, these people have no voice. They—"

"Gee, Claire, sorry to cut you off," I interrupted, "but I'm down in my office and someone's at the door." I rapped a couple of times on the corner of my desk. "I'll pick up the guest list later and get right to work on those thank-yous."

I groaned after hanging up. I felt guilty lying to Claire, but while she might be focused on an upcoming election, I had more weighty matters on my mind . . . like attempted murder. I appreciated Claire's passion—people like her changed the world.

All I wanted to do was save mine.


At four o'clock I ventured out of my office and upstairs. Darci stood at the counter, looking bored.

"Slow day?" I asked, crossing to her.

"Yeah," she replied with a toss of her head. "I think it's too hot for people to venture out today. Did you know school was let out early?"

My thoughts flew to Tink. Did she ride the bus out to Abby's? Another pang of guilt hit me: What kind of mother was I? I didn't even know where my kid was.

I grabbed the phone from behind the counter and called Abby.

"Abby's Greenhouse," Tink answered.

A hand flew to my chest. "Good. Darci just told me that school was dismissed early, and I—"

"Ophelia," Tink interrupted with a tinge of exasperation. "You've got to quit worrying. I'm okay. I rode the bus like I was supposed to."

"Okay, okay," I replied, trying to hide my relief. "How's it going?"

"Hot." She sounded grumpy. "Abby had me repotting plants all afternoon."

"How was your first day of school?"

"All right . . . Mrs. Olson gave us homework. Can you believe it? The first day of school and she assigns an essay."

I gave a low chuckle. "You're in ninth grade now. Your teachers are starting to prepare you for what it will be like when you go to college."

A tiny feeling of loss squeezed my heart as I said the words. Tink had been in my life such a short time, and already we were planning for the day when she'd be on her own.

Her voice in my ear broke the spell. "I don't care what they're trying to do, it's still not fair."

"Is the essay going to be hard?"

"Ha," she said with snort. "It's one of those stupid 'how was your summer' things." She giggled in my ear. "Think I should write about Gert and Winnie?"

"Ah, probably not," I answered with a shake of my head.

The kid amazed me. She was held captive for a week, yet had never been afraid. When we finally found her, she was more annoyed at Gert and Winnie than anything else. Her total lack of fear was just one more reason that I needed to keep her out of the current situation.

"You're right, I guess," she said. "I'll write something about working at the greenhouse." She paused. "What time will you pick me up?"

"Um . . . I've a few errands to run, so it will—"

"What kind of errands?" she asked, breaking in.

*Great, another lie. I sure seemed to telling a lot of those today.*

"Oh you know, get groceries, stop by Claire's, that kind of thing."

"I was going to ask if I could go with you, but forget that if you're going to Mrs. Canyon's. You'll be there for hours," she groused.

"I promise I won't be long."

"Aw, that's okay," she said, her tone abruptly changing. "After we close, Abby's going to show me the journals."

Ah yes, "the journals"—private diaries kept by the women in my family for over a hundred years. They held spells, incantations, folk remedies—things my ancestors had used while living in the mountains of Appalachia.

"That's fine, but don't be getting any big ideas," I warned. "Remember—"

" 'Don't conjure what you can't banish.' Like I haven't heard that before."

In my mind, I could almost see Tink rolling her eyes as she said it.

"Exactly."

"Hey, speaking of conjuring, I've been thinking about yesterday, and—"

*Nope, couldn't let the conversation go there.* "Hey, I've got some work I need to finish before closing," I said in a rush, not letting her finish, "so I need to go. We'll talk later."

"Okay, see ya—love ya."

"Love you, too."

I turned to see Darci watching me with a bemused expression. "Tink busy at Abby's?"

"Yeah," I said with a laugh. "And she's ticked that she's got homework tonight."

"The teachers don't waste much time, do they?"

"No, they don't . . . " *Here was my chance to do a little of my own damage control.* "About Tink and our early conversation—"

Darci arched an eyebrow. "You mean the one where you stated, 'I'm right and I'm going to prove it'?"

"Ah, yeah, that one." I looked down and fiddled with a button on my jacket. "My words were rash. I'd never do anything that might place Tink or Abby in jeopardy."

Darci placed a hand on my arm, and I raised my eyes. "I didn't mean to imply that you would," she said softly.

"I know . . . as I said, my words were rash, and I'm sure a result of Bill and Ethan's attitude. At times it's frustrating." I glanced down, then back up at Darci with a bright smile. "Bill's good at his job. He'll get to the bottom of Stephen's shooting without any help from me."

"Hmmm." Darci tapped her chin with one finger. "While you were in your office, I thought about your dreams, the shooting, and did a little thinking."

"Yeah?" *Knowing Darci's creative mind—this ought to be good.*

"Yeah, I'm not a psychic, but maybe the dreams were only a sign that you'd meet him. Your dreams never indicated any danger, did they?"

I thought about my dream last night and told another lie. "No."

"Maybe the reason you didn't sense any trouble is because what happened has nothing to do with your connection to Stephen."

I nodded my head wisely. "You know, you're probably right," I replied, once again lying through my teeth. "I'm placing way too much emphasis on that connection." I held a finger in the air. "Which is another good reason for me to stay out of the investigation."

"You really think I might be right?" Darci's eyes sparkled.

"Yes," I answered, trying to sound convincing.

"Great." She turned toward the clock hanging on the far wall. "Would you mind if I left early?"

I shrugged. "Might as well. I can close up by myself."

She hustled behind the counter and grabbed her bag. "I've got a date with Jimmy McGuire tonight."

Shaking my head, I watched her hurry to the door and, with a quick wiggle of her fingers at me, disappear outside.

Crossing to the top of the stairs, I flipped the switch, shutting off the basement lights. Darci was amazing—she went through men like Kleenex, but always managed to keep them as friends. She also had a very astute mind.

Did she buy into my lies?

Gosh, I hoped so.

# *Nine*

The sun had begun its downward slide toward the western horizon by the time I left the library, but it was still hot. After throwing my linen jacket in the backseat, I headed for the winery. The shadows seemed to lengthen across the blacktop as I sped down the road. And even though the air conditioner was cranked on high, the heat had my light blouse sticking to my back.

I turned right onto a gravel road that was no more than a path, and into the winery parking lot. A large building holding the reception room and gift shop sat in front of me. Yesterday large crowds had gathered on its wide deck and lawn, but today it was empty. After leaving the car, I was moving toward the steps leading to the entrance when out of the corner of my eye I spied an employee working on the vines. With one foot on the step, I stopped and watched.

The man wore a denim shirt, blue jeans, and a sweat-stained straw hat. Leaning close to the vine, he pruned away some of the leaves hiding the thick clusters of grapes. His clippers paused and he turned, his brown eyes meeting mine across the distance. They flashed with recognition, while suspicion settled on a face wrinkled by too many hours in the hot sun.

Antonio Vargas.

It seemed the perfect time to question him about Stephen. But what would I say? I stepped down, hesitating.

His eyes shifted once more to the vines and he turned his back to me. The moment was lost.

I proceeded up the stairs, and in the gift shop crossed the floor to the young woman behind the counter. The shelves behind her held row upon row of bottled wine gleaming in the late afternoon sun. And wicker gift baskets holding wine and fluted glasses nestled in shredded paper were artfully arranged around the cash register.

"Hi, may I help you?" she asked brightly.

"Yes, I'm looking for Ron Mark."

"I think he was headed to the old church," she said with a smile.

"Church? I didn't know there was a church on the property."

"It's behind the grove of trees to your left as you turn off the main road into the winery."

"Oh."

"It's not far," she said, pointing toward the door. "You can probably find him there. Across the parking lot there's a path behind the trees leading off to the left."

"Okay," I replied, returning her smile.

Once outside, I saw that Mr. Vargas was gone—the vineyard was empty. Taking the path the young woman had indicated led me into the woods across the gravel drive from the vineyard.

Wait a minute, I thought stopping. Wasn't this the same direction Stephen and I had walked yesterday? Would this path lead me to the spot where he'd been shot, only from behind the trees instead of in front of them, where we'd been standing?

Walking down the path, I soon had my answer. Waving up ahead, tied off to the trees, bright yellow crime scene tape marked off the area. I felt my curiosity pull me toward the spot.

*Boy, I'd love to duck under that tape and see what I might find.*

I quickly banished that idea.

*Hey, I'm a psychic, remember? I didn't have to be standing right on the spot to try and sense something.*

Cautiously, I approached the tape and took a deep breath. Shutting my eyes, I envisioned the earth's energy coursing beneath me. I felt its power ease through the ground into the soles of my feet. It edged its way past my ankles into the calves of my legs, up my body, into my torso, until finally I felt the energy pool in the center of my forehead—my third eye. Slowly, I lowered the shield guarding my mind. Images of yesterday flickered there, as if I were watching Stephen and me starring in our own private movie.

I winced as the vision of Stephen's kiss stirred me.

*No, don't focus on that. Focus on the trees behind him.*

The image shifted as if the camera in my head panned the woods. Crows took flight, and for an instant the sun hit the cold glint of metal glimmering just out of reach of the shadows. My body jumped at the crack of gunfire and the picture disappeared.

Opening my eyes, my arms tingled as if hit by a mild shock as the power seeped downward and back into the earth, leaving me. I shook out my hands and inhaled a cleansing breath.

So now I had an idea where the shooter stood. But no face, no sense of his emotions, had filtered through. And I had no motive.

Still shaken by the experience, and off balance, I took a step forward, and the back of my neck quivered. I stopped and whirled around with a feeling someone stood behind me.

Nothing. Only a swarm of gnats drifting in and out of the shade. Must be a little residual energy still playing with my senses, I thought. I took an unsteady gasp and batted at my hair before continuing down the path. Rounding the corner,

I saw a tall old-fashioned steeple rising above the trees. A little farther down the trail, I came out of the grove of trees into a tiny clearing and stood in front of the old church.

Gaping holes marred the faded red-tiled roof and new boards covered the plain square windows. The building had a sad, shuttered look. Its clapboards were aged gray, and in places appeared charred. A stillness wrapped around the church like mourning clothes.

*Something bad happened here.*

It flashed in my head, and without warning, flames flickered in my mind. And with them came a sense of anger, hate, intolerance. I felt my face grow warm as if I stood too close to a bonfire. Stepping back, the smell of smoke seemed to surround me. I heard the cries of women and the wail of children.

I scrunched my eyes, and rubbing my forehead, tried to wipe away the scene. The acrid odor faded while the sounds died away. Opening my eyes, all was as it had been.

Whatever had happened in this quiet glen happened long ago, but the pain of the event still lingered, like a memory too terrible to forget. A heaviness settled in the pit of my stomach, and my throat tightened with sympathy for those who had suffered.

*No, I couldn't let the past deter me from why I was here.*

Stretching my arms wide, I tried to find my center, my core, and allow peace to fill me. And as I did, I raised the shield around my senses that I'd so foolishly forgotten to reinforce after my attempt to "see" Stephen's assailant. The heavy feeling eased and my throat loosened.

Calmer, I approached the new steps leading to the wide double doors as a squirrel chattered at me from a branch hanging low over the roof. One door was opened a crack, and I cautiously pressed it wider.

"Hello? Anyone here?" My voice echoed in the empty sanctuary.

I crossed the threshold and peered in. Fading sunlight

shone down from the holes in the roof, dimly lighting the church. Long benches covered with ghostly white tarps sat along the wall, out of the light. A pile of discarded water bottles and food wrappers sat on top of a moth-eaten blanket to my left. Another white tarp draped over what I presumed was the altar marked the back of the church. On either side, swags of thick, dusty cobwebs hung from the corners. From behind the altar I heard the sound of rustling in the dried leaves littering the floor.

Mice, or at least I hoped it was mice and not something bigger. Like a rat. I shivered.

I took a step forward, and at the same time a loud crunch reverberated through the room. Startled, I pulled back and looked down. What seemed like hundreds of acorns lay scattered amid the leaves. I nudged away the debris with the toe of my loafer. Starting forward again, a sudden hand on my shoulder brought me up short.

With a shriek, I spun around to see the owner of the winery, Ron Mark, standing behind me.

"My God, you scared me," I exclaimed.

"Sorry, I didn't mean to startle you," he replied. "Are you okay?"

"Yeah." I swallowed nervously as I inched a step backward.

"Shannon said you wanted to talk with me."

"Ah, yes," I said with another step back.

"Aren't you the woman who was with Stephen Larsen yesterday?"

I nodded, with a nervous glance around the church. "Who built this place?"

"A group of immigrants from Hungary in the late 1860s," he answered, turning his head while his eyes roamed the old building. "They were a devout religious sect that never allowed themselves to be assimilated into the community. And . . . " His eyes met mine. " . . . the first ones to cultivate grapes in this part of the state."

"What happened here?"

"The outbreak of World War One. Tensions ran high and everyone who had ties to the Central Powers were suspected sympathizers." He shook his head sadly. "Not only were these people of Hungarian descent, their neighbors believed they had Gypsy ties." Walking past me, he headed toward the shrouded altar and turned. "One night, in the summer of 1917, this church mysteriously caught fire."

"Arson?"

Shoving his hands in his back pockets, he nodded. "Yeah, and about the same time, some of the families had their crops destroyed, their wells poisoned, and their livestock stolen."

"All because of their ethnic background?"

Again he nodded. "When we bought this place, we found a diary in an old house we tore down. The woman who kept the diary wrote that everyone had vowed to rebuild."

"Did they?"

"No, they never got the chance. The Spanish flu pandemic started in 1918, and whomever it didn't kill, either moved away or was finally absorbed into the community."

"What people don't understand, they destroy," I murmured to myself.

"What?"

"Nothing," I replied while making a 360 turn. "What are you going to do with this old building?"

"Restore it. We've already started." He pointed to the pile of trash. "The crew Krause recommended isn't good about cleaning up, but they're fast."

"You know Chuck Krause?" I asked, surprised to hear that name twice in the same day.

"A little . . . His aide used to work for me," he answered with a puzzled look. "And before Chuck entered politics, he was in the building trade, and still has a lot of connections. Why? Do you know Chuck, too?"

I focused on the acorns at my feet. "No. I just heard someone else mention his name today."

"I imagine people all over the state will be talking about him before this campaign is over. He has big plans."

"So I heard." My eyes traveled over the old plaster walls. "When will you be finished?"

"Another four months," he said with a big smile. "We're planning on using it for Christmas celebrations, like choral events, weddings. That type of thing. It's going to be very folksy and old-fashioned."

I could envision the old church draped with boughs of evergreen and holly. It would be lovely once again. And maybe the building being used for something positive would banish the old memory of what once happened there.

"I'm sure it will be beautiful," I said, grinning back at him.

His smile suddenly faded. "I have a question for you— why are you here?"

I jumped right in. "Do you know Stephen?"

Surprise widened his eyes. "No, as I told Sheriff Wilson yesterday—I'd never met the man before in my life."

"Did he mention why he was here?"

"No. We talked briefly about the wine industry in Iowa. He was very interested in the production angle—how many workers it took to run an operation like this, what kind of skilled labor I used, that type of thing. When he mentioned he was writing a book, I presumed it would be one of those 'coffee table' type books." In the dim light, I saw his eyes narrow. "If you're his friend, don't you know all of this?"

On the spot, I squirmed. "We're not actually friends—I'd only met him myself yesterday, but after witnessing what happened, I'm . . . " My voice trailed away.

"Curious?"

"Sort of."

"I understand, but don't you think questioning people is better left to Sheriff Wilson?"

"Yes, but Stephen asked me to contact his assistant, and I'd like to be able to give her some answers."

That reply was kind of true.

Ron crossed his arms and stared at me. "I thought Larsen was in a coma. When did he ask you for this favor?"

"Um, well, right after the shooting, before the ambulance transported him to the helicopter."

I felt him shut down as he cast a hurried glance at his watch. "I need to get back to the main house. We've an event scheduled—a fund-raiser—for this evening." He motioned toward the wide double doors. "Why don't you let me walk you back to your car?"

The conversation about Stephen was finished.

Taking my arm, he began to lead me out of the church. We'd taken three steps when we heard a crack from above. Startled, we both looked up in time to see tile hurtling down from a hole in the ceiling. Ron yanked my arm and shoved me toward the entrance of the church.

Behind me, the tile crashed to the floor and the air filled with dust as he hustled me out. Standing in the safety of the doorway, I looked over my shoulder to see broken chunks of old red tile lying right where I'd been standing.

# Ten

Tight-lipped, and not very talkative, Ron escorted me back to my car. The only statements he made were, "Are you hurt?" and, "I'm blocking that area off to visitors." The rest of the communication hinged on body language, and by the way he stiffly marched me down the path, I didn't think I'd be welcome back to the winery anytime soon. After all, who wants a woman around who only seems to bring trouble?

On the drive to Abby's, I tried to reach Karen Burns again. My fingers trembled and I felt my right eyelid twitching as I dialed her number.

Again—no answer. It was just as well. After the tile incident, I really wasn't up to questioning some stranger.

I pulled into the long driveway leading to Abby's house and stopped.

"If you're going to run a bluff, Jensen, you'd better get control," I muttered to myself.

I just sat there for a minute looking toward the house.

To my left sat Abby's vegetable plots. In spite of the recent hot weather, all the plants flourished. Stems, holding red ripe tomatoes, bent low to the ground, while pumpkin, muskmelon, and squash vines snaked across the ground a few feet away. And the watermelon vines—I caught myself smiling in my rearview mirror.

Abby's watermelons were known throughout the county as being the best . . . and the most desirable to snitch in the middle of a hot summer's night. Light green with dark green stripes, at maturity these melons weighed almost thirty pounds. A young thief not only had to be fast, but strong, to run with a couple of thirty pound melons tucked under his arms. Every year Abby always allowed a few melons to be taken, but when she'd had enough, little blue bags with sunflower seeds sown inside would appear hanging from the fence posts, a spell to ward off trespassers that she'd learned in the mountains. After that, no watermelons disappeared in the middle of the night.

Abby's large white farmhouse sat at the end of the lane. Her wide porch with its swing invoked childhood memories of nights catching lightning bugs and letting them go; drinking tall glasses of cold lemonade on a hot summer's day; putting on my bathing suit and darting in and out of a sprinkler while Abby and Grandpa sat on the swing watching and laughing.

I draw strength from this place, I thought, and felt that strength fill me.

I drove the rest of the way to the house and parked. As I walked up to the wide steps leading to the porch, I heard the rat-a-tat-tat of Abby's sprinkler and the call of a meadow lark. I'd turned to see if I could spot the bird when the front door flew open and Tink came tearing down the sidewalk with T.P., her puppy, scampering after her. She'd changed into navy cutoffs and a navy T-shirt after school, and wore her much-loved pink baseball cap. Her blond ponytail bounced as she ran.

Lady followed at a more sedate pace.

With violet eyes wide, Tink ran up to me and grabbed my arm. "It was sooo cool," she exclaimed. "Abby let me witch for water."

T.P., picking up Tink's excitement, ran circles around us, yipping and barking.

"T.P., hush," I said sternly.

Lady sat calmly on the sidewalk and gave me a look that said, *Good luck with that one.*

"Oh yeah," she said with a glance toward the dogs, "Abby and I drove over and picked them up."

Tugging me up the sidewalk, Tink skipped along. "She showed me how to make a dowsing rod out of willow." She stopped to catch her breath. "And guess what, I found the old well out by the summer house. I didn't even know it was there."

"That's terrific, Tink." Laughing, I let her lead me through the doorway and down the hall into the kitchen.

The crystals on the windowsill caught the light of the dying sun and made rainbows across the oak floor as Abby stood in front of the old wood-burning stove mashing potatoes. She stopped for a moment and stirred the gravy simmering on the burner next to the pot of potatoes. On the counter to her left sat a big platter of fried chicken. A loaf of fresh baked bread, with a crock of sweet butter, had already been placed on the scarred wooden table.

"Hey, something smells good." I crossed to her and gave her a light kiss on the cheek.

My stomach chose that time to give a low rumble.

With a chuckle, Abby smiled and brushed a silver tendril out of her eyes. "Would you like to stay for supper?"

The twinkle in her eye told me she already knew the answer.

"Sure, better than the frozen pizza at home, huh, Tink?" I called while moving to the cupboards to get three plates and three glasses.

Tink came up beside me and, pulling open a drawer, took out silverware.

I shot a look over my shoulder at Abby. "Dowsing?"

Giving Tink a fond glance, she picked up the platter of chicken and carried it to the table. "She can't get in trouble with that skill," she replied, placing the chicken next to the bread. "And it's a good lesson in sensing the rhythms of the earth."

"And I did good, didn't I, Abby?" Tink asked with pride.

"Yes, my dear, you did." She returned to the stove and took up the mashed potatoes and gravy while I laid out the plates and glasses.

"That's great, Tink," I said, putting a hand on her shoulder as she set the silverware on the table. "I was never any good at it."

"You lacked patience, Ophelia," Abby said. Crossing to the table with the bowls, she stole a sideways glance at Tink. "Take off your hat, dear."

"I didn't," Tink said to me, referring to my lack of patience. "I walked really, really slow until I felt the willow branch tremble in my hands. It was awesome . . . " She paused and turned her fists down as if pulled by an invisible force. "I was dead on the spot," she finished with a little swagger.

Abby caught the swagger and arched an eyebrow. "Tink," she gently chided, "what did I tell you about the power?"

Tink's cockiness fell away. "It isn't mine—I'm only the instrument."

I hid my smirk. *Jeez, how many times had I heard that statement growing up? It was one of Abby's favorites.*

I pulled out a chair for Abby, then Tink and I took our seats at the table, too. "How did you like the journals?" I asked, placing my napkin on my lap.

Tink's fork stopped in midair. "Oh, wow! I read some really weird stuff. One said to mix pulverized rabbit droppings"—she let out a giggle—"with bran and feed it to your chickens. It makes them lay lots and lots of eggs."

"Works, too," Abby said with a wink.

"Yuck." Tink shoved a forkful of food in her mouth. "If I had to do that, I'd rather not have so many eggs," she mumbled with her mouth full.

"Swallow, dear, before speaking," Abby said gently, and filled Tink's glass from the pitcher of ice water already on the table. "When I was a girl, the egg money bought food that we couldn't grow. More eggs—more food."

"Hmm." Tink cocked her head thoughtfully. "So I should be thankful we don't have to do that, right?"

Abby patted her hand and smiled. "Yes, you should."

For a few moments the only sound was the clink of our silverware on the stoneware plates as we dug into Abby's excellent meal.

"What happened today?" Abby asked, breaking the lull.

I almost dropped my fork at her sudden question. Did she sense something, or was it normal curiosity? Had Darci talked to her?

I laid my fork down and folded my hands in my lap in case they twitched. "Stephen's in critical condition and the doctors are worried about pneumonia. I ran into Bill, but he's as closed-mouth as ever about the investigation."

My concise report wasn't everything that happened, but omission wasn't lying, was it?

Abby sipped her water. "Do you intend to carry through with your plan?"

Tink perked up in her chair. "What plan?"

I felt my mouth tense. "I had this crazy idea that I'd approach this as a psychic."

"Cool—can I help?"

"No," Abby and I replied simultaneously.

Tink's face fell. "Shoot. Why not?"

"Tink, dear, you're a medium, and although you're coming along nicely in your training, the skill needed is clairvoyance."

"I can talk to the spirits," she argued, settling back in her chair. "They might give me clues, and I bet Mr. Larsen has family that's passed over. I could try and reach one of them."

Abby shook her head. "I know you want to help, but that's not a good idea. Ophelia needs to handle it—she needs to prove to herself that she can do it."

Wise woman, my grandmother, which made me feel crappy for what I said next.

"I've changed my mind, Abby." I kept my head down.

Out of the corner of my eye I saw her push her plate back. "You seemed so determined this morning."

"I've had second thoughts," I replied, looking straight at her, hoping my face didn't give me away. "How often have you witnessed an event without there being some great cosmic plan to involve you?"

Abby studied me carefully. "Many times. As I told you last night, there are situations beyond our control. We've all had to accept that. We do what we can—when we can."

"Abby," I said with a bright smile, "that's excellent advice." Under the table, for the second time that day, I crossed my fingers as I told another lie.

# Eleven

Tink was unusually quiet on the way home. It didn't bode well for me—it meant she was thinking something up.

"You don't have much to say," I commented, stealing a glance her way and turning the radio down. "What's up?"

She tugged her baseball cap lower on her forehead and slumped in the seat. "Nothing."

"Okay," I replied cheerfully, and reached for the radio dial, intending to turn the volume louder.

"All right, all right, I'll tell you," she said in a rush, as if I'd been using a rubber hose on her. "I don't see why everyone else can use their gift and I can't."

"'Cause you're a kid," I said, smiling, "and you're still learning how to control your abilities."

"Ha—Aunt Dot," she replied, referring to my great-aunt who'd recently paid us a very memorable visit, "said Great-Aunt Mary started contacting the spirits when she was only ten. I'm almost fourteen now." She held up a hand and spread her fingers wide. "I'm three years older than she was."

"That may be, Tink, but I don't know if I'd start quoting Aunt Dot if I were you." I gave her another glance. "Remember, she claims she also talks to fairies."

Tink crossed her arms. "How do you know she doesn't?"

That was the problem when it came to Aunt Dot—I

didn't. When Dot first showed up for her visit, I'd scoffed at her ramblings about her fairies. But after everything that happened, I wasn't so sure anymore.

"Tink," I said, switching tactics, "Aunt Mary and Aunt Dot live in the Appalachian mountains. Things are different there."

She squirmed in her seat, turning toward the window. "Humph."

I searched for some of the stock answers Abby had given me when I was a kid and being a psychic was something exciting. "You need to respect your ability," I lectured. "Being a medium isn't some parlor game, or a toy that's been given to you for your amusement."

"Like I don't know that?" she shot back with a tinge of sarcasm.

Thinking of the ghost she'd conjured—one we'd a heck of a time banishing—I nodded. "I guess maybe you do."

"I wouldn't try anything without supervision," she pressed, sensing a change in my attitude.

"Abby and I aren't mediums. Part of your training has been guesswork."

"Can't you call Great-Aunt Mary and ask her advice?"

"No."

She shoved back in the seat with a pout. "When we go to Appalachia this fall for her hundredth birthday, I'm asking her hundreds of questions."

I laughed. "Sure you will. You don't know Great-Aunt Mary. She's not the friendly, little pixie Aunt Dot is." My voice grew heated. "That woman can sour milk with just one look."

"You're teasing," she scoffed.

"Well," I replied as I whipped into our driveway, "I haven't actually seen her do it, but it wouldn't surprise me."

Tink didn't understand. Great-Aunt Mary scared the pants off me, and the less contact I had with her, the better. I was *not* looking forward to our upcoming trip.

Once inside the house, Queenie greeted us by ignoring us. I imagined she was out of joint over the fact that she'd been left behind when Abby and Tink picked up the dogs. Curled up on the bottom step of the stairs, she groomed herself with her pink tongue, making long, leisurely strokes over her black fur. She paused and looked up with narrowed eyes to let me know that she was aware of our presence but could care less.

Scooping her up, I chucked her under her chin. "Poor baby—how about a treat?"

I walked into the kitchen, with Lady and T.P. following. After all, if Queenie received a treat, so should they. After handing out the goodies, I went upstairs and showered, changing into shorts and a T-shirt.

Padding down the hall in my bare feet, I knocked on Tink's bedroom door. "Hey, don't be on the phone too long—"

The door opened a crack to reveal Tink standing there with her cell phone to her ear. "How did you know I was on the phone?" she asked, eyeing me skeptically.

"You're always on the phone. Tell Nell hi, and remember your essay."

With a roll of her eyes and a nod of her head, she went back to her conversation.

I shut the door with a chuckle and went downstairs to the kitchen. While I tried Karen Burns again, I poured a glass of lemonade.

Still no answer. Maybe I was dialing the wrong numbers.

I carried it with me back to my office. Standing in the doorway, I took a deep breath and surveyed my room.

This was my place, my place of magick. Crystals lay scattered on my desk and on the end table near the wing chair sitting by the windows. They seemed to radiate a soft glow from their position on the bookcases lining the walls.

I crossed to my desk and checked Stephen's date book for Karen's number. Nope, I had the right one.

I lit a white candle and propped my feet up on my desk. I reached out and picked up a piece on amethyst lying to my right. Rolling the stone over and over in my hand, I watched lightning bugs flicker on and off in the backyard as I thought about the past twenty-four hours.

I felt a strong need to talk with Karen Burns. Since she worked closely with Stephen, she would know about his life. If I could talk with her, I had a feeling some of those pieces would fall into place. *But how could I talk to her if she wouldn't answer her freaking phone?*

My thoughts moved on to that afternoon. Could the falling tiles have killed me? I suppose—if one would have hit me on the head. But no matter where they landed, I would've been hurt. I stroked the crystal with my thumb. What had caused their sudden fall? Ron hadn't offered any explanation. Could a squirrel, or something larger like a raccoon, skittering across the roof knocked the tile through the hole?

I still pondered my last question when the phone rang. Picking it up, Darci's voice greeted me. "Turn on the TV," she said without preamble.

"Why—"

"Never mind, just do it," she insisted, cutting me off. "Hurry."

I ran to the living room, grabbed the remote and hit the power button. "What channel?"

"Thirteen."

Punching the buttons, I watched as the channel came on.

My face, with the expression of a deer caught in the headlights, suddenly filled the screen.

Peachy.

After a brief conversation with Darci, bemoaning my bad luck at getting caught on camera, I checked on Tink and wished her a good-night. Returning to my office, I crossed to the window and stared out into the night.

No stars or moon lit the sky. Clouds moving in from the

west had hid their light. *Good. Maybe the clouds would bring rain and much cooler weather.* They had shrouded the backyard in complete darkness. Even the lightning bugs were gone now.

With a sigh, I turned back to my desk. I was upset about appearing on the news. If the whole town hadn't known I was present when Stephen was shot, they would now. I'd be fending off questions from curious old ladies all day tomorrow. I was willing to bet that Edna Simpson would be the first to arrive. The heat had kept her home today, but tomorrow I wouldn't be so lucky. The woman loved reading true crime, and now she'd have a chance to hear about one firsthand. She'd want to know how much blood, how much gore. But most of all she'd want to know what Stephen had said.

It was apparent in the interview that I'd lied to the reporter. The way I clutched my purse, the way my eyes widened when I was asked the question, a person would have had to be an idiot not to see that I wasn't being honest. And though Edna Simpson might be old, she was *not* an idiot. She also loved to embellish whatever tale she heard. By the time she finished repeating *her* version of the story, I wouldn't recognize it when I heard it.

*Shake it off, Jensen, there isn't anything you can do about it now.* Leaning forward, I spun the amethyst. *You have more pressing questions on your mind.*

My eyes traveled to the old leather pouch lying on the corner of the desk. My runes. They had originally belonged to my great-grandmother, Annie. Picking up the pouch, I shifted their weight back and forth in my hands.

*Well, if ever there was a time for clarity, it's now.*

Placing the bag back on the desk, I opened a drawer and removed an abalone shell, a bag of Abby's homegrown sage, and a square ceramic tile. Normally, before I did a rune reading, I'd do a lengthy cleansing ritual—bathing in sea salt, dressing in one of my long white robes—but tonight I didn't have the time. Smudging would have to do.

Opening the Baggie, I broke off some sage leaves and rolled them into a tight ball. After putting the abalone shell on the ceramic tile, I laid the ball of leaves in the center of the shell. I struck a match, lit the sage, and blew softly until a thin plume of smoke rose in the air.

Leaning forward, clearing my mind, I gently wafted the smoke toward me with both hands.

*May I only hear the truth,* I repeated in my head as I brushed the smoke toward my ears.

*May I only see the truth.* I sent smoke toward my closed eyes.

Inhaling deeply, I swept smoke around my mouth. *May I only speak the truth.*

A slight groan escaped. *Considering how many lies you told today, maybe you'd better repeat that one.*

I tapped down my errant thoughts and repeated the ritual. Satisfied that I was ready, I stood, and picked up the tile with the smoldering shell, walked over and placed it in the center of the room. After flicking the lights off, the white candle that I'd lit earlier followed. Removing a box of sea salt from my desk drawer and starting clockwise, I carefully sprinkled a wide circle of salt around the candle and shell. The pouch, a notebook and pen, and a linen square joined the circle. Stepping over the salt, I eased down to a cross-legged position in front of the candle and shell. I laid out the square and thought of my question.

*What should I ask? The shooter's name? Nope, the runes didn't work out that way.* Even though each rune also represented an alphabetic letter, I didn't expect them to spell out a name for me.

What did I want to know—what was going on—sprung to mind, but that question was too generic. I needed to be specific. How about, *Was Stephen the intended victim?*

I held that question in my mind while I concentrated on the energy above, below, and around me. Once safe and secure in my bubble, I cast the runes on the linen square.

I'd do a reading that was commonly called a Celtic cross. The first three runes, placed in a straight line, represented the past, present, and future. Above the "present" rune, sitting at twelve o'clock, would be the rune indicating what help I could expect. The last rune, directly below the "present" and at six o'clock, would show me that which can't be changed.

Slowly, I let my hand move over the runes, sensing their power. When it tingled sharply, I picked up the rune and placed it on the square in front of me. I repeated the process four more times until the shape of the cross was laid out before me.

Scooping up the remaining runes, I returned them to the pouch and focused on the ones I'd selected.

I turned the middle rune, the one in the "present" position.

*Laguz.* "Law-gooze," I said softly.

It represented intuitive knowledge. A female capable of dealing with challenges. Good—that made sense. I was female and a psychic. It told me I was up to facing my problem, and I felt my confidence lift.

I flipped over the rune to the left. *Hagalaz.* "Haw-gaw-laws," I said aloud. This showed the past and how it affected the current situation. Hagalaz represented elemental forces—detached and impersonal—that could cause a disruption beyond anyone's control. It also indicated that some official had held fate in their hands. Another meaning—someone was contemplating taking a risk.

I didn't know enough about Stephen's life to give a correct interpretation of what this rune might mean. Had he taken a chance at some point and set the wheels in motion?

Looking at it from my perspective, it certainly applied. My life had been disrupted by fate. An official who'd controlled my life? Easy—Bill. And the risk factor? Duh, who knew what might happen if I pursued my current course? An unknown assailant was running around with a gun.

The next rune I turned over was in the twelve o'clock position and indicated what help I could expect to receive. The glyph was upside down.

*Not so good. Algiz.* "All-yeese," I muttered.

Reversed, the rune spoke of betrayal and deception by others. And I would be vulnerable to it. *Did it mean Stephen had lied to me? Had Ron lied to me? Or was it someone closer to me?* One thing I knew for sure, it indicated that I needed to proceed with caution and be skeptical of those who appeared to offer aid.

I flipped the rune placed in the fifth position, the one at six o'clock.

*Oh, that's just great!*

My heart sank. The rune showed that which could not be changed.

*Thurisaz.* "Thor-ee-saw, reversed," I whispered with eyes wide. The hammer of Thor; backward, it meant thorns, torture, and again, betrayal by a man. Well, at least I now knew it would be a male who let me down. And it was another warning that I needed to be careful and think things through before I blindly rushed in.

One more rune to go, the rune farthest to my right. The future.

I gave a sigh of relief. *Jera.* "Yare-awe."

The harvest. On the whole, a positive rune. It related to karma, and if the seeds sown were good deeds, the reward would be positive. But if negative thoughts and actions had been seeded, the result would be just as negative. It also showed that all things have a season, and seasons can't be rushed. The harvest would be reaped in the fullness of time.

Not necessarily comforting to someone who lacked patience. Someone like me. I wanted answers and I wanted them now.

I picked up the pad of paper and the pen. Carefully, I drew each rune in its specific position on the paper. As I did,

I tried to think of them in relation to each other, the over-all pattern. It seemed the runes were more about me than Stephen. Did it mean Bill *was* right after all—I was the intended victim?

No, that still didn't feel right. They spoke of my ability to handle whatever it was I faced, but that I needed to exercise caution. Not to go rushing in without careful consideration.

True, I hadn't always listened to my instincts, had second-guessed myself and as a result reached the wrong conclusion. They warned me not to do that this time. To listen to my feelings.

What puzzled me most was Thurisaz—that which can't be changed. Was it something from my past? Would a past betrayal by a man reach out and affect what was happening now? Or was the betrayal yet to come?

Perplexed, I looked at the rune again. Sure, I'd experienced my share of letdowns, but nothing major. Nothing I could see that applied to the now.

Reversed, the rune also indicated a habit of blindly following my own wishes—again rushing ahead—of being stubborn.

Okay, I thought with a grimace, maybe a little.

My eyes moved to the last rune, Jera. *A karmic debt I owed?* Boy, if that were the case, I hoped the debt wasn't a bad one. I'd learned in my thirty-some years that redemption didn't come easy.

Feeling a little fried, I placed the pad and pen down and rose to my feet. Crossing to the edge of the circle, I walked counterclockwise, letting the energy slowly leave the room. When I arrived at my starting point, I got on my knees and crawled along in the same counterclockwise direction, sweeping up the salt in my hand. Once I gathered it all, I dumped it in the shell and mixed it with the ashes of sage. Then turning the lights back on, I quietly left the room and went out into the backyard.

I paused at the edge of the patio and waited for my eyes

to become accustomed to the darkness. Enough light spilled
in a pool from my office window so I could get my bearings.
Walking toward the light, I stopped outside of its circle.

I began by facing the north. Taking a small amount of
the ash and salt, I sprinkled it on the ground, returning it to
the earth from whence it came. I turned to the east and cast
a small amount to the wind. With a quarter turn, I looked to
the south and thought of the cleansing fire that had burned
the sage. As I did, I dropped ashes and salt. Another turn
and I faced the west. At my feet, the grass was damp with
dew. I dumped the remainder on the ground and used my toe
to mixed the ash and salt with the moisture.

Finished, I took one step toward the patio, when a neigh-
bor's dog began barking furiously. Startled, I dropped the
shell in the wet grass. As I bent to retrieve it, I heard a loud
pop, followed by the sound of shattering glass and the roar
of a motorcycle.

Stunned, the sounds melded together in my mind, making
sense.

Damn, somebody had just tried to shoot me!

# *Twelve*

The promised rain hit with a vengeance. Through the window, I saw lightning cut across the sky in bold flashes. And thunder rattled the pictures hanging on the wall. Inside the house it wasn't much calmer. Cops crawled all over my cottage, looking for evidence.

My first call had been to Bill, my second to Darci to please come and pick up a wide-eyed Tink and get her out of harm's way, and my third was to Abby. Darci had evidently broken every traffic law to arrive at my house in record time. Even though I could see that she hated missing out on the excitement, she packed up Tink and tried to overcome Tink's reluctance at leaving with promises of homemade banana splits waiting for them at her house.

While I sat on the couch in the living room with Lady curled up at my feet and Queenie resting on the back, Abby bustled around in the kitchen making tea. Ha—tonight I had no intention of drinking any, no matter what she said. I didn't need Abby's home remedies floating around my system.

Bill sat on the other side of the coffee table in a wingback chair, and, at the moment, didn't look too pleased with me.

"Now do you believe me?" he asked in a taut voice.

"Believe what?" Abby asked entering the living room. She carried a tray full of steaming cups. After offering a cup to Bill, she held the tray toward me.

"No thanks," I said, giving her a knowing look.

An expression of innocence flashed in her green eyes, but I wasn't buying it. I shook my head and waved the tray away.

Turning back to Bill, she said, "I'll take the men in Ophelia's office some tea, and when I return, I want an answer to my question."

After watching her leave over his shoulder, he focused his attention back on me. "You didn't tell her?"

"No, I didn't want her to worry."

"Not telling her wasn't smart," he said with a frown. Pulling out his notebook, he flipped it open and removed a pen from his shirt pocket. "Tell me everything that happened today."

I held up a hand. "Wait a second. I don't want to sound snitty," I said carefully, "but I live within the city limits of Summerset, and this isn't your jurisdiction. Why isn't one of the police questioning me?"

Bill's hand stole to his head and he gave it a quick rub. He looked exasperated. "I'm doing the chief a favor while he's on vacation. These officers are new—they haven't even been to the academy yet—so Tom asked me to cover anything unusual while he's gone." He poised his pen over the notebook. "And residents getting shot while standing in their backyard is definitely unusual." Giving the pen a click, he rolled his shoulders like a wrestler going into the ring. "Any more questions?"

"No." I tucked my feet underneath me and waited.

"Let's start with the shooting." He glanced down at his notebook. "Your call came in at 11:45, so the shooting happened after eleven-thirty. Are you normally outside that time of night?"

"Of course not," I huffed. "I'm usually fast asleep in my bed."

"What was different tonight?"

"I'd been doing a little . . . ah . . . work in my office, and—"

"Were the lights on in your office?" he asked, cutting me off. "Could you be seen through the window?"

I thought about it. Someone could have watched me while I sat at the desk, but I wouldn't have been visible sitting on the floor with my runes. *Did I want to try and explain that one? No.*

"Yes, the lights were on and, yes, I suppose someone would've been able to see me most of the time."

I felt a little shiver at the idea of being watched in my own home.

"So you finished working and went outside." Bill scribbled in his notebook then looked up. "Why?"

I focused on a spot over his shoulder. "Um, well, I needed some fresh air before I went to bed."

"How long were you outside before the gunshot?"

"Not long—no more than ten minutes."

"What happened next?"

"I'd started to walk back to the house when a dog barked. It startled me and I dropped something—"

He didn't let me finish. "What did you drop?"

Just then Abby came strolling back into the living room, carrying an empty tray. She took a place next to me on the couch but said nothing.

"What did you drop?" he asked again.

"A shell."

"You were walking around the yard, in the dead of night, carrying a shell?" He looked first at me, then at Abby. "Never mind. I don't think I want to know," he muttered to himself while clicking his pen rapidly. "What happened next?"

"When I bent to pick up the shell, I heard a pop and the shattering of glass. Then I heard a motorcycle."

"Did you see anything? Any movement?"

"No, it was too dark."

"Where did the sound come from?"

"The dog or the motorcycle?"

"Motorcycle."

"I think it came from behind the trees at the back of the yard. Maybe toward the west side."

Bill flicked the switch on the small radio clipped to his jacket and it crackled to life. "Ben, have someone check the west side of the property for tire tracks."

A garbled voice answered him, but from where I sat, the only word I caught was "rain."

"Yeah, I know," Bill answered into the radio. "They've probably been washed away, but maybe we'll get lucky." With a flip of his finger, he turned the radio off.

"Bill, I don't mean to interrupt, but would you please explain to me what's going on?" Abby asked in a calm voice that belied the tension I felt emanating from her.

"Your granddaughter is determined to mess up my investigation," he said unkindly, "and in the process, get herself killed."

Squaring my shoulders, I opened my mouth to defend myself, but one look at his face and I snapped it shut.

He proceeded to give Abby a rundown of his theory with me as the victim. While he did, Abby grew visibly paler and her hand stole out to clutch mine.

I didn't appreciate how his recitation was affecting her. "Do you think it's necessary to give her a blow by blow, Bill?" My fingers squeezed Abby's hand.

"Yes, I do," he replied, his head bobbing empathically. "Maybe she can talk some sense into you." Picking up his cup, he sipped his tea as he skimmed over his notes. "Did anything out of the norm happen today?"

*Well, let's see . . . Was almost getting conked on the noggin with falling tile out of the norm?* Yup, I'm sure Bill would have considered it unusual. But I didn't want to tell him about the visit to the winery. I lowered my head and plucked at the hem of my shorts while I argued with myself. *Suck it in, Jensen, and get it over with.*

When I raised my head, the words flew out of my mouth. "I went to the winery after work, paid a visit to the old church, and about got beaned by some falling tile. I—"

"You what!" Bill jerked the hand holding the tea, making it slosh over the rim and down the front of his shirt. He set the cup down, grabbed his handkerchief and dabbed at the wet spot.

"Here, let me," I said, standing.

"Sit," he barked, jabbing a thick finger at the spot I'd just vacated.

I sank to the couch.

"My God, Ophelia, you *are* trying to get yourself killed!" He scrubbed at his chest furiously, sending the notebook on his lap flying to the floor.

"I am not," I replied hotly. "It was an accident. Right before I went inside the church, I saw a squirrel. It probably ran across the roof and knocked the tile through the hole."

Bill scowled at me.

"Look, I'm telling you I *know* I wasn't the intended victim yesterday—"

"What about tonight?" he asked, challenging me.

"Okay, tonight somebody took a potshot at me, but whatever is happening right now—it's not about me, it's about Stephen."

"You're sure?" he sneered.

I ignored the sneer. "I know you don't think I can help you, but I can," I blurted out. "I took a look at the crime scene—"

His eyes narrowed even more. "Did you cross that tape?"

"No." Clenching my hands in my lap, I stared at him defiantly. "I stood on the other side and tried to get a reading on what happened."

He wadded up his handkerchief and shoved it in his pocket. "And?"

"Not much," I admitted reluctantly. "The shooter stood in the shadow of a tree, so I couldn't *see* his face." My voice brightened. "But I could probably show you which tree."

"No, thanks," he said, picking up the notebook. "We know where he was standing . . . we found the shell casing."

"Bill," Abby said, the soft rhythm of the mountains thick on her tongue. "I know you don't fully believe there is such a thing as a sixth sense, or what Ophelia is telling you, but I do." She patted my tight fists. "If my granddaughter's instincts tell her you're on the wrong track, you'd best believe her." Abby's eyes traveled to the wet spot on Bill's shirt. Raising them to his face, she smiled sweetly. "Care for more tea?"

After all the cops had finally left, I locked the door and turned to find Abby standing right behind me. "Let's talk," she said in a firm voice.

I snuck a longing look over her shoulder for a possible escape route. "Gee, Abby, I'm kind of tired."

Her eyebrow arched and she crossed her arms. "You weren't tired when you were creeping around the backyard in the middle of the night."

"But," I motioned to my front door, "there's been a lot of excitement, and—" Her lips tightened and I gave up. "Okay, but I'm not drinking any tea," I said vehemently. Trudging behind, I followed her into the kitchen and yanked out a chair, then sat down and waited for her to pour *her* tea and join me.

She got right to the point. "Whether or not you were a target at the winery yesterday and today, you're a target now and—"

My thoughts leapt ahead of her words. "Tink," I said with a soft whisper.

She leaned forward and stared into her cup. "We need to protect her."

"I agree. And with school in session, it's going to be hard." I tugged on my bottom lip. "I don't think she'd care for one of us attending her classes with her."

Abby softly chuckled. "No, I'm sure she wouldn't . . . " She paused and traced a delicate flower painted on the side of her cup. "I have an idea."

"Not police protection." My voice rang with certainty. "She won't like that either."

Abby looked up and her eyes drilled into mine. "Send her to the mountains."

"What?" I jumped out of my chair. "To Great-Aunt Mary's? Are you nuts?"

"Aunt Dot lives there, too," she answered defensively, and sat back in her chair. "She and Tink formed a tight bond during her visit. They'd love to have her."

I paced over to the counter and whirled. "What about school? We don't know how long this investigation is going to take."

"Aunt Mary was a country schoolteacher for forty years," she scoffed, scooting around in her chair to face me. "She's more than capable of home-schooling Tink while she's there."

Leaning back, I gripped the edge of the counter. "Abby, the woman's almost a hundred years old," I said, shocked at the idea of Great-Aunt Mary keeping up with a fourteen-year-old.

"True, but Aunt Mary is as spry now as she was fifty years ago. She can handle Tink."

"What if she can't?" I argued.

"I have cousins in the area. I'm sure they'll help Aunt Dot and Aunt Mary keep Tink occupied." She gave me a smug look. "It will be good for Tink. She can learn a great deal from Aunt Mary."

"That's what I'm afraid of," I grumbled.

"Ah, you mean her gift—there's that, too." She thought for a moment, then nodded. "Aunt Mary shares Tink's abilities—we don't. She'll be a good guide for Tink."

With a scowl, I loosened my grip and turned toward the window. I didn't know if I wanted the mean, prickly, old, Great-Aunt Mary as a guide for my sweet young daughter. How did I know what she might teach Tink? What if Tink came home ready to pulverize rabbit poop, carry the right eye of a wolf inside her sleeve for protection, tie the heart of a bat with a red string to ensure she won at games. *I'd* read those journals, too.

From the window, a car driving slowly down the street caught my attention. I took a step back and watched as it stopped under the street lamp at the intersection. Through the pelting rain, the light bar on top of the car reflected back at me.

Bill had assigned officers to do drive-bys.

With a sigh of resignation, I crossed the kitchen and stood by Abby's chair. "When you talk to them, please ask Aunt Dot to lay off the fairy thing, okay?"

# Thirteen

The dreams, when they came, left me breathless. The scent of expensive perfume surrounded me as I sat in a car speeding past houses, the windows either shuttered or the curtains drawn. I wasn't happy—I *did not* want to be here, but something told me I'd had no choice. Looking down, I saw I wore an evening gown—black lace covered flesh-toned silk on a bodice that dipped dangerously low, showing cleavage I didn't know I had. A satin skirt with tucking covered my legs down to my ankles. Something dug at my waist, and I shifted uncomfortably. My whole torso felt like I was bound by elastic.

*My God, I'm wearing a girdle. I've never worn a girdle in my life.*

My hand stole up to my hair. I fingered loose curls covering the top of my head and spilling down onto my forehead. The rest was held up and off my neck by combs. I felt the soft petals of a flower attached to one of the combs. Turning my head, I caught my wavy reflection in the car window.

Amber eyes, slanted slightly up in the corners, stared back at me from a pale face crowned with dark red hair. *I'm a redhead?* A small, well-shaped nose sat above lips almost too big for the face. I didn't know who stared back at me, but it wasn't Ophelia Jensen from Summerset, Iowa.

"Madeleine?"

*Right—I'm supposed to be Madeleine.*

"Huh?" I turned back to the woman sitting next to me on the smooth leather seat. I recognized her as one of the tall, thin women from my last dream. She, too, wore an evening gown in red with fine quilting around the top. *Had she forced herself into a girdle, too?* The name "Giselle" popped into my head.

She picked up a small evening bag lying beside her on the seat and removed a tube of lipstick and a compact. Opening the compact, she uncapped the lipstick and, after a couple of deft turns, began applying the bright red cream to her lips.

I saw the driver glance back at us in the rearview mirror.

"You'd better change your attitude," she said under her breath, using the compact to block the driver's view of her lips.

"I hate these parties," I replied, settling back in the seat. *That comment sounded like me.*

"Shh," she hissed, with a jerk of her head toward the driver.

I knew what she meant—keep my mouth shut or I'd be reported. How did I know that? How did I know I was being forced to attend a party? Yet I did.

Staring out the window again, I watched darkened monuments, parks, churches flash by. The car's headlights, partially covered with tape to lower their brightness, reflected dimly off signs, once in French but now in German. Everywhere, the presence of the Nazis scarred our streets.

*This is so weird. I'm still me, Ophelia Jensen, but at the same time, I'm someone else—the woman everyone calls Madeleine. I know what she knows, I feel what she feels.*

A sudden bizarre realization hit me.

*I'm speaking French, and I don't know French.* When

I woke, would I still be able to converse in the language? Somewhere in the recesses of my mind, I felt like giggling.

*Wait, I never giggle.*

*What's going on? Am I under so much stress that I've begun to suffer from multiple personality disorder? That I'm developing a new persona called Madeleine? What if she decides to make an appearance while I'm awake?*

The thought scared me and I tensed—I had enough problems.

*Relax*, said a voice in my head, *go with the dream.*

I tried, and as I did, I felt the "Ophelia" part of me fade away as if going into a deep sleep, and the "Madeleine" part take control.

Looking at the back of the driver's head, my hatred of the Nazis filled me, but I schooled my expression to show nothing. Like so many others, my life depended on my ability to hide my true feelings. The effort turned my mouth to dust.

The car slowed as it approached a grand house with iron gates. The gates opened and we pulled into a paved drive. At the entrance, the car stopped and the driver got out and opened my door as a servant opened Giselle's. Pulling my stole around my shoulders, I exited the car as gracefully as possible in my tight gown. With a smile, Giselle linked her arm with mine, and we climbed the wide steps leading to the heavy doors. As if by magic, the doors swung wide at our approach, revealing a magnificent entry, light and bright. A sharp contrast to the black shadows that hung over the city now.

Antique Persian rugs lay scattered on marble floors polished to a mirrored shine. Fine art by some of France's most well-known impressionists hung on the walls. From the salon on my left, I heard laughter and the sound of clinking glasses.

I thought of the poor gathering in dark rooms, around their meager meals, and my lips twisted with bitterness. A sharp jab in the ribs from Giselle made me remember where I was, and, as I crossed the threshold, I forced myself to smile at the servant taking my stole.

As an officer strode out of the salon toward us, Giselle stepped forward and offered her hand.

Taking it, he dipped his head stiffly. "Mademoiselle, so kind of you to join us," he said in a clipped voice as his cold green eyes appraised her.

Giselle rewarded him with a gracious nod. "Colonel Vogel, it's our pleasure. Thank you for the invitation."

The colonel's focused his attention on me.

Striving to mimic Giselle, I nodded, too. "Yes, thank you, Colonel."

"Ah, Madeleine, no need to be so formal," he replied, lifting my hand and pressing it to his lips. Releasing it, he motioned toward the salon. "Ladies, please join us."

As I followed the colonel and Giselle across the polished floor, I still felt the pressure of his lips on the back of my hand. I fought the desire to wipe away the feeling on my expensive gown.

The salon was much like the entryway. Priceless paintings adorned the cream-colored walls, and heavy crystal chandeliers sparkled in the candlelight. Women, powdered and rouged, lounged gracefully on antique furniture covered in satin, chatting with men dressed in uniforms. Servants, carrying trays laden with glasses filled with dark red wine, mingled with the guests.

*This house was fit for a king . . . or a conqueror.*

We joined a group gathered by the fireplace. And as we approached, I overheard the words "Russia" and "Leningrad."

The colonel's voice rang out over the conversation. "With such charming company," he chided, "let's have no talk of war tonight."

He stopped the servant nearby, and seizing two glasses from the tray, handed them to Giselle and I. Taking a glass for himself, he raised it high. "To the Fuehrer," he toasted in a loud clear voice.

Giselle lifted her glass, and after a warning glance at me, took a drink.

Reluctantly, I tipped my glass toward her, but holding it to my lips, only pretended to sip. I would *not* drink to Hitler.

After the colonel's warning, the conversation shifted to the latest gossip from Berlin. Caring nothing about the quirks of the Third Reich's upper echelon, I tried not to look bored.

"Madeleine, you seem very quiet tonight," the colonel whispered at my elbow.

I carelessly lifted a shoulder in reply. *Be charming, be witty,* insisted the voice in my head, but it was impossible.

"When is Henrick returning?" he asked.

A moment of disorientation threw me. *Henrick? Who's Henrick?* Then it hit me, Madeleine—me—we had a lover. *Wow—a lover!* A Swedish businessman involved in selling much needed iron ore to the Third Reich. I hid the surprise on my . . . Madeleine's face.

"Next week," I answered quickly to cover my confusion.

Colonel Vogel smiled. "Good. I miss his dry humor." His expression turned to a slight leer for an instant as his eyes wandered to the flesh spilling out the top of my dress. "I'm sure you miss him, too, but maybe for other—"

The colonel's remark went unfinished as one of the servants announced in a loud voice, "Dinner is served."

Offering me his arm, Vogel escorted me to the dining room.

A sideboard laden with food sat along one wall, and the various aromas filled the room. Again I thought of the families doing without tonight while Vogel fed his guests a sumptuous meal. Any appetite I had slipped away.

Vogel led me to the head of the table and pulled out the chair on the right. Masking the disdain I felt, I looked down the table, over the expensive china and crystal, at the other guests. The wine had flowed freely in the salon, and the conversation was becoming louder and louder as they continued to drain their glasses. The din hurt my ears, and I tried blocking it out by concentrating on the courses spread out before me.

Foie de gras followed by rich onion soup; rack of lamb with roasted potatoes; green beans in a heavy cream sauce; thick, crusty bread; cheeses. I picked at the food that was placed in front of me in rapid succession.

Vogel leaned to his right. "Madeleine, aren't you feeling well?" he asked in a hushed voice.

I grabbed my goblet of water and drank thirstily. Finished, I put the goblet down. "My apologies, Colonel," I replied, giving him a stiff smile. "The room is becoming rather warm, and—"

With a snap of his fingers, he had a servant scurrying toward the head of the table. "Mademoiselle is warm. Open a window," he commanded.

"Really, Colonel, that's not necessary."

Before the colonel could reply, I heard the officer sitting two chairs away say "Drancy" over the noise. Vogel's attention immediately shifted from me to the young officer, who quelled at his glare.

"Drancy?" I asked, drawing Vogel's eyes back to mine.

He waved his hand and let it fall on my wrist. "Don't concern yourself, my dear." He shot the young man a last angry look. "It's merely a holding area for enemies of the Reich, criminals, and malcontents," he answered, with a hard squeeze.

It was as if I'd been slammed back into my body. I could still feel the pressure of Vogel's fingers around my—Madeleine's—wrist. Confused, my eyes roamed my familiar bedroom, searching for reassurance that I was in my own body, in my own time.

Sensing my tension, Lady lifted her head and gave a low

growl from her spot by the window. In the gray light, I saw her coarse, white hair stand in a ridge down her spine.

"Shh," I whispered. "It's just me."

*I think it's just me.* I ran a hand over my face. Yup, my nose, my lips. Taking a strand of hair, I held it in front of my face. Brown, not dark red. *Thank God—I'm Ophelia, not Madeleine.*

Scooting up in bed, I pressed back against the headboard. These dreams were so fantastic, and not in a good way. They left me feeling befuddled and disturbed. Rolling my head toward the window, I noticed that last night's storm had abated to a fine drizzle. And with it came an oppressive chill.

Rubbing my bare arms, I grabbed a sweatshirt and pulled it on. I followed it with a pair of sweatpants and socks. My mind drifted back to the strange dream. What had ended it so abruptly? Oh, yeah, Vogel had told Madeleine not to be concerned about Drancy. He called it a "holding area"? Did he mean prison? A niggle of curiosity picked at me. Knowing I wouldn't be satisfied until I looked it up, I went to my office.

One of the officers had kindly tacked plastic sheeting over the broken window to keep the rain out, but it did nothing to keep out the pervasive damp. Stepping over the broken glass, I shut the curtains, hoping it would help, and zipped up my sweatshirt.

A little warmer, I sat at my desk and booted up my computer. Once online, I typed *Drancy* in the search bar. The second search result listed *Drancy internment camp*. In a second I was on the site and skimming the information.

It said Drancy was located northeast of Paris and was originally built as a housing complex but was used as a police barracks. The Nazis converted it to a detention center to hold "undesirables"—Jews, homosexuals, and the Roma people—Gitan, or Gypsies, a term considered somewhat derogatory. The camp was opened in August 1941, when four thousand Jews were sent there. Families were separated and young children were torn from their mothers' arms. Children captured by Klaus Barbie in a raid on a children's home were held at Drancy, too.

Bile rose in my throat as I read the next sentence.

The next stop for the prisoners of Drancy, including all the children: Auschwitz.

# Fourteen

Feeling sick, I stumbled to the kitchen to make coffee. Images of children herded into boxcars and sent to gas chambers haunted me. My hands shook as I poured the last spoonful of coffee into the basket, and the grains scattered across the counter. Frustrated, I hit the On button, and grabbing a dishcloth, wiped up the spilled coffee. While I waited impatiently, coffee cup in hand, for the pot to fill, I stared out the window.

Why were these troubling dreams plaguing me? I could see no connection between them and Stephen's shooting. Pressing on my stomach, I tried to rub the nausea away as I stared at the drizzle running down the kitchen window. The gloomy morning matched my mood. I was more disturbed by the dreams and the images they invoked of lost children than the idea that someone might be trying to kill me. *But, I argued with myself, I couldn't change history, I could only mourn the loss of so many. I need to focus on what was happening now.*

"You look bleak."

Looking over my shoulder, I saw Abby standing in the doorway.

"I am."

She crossed the kitchen and laid a hand on my shoulder. "We'll get to the bottom of this," she said softly.

I didn't tell her it wasn't the shooting that made me feel disheartened, but my dreams. I wasn't ready to ask her advice until I could make more sense of what they might mean.

"You're right," I answered, my voice sounding tinny. "I'm just feeling a little lost right now."

She gave my shoulder a light squeeze. "I take it you're not planning on going to the library today?" she asked.

"No, I'm going to call Claire and request vacation time." I looked at the clock. "But first I'm calling Darci and telling her to keep Tink there—not send her to school." I felt my heart wrench a bit. "Will you call Great-Aunt Mary?"

"Yes. Don't worry," she said confidently. "They'll be pleased to have Tink."

"Well, then," I said, accepting the reality of what I had to do. "I'd better check the airline schedule. What airport?"

"The closest one to the mountain is in Asheville, North Carolina."

Setting my cup on the counter, I hugged myself and stared again at the somber sky. "Tink's not going to be happy."

I'd made the understatement of the century. After picking her up at Darci's, I fended off her questions as best I could and waited until we were home to give her the news that she'd be leaving for the mountains tomorrow.

There's nothing like a fourteen-year-old pitching a hissy fit.

Tink cried and pleaded to stay, and the histrionics led to the biggest argument we'd ever had. It ended with Tink running upstairs and slamming her bedroom door.

The confrontation left me shaken and almost ready to change my mind, until I saw the patrol car make another slow pass by my house. Tink would have to accept my decision and make the best of it. This time tomorrow she'd be in North Carolina.

I called Abby and finalized the arrangements. A cousin

would pick Tink up at the airport and take her to Great-Aunt Mary's.

After waiting about an hour to give Tink time to calm down, I went upstairs and knocked on her door.

No answer.

I rapped again, then pushed it half open. Sticking my head in the door, I saw her sprawled facedown across her bed, with T.P. curled protectively next to her.

"We need to talk, sweetie," I said with a calmness I didn't feel.

Tink lifted her head and shot me a look over her shoulder. Her eyes were red and puffy, and I felt a pang of remorse. Without a word, she turned and lowered her head.

*Okay, maybe you don't want to talk, but I do.*

I crossed the room and sat on the other side of her. Reaching out a hand, I made a move to stroke her hair, but she jerked away.

"I know you're mad, but this is for your own good."

She rolled over and scooted up in the bed. She pulled her knees to her chest and wrapped her arms around them. "Who says?"

"Me," I replied firmly, "and Abby."

Her face softened for an instant. "Abby?"

"Yes, the trip was her idea."

Her eyes narrowed and her lips thinned. "I didn't think *she'd* betray me."

"Come on, Tink," I said with a shake of my head. "This isn't a betrayal. We want to keep you safe."

"I'm safe here," she answered mutinously.

"Right," I scoffed, "with bullets coming through the windows? I don't think so."

"So from now on, every time someone threatens you, you're going to send me to Great-Aunt Mary's?" She gave a derisive snort. "I might as well move out there."

I felt my patience running thin. "Tink—"

"It's the truth."

The conversation was going nowhere. I needed to take a different tack.

"Yesterday you were excited about meeting Great-Aunt Mary," I pointed out.

"So?" I heard the mistrust in her voice.

"So . . . now you'll have the opportunity to ask her all those questions."

She thought for a moment. "How long will I have to stay?"

"I don't know."

"If it's until Sheriff Wilson finds the guy who shot at you, it could be forever and ever."

"It won't be forever and ever," I said with a chuckle. "Haven't we always found out the truth?"

"Yeah." She tucked her legs under her and leaned forward. "But you'd find the truth faster if I helped."

A sigh escaped. "We talked about that yesterday—you're not ready. You need to learn more control."

Her lip curled. "Great-Aunt Mary can teach me."

It killed me to say it, but at that point I'd have done anything to get her cooperation. "There you go." I slapped the bed. "This is your chance to have Great-Aunt Mary train you."

Damp emanated from the plastered buildings on either side as I walked down the narrow sidewalk. In the street, greasy pools of water gathered between the cobblestones. Passing the alley, I heard the low growl of a dog. I glanced over my right shoulder and saw the scrawny animal curled protectively around a precious bone, gnawing furiously. Spotting me, he jumped to his feet, the bone still in his mouth, and ran deeper into the alley.

Too many people lived too close together in this poor section of Paris. A sense of futility hung in the air. It had been bad before the Germans came, but now, with the food shortages, the occupants here rose every morning only to face another hopeless day.

*Paris? Ah, I'm dreaming of Madeleine again.*

I felt Ophelia slide away to a corner of my mind.

I stopped in front of a thick oak door, scarred by centuries of use. Looking up, I saw the small stained-glass window depicting the trials of Saint Flora of Beaulieu.

How appropriate—the patron saint of the betrayed, the abandoned—having a church named for her in this section of the city where people lived in such wretchedness.

Feeling the sadness weigh me down, I lifted heavy hands and pulled my scarf tighter around my head. With a shove, I pushed the door open and stepped inside.

The smell of the streets was replaced by air clouded with the smoke of burning incense and beeswax candles. The small stained-glass window and candles provided little light, and it took a moment for my eyes to adjust to the quiet darkness. Slowly, I made my way down the short aisle and took a seat on one of the simple pine pews. Bowing my head, I waited.

I heard soft footfalls coming from behind me and felt the weight of another body join me on the pew. From the corner of my downcast eyes I saw legs encased in black slide next to me. He shifted forward onto the kneeling rail and raised his hands in prayer. I joined him, mimicking his supplication.

"Have you picked up the package yet?" he whispered, not looking at me.

"Not yet. I wanted the key first," I murmured.

In profile, Brother Sebastian frowned. "It's getting late. Curfew will be starting—you could be stopped."

"I have my authorization papers," I replied confidently.

"Don't be foolish, Madeleine. Once you have the package, it could be fatal if the police or the Germans stop and question you."

"All right, tomorrow, then," I replied, bowing to his wishes.

With a nod, he stuck his hand in the pocket of his cassock,

then withdrew it. Taking my hand in both of his, he pressed a small piece of cold metal into my palm as he whispered a blessing. When he released my hand, my fingers curled around the key. Without a word, he rose and slowly walked down the aisle to the front of the church. He disappeared seconds later through an arched doorway.

I waited a few minutes, then rose myself and left the way I'd come. Opening the door and stepping outside, the bleakness of the streets hit me like a hammer.

I groaned.

My moan wakened me.

Okay, now I'm Ophelia, I thought, combing my hair back from my face and staring at the dark ceiling.

Package? Key? Pulling the blankets up to my chin, I wasn't surprised. In the last dream, I'd felt Madeleine's hatred of the Germans, so it made sense that she'd been some kind of courier.

Wait a minute, I was acting as if this actually happened. This was only a dream—the random wanderings of my subconscious.

Wasn't it?

Shaking my leg nervously, I sat in the airport next to Tink and watched the board announcing the flights. "Do you have your jacket? You know it gets chilly in the mountains at night."

"Yes."

I turned my head and studied her. "Do you have enough underwear to last at least a week?"

Her eyes flew wide and she glanced quickly to the right and left. Satisfied that no one had heard me, she looked up at the ceiling. "Jeez . . . yes."

Offended by her reaction, I crossed my arms. "For all I know, they're still using a wringer washer." Leaning sideways toward her, I said in a hushed voice, "You're not going to like feeding your undies through it, piece by piece, while the wringer squeezes out all the soap. I watched Abby do laundry that way when I was a kid. It takes forever."

"I'll be okay," she grumbled.

"What about shampoo and toothpaste?" I asked.

Tink scrubbed her face with her hand. "I'm not going to the moon. They have stores in the mountains."

"A general store. And they go once a week, on Saturdays. Plus, I doubt the store carries the shampoo you like."

"I'll get by."

I uncrossed my legs and looked down at my watch. The minutes were flying by. Soon I'd be putting her on the plane and sending her hundreds of miles away. I felt torn. My first priority was to keep her safe, but the idea of being separated, even for a short time, hurt. My thoughts flew back to the families I'd read about at Drancy. How did they stand the pain? Many never survived, and those that did might have never learned what happened to their families. How did someone live with that? At least I'd know where Tink was, that she was safe. I could call her whenever I wanted.

Pinching the bridge of my nose, I tried to stop the tears I felt prickling my eyes.

"I'll call," I said abruptly, my voice thick.

Tink nudged me with her shoulder. "Quit worrying about me. Now that I think about it, staying with Great-Aunt Mary might be fun. And it's going to be great to spend time with Aunt Dot again—"

Remembering the trouble the two of them caused during Aunt Dot's visit, I nudged her back, cutting her off. "Hey, don't be getting any crazy ideas while you're out there."

She giggled. "I won't." Her smile fell away. "It's time."

The tears sprung to my eyes, and I felt an empty spot form in my heart. Rising, I picked up Tink's carry-on and followed her to the escalator.

At the top, she turned to me. Violet eyes shimmered. "This is it."

"Yeah," I replied, not trusting myself to say more.

"I'll call as soon as I get there." A tear trickled down her cheek.

"Great," I said, touching my own wet cheek. "Be good." I laid a hand on her smooth face. "Mind your manners, okay?"

She nodded and threw her arms around me, burying her face in my shoulder. Placing my free arm around her, I hugged her to me.

"I love you, Titania," I said, using her real name as I stroked her hair. "I'm going to miss you."

"I love you, too," she said, her voice muffled by my shoulder. "Hurry up and catch the bad guys so I can come home, okay?"

With tears running freely, I nodded.

Stepping back, she took her carry-on and joined the line of passengers waiting to go through security.

Unable to take my eyes off of her, I watched the guard check her ticket and motion her through the scanner. She removed her shoes and placed them, with the bag, onto the conveyer belt. When she'd reached the end, after grabbing her bag and putting on her shoes, she craned her neck trying to spot me.

I gave her one last, weak smile and a wave.

She lifted her hand, and with a thumbs-up vanished in the crowd of departing passengers.

# Fifteen

Once home, I let the dogs out and, reluctant to go back inside the empty house, watched them chase around the backyard. T.P. ran off his puppy exuberance, while Lady paraded at a more sedate pace. T.P. continually tried to engage her in a game of "catch me if you can," but Lady was having none of it. She seemed to sense my melancholy and kept running to my side.

"You know something's up, don't you?" I asked, scratching her ears.

Laying backing her ears, she rubbed my leg with her nose.

"Everything will be fine," I whispered, trying to convince myself.

Going back inside, I was struck at how quiet the house seemed. Amazing how much noise one teenager made.

"It's okay, it's okay," I kept repeating while wandering the house, at a loss of what to do.

And it was okay . . . unlike when Tink was kidnapped. I knew she would be safe with Great-Aunt Mary. Both she and Aunt Dot were elderly, but as Abby had pointed out, close relatives lived in a little cluster on the mountain around them. They'd offer Tink protection, too. And, I thought I wasn't the only one intimidated by Great-Aunt

Mary. Abby had spoken often about how most of her neighbors thought twice about crossing her. *Yeah, Tink would be fine.*

"Well," I said out loud, putting my hands on my hips and scanning the living room. "I'm not accomplishing anything just moping around."

I went upstairs and pulled out the copies I'd made of Stephen's date book. I tried Karen Burns again and left a voice mail. Flipping through the pages, I then found the entry listing the Vargases' phone number. I picked up the phone and dialed. A man answered.

"Mr. Vargas?"

"Yes?"

"Hi, this is Ophelia Jensen from the library. Would it be possible to talk with you this afternoon?"

"Why?" He sounded suspicious.

"Ah, it would be better if I explained in person."

"Has Evita done something?"

Hearing the tinge of panic in his voice, I knew I could use his concern to my advantage. But lie about a kid? Nope, I couldn't do it. "No, we love having Evita at the library. It's about another matter."

"Okay." I heard the relief in his voice. "I'm home—it's too wet to work."

"I'll be right over," I said in a rush, before he could change his mind.

Fifteen minutes later I pulled into the yard at the old Murphy place. A vegetable garden grew a short distance from the small white clapboard house. Peppers, tomatoes, and squash flourished in tidy rows, and the overall appearance of the home was neat and well cared for.

The Murphys had to be relieved to have responsible renters, I thought.

I walked to the small front porch and knocked. A moment later Mr. Vargas appeared at the screen door. Over his shoulder I spied Deloris Vargas standing in the doorway to what I assumed was the kitchen. Her hands were clasped tightly in front of her, and her face was drawn with worry.

Mr. Vargas opened the door and motioned me inside. Looking at his wife, he said something in rapid Spanish, and after a glance at me, she disappeared into the other room.

I shook his hand as he nodded toward the faded couch. "Mr. Vargas, thank you for seeing me." Crossing the room, I took a place on the couch, while he sat in an old recliner.

"Why did you want to see me?" he asked, studying me closely.

"Well . . . " I crossed my legs and folded my hands in my lap. "I'm a friend of Stephen Lar—"

His posture turned rigid. "I've already talked to the police," he broke in.

"I'm sure they were here." I nodded my head and tried to look nonthreatening. "Um, they have Stephen's date book, and your number was listed . . . " I paused as I struggled in the face of his stony expression. "Ah, I was just wondering if you did speak with him before the shooting?"

"Yes."

He wasn't exactly forthcoming with information. I was going to have to pull it out of him.

"Could you tell me what you talked about?"

"The winery."

"Did he mention the book he's writing?"

"No."

I felt frustrated. "Do you remember his questions?"

"Why do you want to know?"

Tucking a strand of hair behind my ear, I searched for an excuse other than being snoopy. "I wanted to pass the information along to his assistant. Maybe she could continue his research while he's in the hospital."

*Brilliant, Jensen, brilliant.* Even I almost believed the bs I was handing out.

"He asked me how long I'd been in this country, how long I'd worked at the winery, if I've been treated fairly." He stopped abruptly.

"That's it?"

Stiff lines formed around his mouth. "Yes."

*I'm not the only one passing around the bs—he was lying.*

"But—"

The front door slammed open and Evita danced into the room. Her eyes widened and her mouth formed a small O when she saw me sitting on her couch.

"Miss Jensen," she said, hurrying over to me, "did you come to visit me?"

Stealing a look at her father, I saw his body relax and his expression become tender as he watched his daughter.

I turned my attention back to Evita and chuckled. "I really came to talk to your father—"

Her exuberance slipped a little.

"But I'm glad that you're here," I said with a grin. "How do you like *Because of Winn-Dixie*?"

She bounced back on the couch as her little fingers plucked at my jacket. "I love it!" she exclaimed. "I asked Papa if *I* could get a dog that smiles."

"Ah, a smiling dog," I said with a laugh. "Everyone should have one of those."

Her head bowed. "Papa said no." Her voice was suddenly sad. "He said we might move once my aunt comes from—"

"Evita!"

She jumped and focused her eyes on the worn pattern of the old couch. "Sorry, Papa," she said, not meeting his stern frown.

Mr. Vargas abruptly stood. "That's all I can tell you, Miss Jensen."

He sounded determined, and I knew the conversation was finished.

Rising myself, I looked down at Evita. "I've got to run now, sweetie."

When she raised her eyes to mine, a sheen of tears dulled their brightness.

Fighting the urge to stroke her brown curls, I gave her a wink. "I'll see if I can't find more books with smiling dogs, okay?"

With a small grin, she bobbed her head, then scrambled off the couch and headed toward the kitchen.

I turned toward her father and extended my hand. "Thank you for your time, Mr. Vargas."

He shook my hand but didn't reply.

Accepting defeat, I walked out the door and down the porch steps. As I reached the bottom step, I heard the screen door swing shut, followed swiftly by the sound of the Vargas's front door closing.

The next sound? The click of the dead bolt being shot home.

Unwilling to face my empty house, and troubled by the scene at the Vargas home, I took a detour by Darci's, and as I drove I dialed Karen Burns again.

Still no answer—I left another message.

Darci answered the door shoeless, dressed in blue jeans and a sweatshirt. A pen stuck out from behind one ear and she looked a little frazzled.

"Hey, come on in," she said with a hug. "Is Tink on her way to North Carolina?"

"Yeah," I replied dejectedly, and followed her into the living room.

Textbooks lay in a pile on the couch, and papers scattered the floor. Her laptop hummed from the coffee table.

"I'm disturbing you," I said, taking it all in.

"Ahh, that's okay." She waved her hand toward the mess. "I'm finished. I've been studying all afternoon for my Humanities test tomorrow. If I haven't learned it by now, it's too late," she said with a giggle. "Want a beer?"

Just then, a beer sounded pretty good. "Sure."

I stacked the textbooks on the coffee table and sat on the couch. Darci returned a moment later carrying two bottles and handed me one. I thanked her and took a long drink of the cold, amber liquid.

Settling at the other end of the couch, she tucked her legs underneath her. "Have you heard from Bill today?"

"Nope," I replied with a shake of my head. "He's been suspiciously quiet. The only activity has been the patrol car cruising by now and again."

"You haven't called him?"

"No," I said, leaning back. "I decided it's best to let *that* sleeping dog lie." I sipped my beer and mulled over a tactful way to bring up the Vargas family. Darci had lived in Summerset all of her life, and thanks to her friend Georgia, she knew the dirt on everyone. "What do you know about the Vargas family?"

*Smooth, Jensen, very tactful—not.*

"Not much," she said, tilting her head and gazing at me. "Why?"

"How long have they lived here?" I asked, ignoring her question.

"Hmm." She regarded me thoughtfully. "About ten years. I might be wrong, but I think they came to Summerset shortly after the winery opened. From Texas."

"Good memory."

She lifted a shoulder. "They were the first Latino family to move here."

"Were there any problems?"

"Maybe when they first came." Darci narrowed her eyes. "I remember overhearing Mom and Dad talking about an incident at Stumpy's . . . some redneck shooting off his mouth."

"Were they harassed?"

"Not that I heard." She paused and drank a long swallow

of beer. "You know how it is—any change and there's a lot of talk at first, then it all dies down and people move on to the next thing."

"Were Mr. and Mrs. Vargas born in the U.S.?"

"How would I know?" She giggled. "Why all the questions?"

"Oh, I don't know." I struggled to come up with an excuse, without telling Darci about Stephen's date book. "Ah, the shooting happened at the winery, Mr. Vargas works at the winery."

Her eyes shot wide with surprise. "You think he's a suspect?"

"No," I replied, doing some fast backpedaling, "but there might be a link. You said the Vargases were originally from Texas—"

"I said I *think* they moved here from Texas," she interjected.

"Yeah, well, Stephen said that from here he was headed to Texas."

Darci studied me with skepticism written on her face. "That's pretty weak."

I gave my hand a toss. "I'm just trying to make sense of what happened."

"I see." Darci threw an arm over the back of the couch and arched an eyebrow. "I thought you were staying out of it."

"I am," I explained, nodding vigorously, "I am. But I can't help wondering . . . " I let my voice trail away.

"Speaking of Stephen—how's he doing?"

"No change."

"Have you ever read one of his books?" she asked, making a sudden shift in the conversation.

"No. Have you?"

"Yeah, I'm reading one right now. You know what I noticed?" she asked thoughtfully.

"What?"

"He does meticulous research." She held up one finger.

"Okay." I wasn't sure what point she was trying to make, but knowing Darci, there was one. It would just take some time for her to make it.

Holding up a second finger, she said, "He quotes numerous sources."

"That's good," I replied, at a loss what to say.

Her third finger shot up. "He takes on some tough subjects. The book I'm reading now deals with the mob." She scooted forward, dropping her hand. "Think about it—the subjects he's covered—I bet he has more enemies than you do."

I started to raise my bottle to my lips, then lowered it. "Thanks a lot."

"You know what I mean. He's been writing a long time. He's had more opportunity to tick people off. You just started a couple of years ago," she said brightly.

Rolling my eyes, I finally connected her dots. "And one of these enemies followed him to Iowa and shot him?"

She nodded her head emphatically. "Right."

"So now I have a hit man after me?"

"Yeah."

"That's comforting," I muttered. "Why?"

She cocked her head. "Why what?"

"Why would the hit man be after me?"

"Hmm, well . . . " Her pretty face puckered in a frown. "I haven't figured that out yet."

# *Sixteen*

After leaving Darci's, I still didn't feel like going home, so I decided to visit Stephen. Or at least try to visit him.

With one eye out for anyone who looked like a reporter, I hurried across the parking lot and into the lobby of the Regional Medical Center. I knew where Stephen was, and my plan was to just brazen it out—to walk into the Cardiac Surgery Intensive Care Unit and into his cubicle. The worst that could happen would be they kicked me out. It wouldn't be the first time my presence wasn't welcomed.

I marched through the lobby and followed the route Bill and I had taken on Monday, only this time I prepared my defenses before entering through the swinging doors. I didn't need to be caught off guard as I had been before. With my head down and eyes averted, I walked past the nurses' station toward Stephen's cubicle. I stopped short at the door.

A tall blond woman stood next to Stephen's bed, her eyes glued on his face. Her shoulders hunched forward as one hand gently stroked Stephen's arm. She looked rumpled and her whole body tired.

Oh my gosh, it was Stephen's mother. I didn't feel any guilt at worming my way around the hospital rules, but I did at intruding on this poor woman.

I pivoted on my heel and took a step before she spotted me.

"Wait," she said, leaving Stephen's side and coming toward me. "Are you here to see Stephen?"

I felt a blush creep up my face at getting caught. "Yes," I mumbled.

Her eyes narrowed as they studied me. "You're not with the press, are you?"

"No, ma'am. I'm Ophelia Jensen. I—"

Her hand darted out and grabbed my arm. "You witnessed the shooting."

"Yes, I did. I'm so sorry." I glanced over her shoulder toward the bed. "Is there any change?"

"No." Her eyes flitted back to the still figure lying in bed. "He's not making any improvement, but his condition isn't deteriorating either." Her focus returned to me. "I'm thankful for that." She tilted her head. "Would you mind answering some questions for me?"

She took me by surprise. "Ah, no," I stuttered.

Giving me a wisp of a smile, she nodded. "Thank you. There's a garden café outside, at the end of the hall. I'll just be a minute," she said, motioning toward the nurses' station. "I need to let the nurse know where I'm going."

She walked quickly to the station and, in a low voice, explained that she'd be at the café if they needed to reach her.

Together, we left the intensive care unit and walked down the hall and out the double doors to the café. Mrs. Larsen offered to buy me a coffee, but I declined. While she ordered hers, my eyes wandered the small area.

Above me, leafy branches formed a shady canopy. Dappled sunlight filtered through the leaves. At one plastic table, hospital staff dressed in scrubs sat on plastic chairs. Near them, an elderly gentleman, accompanied by a young man and woman, tottered over and took a seat at another table. I watched as the young woman leaned forward and gently rubbed the old man's arm. Feeling as if I were intruding on a private moment, I averted my eyes.

When Mrs. Larsen took a seat opposite me, she got right to the point. "Can you tell me what happened?"

"Hasn't Sheriff Wilson talked to you?" I asked, surprised by her directness.

"The sheriff seems to be a very nice man, but he wasn't a fount of information."

"Well, ma'am—"

"Please, call me Louise," she said.

"Louise . . . there isn't much to tell. I'd just met your son, and it seemed we had a lot in common, so . . . " I paused and shifted in my chair. I didn't want to try explain the connection I'd felt. "Um, we went for a walk. We were standing near the woods when it happened. The shot seemed to come out of nowhere." I hesitated, knowing this had to be painful for her to hear. "I'm sorry, I didn't see anything."

"Did Stephen say anything about his work?" Her lips formed a tight smile. "No, of course he didn't. He's terribly close-mouthed," she commented, answering her own question.

"Do you think the motive is tied to one of his books?"

"I can't think of any other reason. As far as I know, Stephen doesn't have any jealous ex-girlfriends, he doesn't have any overzealous fans, and I'd be shocked if he were involved in anything illegal." Her face took on a faraway look. "He's always had such a strong sense of justice."

"But he does have enemies?" I quizzed.

"Oh, yes," she exclaimed, and lifted the cup to her lips with a trembling hand. "He's done exposés on the mob, crooked CEOs, shady politicians—any one of them might want revenge."

Hmm, maybe Darci was on to something. Maybe the motive wasn't related to his current book, but one he'd already written.

"Were you able to give Bill any specific names?" I asked. "Did Stephen ever receive any death threats?"

"If he did, he wouldn't have told me, and he's never mentioned anyone who's wanted to harm him. The person who'd be able to answer those questions is his assistant, Karen Burns."

"Have you spoken to her?"

"No." She shook her head. "And that surprises me. She and Stephen work closely together. I'm a little shocked she isn't here." She blew on her coffee and took a sip before continuing. "Stephen's always been a fighter, always cared about the underdog. Even as a child. He's never backed down." Her breath hitched in her throat. "And now it's led to this."

"Louise," I said, patting her frail hand. "It's very admirable that he's used his talent to help people by exposing the truth."

"I know," she said with a sigh. "His father and I had always hoped he'd go into the law. We saw him working in civil rights, but no, he wanted to write." Her eyes shimmered with tears. "And now look at the price he's paid."

"Bill's very good at his job," I interjected. "He'll find who did this."

Her mouth turned to a bitter smile. "I hope so, but what about the next time? I don't see Stephen ever changing. He's so devoted to his work that he's led a solitary life. No wife, no family of his own—all those things a mother wants for their child, he lacks."

Two years ago I wouldn't have understood how she felt, but now I did. Someday I wanted those things for Tink, too. Home, family, success, all the good things life has to offer. I searched for words of comfort but could think of nothing to say.

Her eyes suddenly widened and she quickly wiped her cheeks. "Oh no, don't look, but here comes that awful man," she gasped.

So I did exactly what she told me not to do. I spun around in my chair, searching for the man. "Who?" I asked, my gaze roaming the tables.

"That politician . . . Chuck Krause," she hissed.

My eyes flew back to Mrs. Larsen. "Chuck Krause is—"

A shadow fell across the table. "Good evening, Louise."

Mrs. Larsen lifted her head. "Mr. Krause," she answered in a tight voice.

I didn't want to get involved in this conversation, so I tried to pretend that I was invisible. It didn't work. I felt Krause's eyes on me and looked up.

"I'd like to introduce Ophelia Jensen," Mrs. Larsen said graciously. "She's a friend of Stephen's."

"Ah, Ophelia." Krause's face fell into an expression of feigned sympathy. "You were with him at the time of the accident."

Attempted murder—an accident? *Okay, Jensen, cut him some slack. Maybe he's trying to spare Mrs. Larsen's feelings.*

Evidently, Mrs. Larsen didn't feel the need to have her feelings spared. "Mr. Krause, someone tried to kill my son," she replied with a tinge of sarcasm. "I'd hardly call that an accident."

Krause slipped into the chair next to her and laid a hand on her shoulder. She shrank from his touch, but he seemed oblivious. "Louise, I want you to know I'm taking a personal interest in your son's case. Stopping this kind of violence is a promise I've made to the voters if elected." His voice rose as he glanced quickly over his shoulder to see if he had an audience. "I will bring pressure to bear until the guilty are brought to justice."

Unwilling to watch Krause's performance, I lowered my eyes. *Man, enough hot air was coming out of him to evaporate water.*

"I appreciate your efforts, but my main priority is Stephen's recovery," she said shortly.

"Perfectly understandable. Your days must be very long, though, Louise. Nothing more tiring than sitting around a hospital day in and day out." He patted her shoulder again. "You need to take care of yourself, too. I'm having a fund-raiser next week, and I'd love for you to be one of my honored guests. It would be good for you to get away from the hospital for an evening."

My head popped up. *Her son's fighting for his life, and this bozo wants her to come to a fund-raiser?*

"Mr. Krause, the only thing *good* for me right now would be for my son to recover," she answered in a voice dripping with ice.

Krause's eyes widened imperceptibly as her put-down penetrated his thick skin. "Naturally," he said, rising and pressing a hand on her shoulder. "I just stopped by to see if there's anything I can do. If there is, please let me know."

"Good-bye, Mr. Krause," she said without looking up.

Mrs. Larsen waited until Krause was out of earshot. "Humph," she whispered, leaning across the table. "The only reason *he* stopped by was to check on free air time."

I gave her a puzzled look. "Huh?"

"The reporters have been such pests," she answered in disgust.

"I know they've been hanging around—one waylaid me leaving the hospital Monday. Have they been bothering you?"

"A little," she conceded. "Security has tried to keep them away from me, but Mr. Krause . . . " Sitting back in her chair, she gave her head a disgusted shake. " . . . he's sought them out . . . and not only that, he wanted me to join him."

"You're kidding?"

"No, I'm not. And this fund-raiser . . . I may be old, but I'm not stupid." She sniffed indignantly. "He can't fool me.

He wanted to parade out the grieving mother to make some kind of political point."

"So," I said with an evil grin, "he's not only smarmy as hell, he's a political ambulance chaser."

A true smile lit her face. "Very well put, Ophelia."

# *Seventeen*

I loved the Internet. Anything you wanted to buy was only a click and a credit card away. Like plane tickets. I'd decided if Karen Burns wouldn't answer her phone, I would fly to St. Louis and talk to her in person. Unfortunately, because of my late booking, the only flight I could get had a three hour layover in Detroit. It would take me almost seven hours to reach my destination instead of the six if I drove.

*But this is better*, I told myself. If I'd driven and Bill got wind that I left town, he could've had me apprehended. By flying, I could slip down to St. Louis and be back before anyone knew I left. I'd covered my bases with Abby by calling and telling her that I planned on a hot bath and then retreating to my bedroom. She wouldn't try and contact me until that evening. By then I'd be at the hotel, and pretend I was home. Thank goodness for cell phones—she'd never know that I was six hundred miles away.

*I think.* A little flutter of doubt shook me. *No, this would work.*

*And if it didn't?*

I shrugged. It wouldn't make a difference. I'd be in Missouri—she'd be in Iowa. The worst that could happen would be the hell of a lecture that I'd receive when I arrived home.

As I dug my needlepoint out of my carry-on, my thoughts

drifted to the conversation I'd had with Tink. She sounded happy and excited. It appeared she now saw the trip as an adventure instead of a banishment. I had also spoken briefly with Aunt Dot, who wanted to know all the details of the latest family "problem." I'd blanched a bit when she mentioned maybe it would be good for her to pay another visit. Just to help, of course.

*Right.*

I dearly loved Aunt Dot, but the thought of her on the loose again in Summerset gave me the shivers. I emphatically told her we needed her to protect Tink. With that, she chortled and told me all about the forgetful spell Great-Aunt Mary had placed around the property—any stranger without an invitation would have a hard time finding them.

I didn't question the spell, nor did I question the fact that, according to her, the fairies were happy to see Tink.

Whatever—as long as Tink was safe, it was all that mattered.

Paying attention to my needlepoint, I saw that I'd, once again, balled the thread into a tight little knot. I gave up and shoved it back into the carry-on. Next, I picked up my latest J. D. Robb paperback, but even the exciting adventures of Eve Dallas couldn't keep my mind from wandering.

Tapping my foot, I checked my watch for the hundredth time. *Crap, I still had two more hours before the flight. I'll call Karen again.*

I hit the now memorized numbers and listened as it rang and rang. It was weird. Surely she knew that her boss had been shot. One would think she'd have contacted someone by now. Could she have spoken with Bill? Finally, the voice mail clicked on and I left another message. One way or the other, I intended to track the woman down and question her about Stephen. I had her address—I'd camp out on her doorstep if I had to.

Bored beyond belief, my eyes traveled around the airport. Maybe I could amuse myself by people watching? Businessmen sat with their Bluetooth headsets clipped to their ears while they tapped away on their laptops. *Not much of interest there.* In the next row, a mother tried to keep her toddler entertained. I could relate—he appeared as bored as I was. He caught my eye from over his mother's shoulder and gave me a toothy grin. I smiled. Satisfied he'd been noticed, he returned to tugging on his mother's hair.

I stole another look at my watch. *Well, that took all of fifteen minutes.*

Bouncing my knees impatiently, I glanced toward the gift shop. *Okay, let's give that a try.*

I stood up, slung my carry-on over my shoulder, and strolled over to the wide doorway. Travel pillows, lap rugs, candy, souvenirs of Detroit, magazines—everything a weary traveler would want lined the shelves. Taking my time, I browsed the magazines, studied the selection of candy, fingered the soft lap robes. From behind me, I felt someone staring at my back and my nerves jangled. With a sideways look, I noticed one of the clerks watching me, suspicion written on her face.

*Oh man, she thinks I'm a shoplifter.*

Crossing to the counter, I picked up a pack of gum, paid for it, and beat a hasty retreat out of the shop.

From across the way, I caught sight of a bookstore. Tucking my gum in my pocket, I wandered into the store. Immediately my attention was drawn to the display of the latest best-sellers. Placed in a prominent position was *Terror on the Seine* by M. J. LaSalle. Striding over, I picked up the hardcover and skimmed the blurb on the back.

As I read, icy fingers tickled up my spine.

The novel told the story of a man hunting a group of neo-Nazis as they tried to build a new Third Reich à la Frankenstein's monster.

Was Stephen a World War II buff? If so, had my connection with him been so strong that I sensed it on some level? Was it why I'd suddenly started dreaming about Paris and the German occupation? What if the dreams were not mine, but his?

Clutching the book, I hurried over to the counter and paid for it. I rushed back to the waiting area and flipped the cover open.

For the next hour I sat lost in the story. No doubt about it—Stephen spun a good tale. One scene that drew my attention portrayed a dinner party eerily like the one in my dream. The one I'd experienced as Madeleine. Stephen had even mentioned Drancy and Auschwitz in the dialogue.

Was that the connection? What if somehow, while his body was in a coma state, his mind was reaching out and touching mine?

I grimaced. If his mind was indeed invading mine, I wished his message would be a little more specific than showing me the life of a Parisian model living over sixty years ago.

Tangled up in all the questions, I almost missed the boarding call for my flight. Hurrying, I shoved the book in the pocket of my bag and joined the other passengers.

Once strapped in my seat, I entertained myself by looking out the window. In a short time we were in the air, flying through cloudless skies over the Midwest, back toward St. Louis.

I leaned my head against the window and watched the earth below. The fields resembled the patchwork quilt lying on Abby's bed. Squares in shades of light and dark green marked the pastures and growing crops, while brown rectangles showed fallow land. Scattered amidst the fields were houses and farmsteads, reminding me of the little pieces to a Monopoly game.

Lost in my fanciful imaginings, I felt my eyes grow heavy.

The sound of the flight attendant pushing an empty cart up the aisle woke me with a start. *Dang, I'd missed the free peanuts.* Turning toward the window, I spied the city of St.

Louis and the Gateway Arch gleaming in the early evening sun.

*Good, I'm almost there. I can get on with my mission to find Karen Burns.*

Thirty minutes later I stood at the baggage claim waiting for my luggage to shoot down the ramp onto the carousel. As I did, I went over my list in my head. *Call Abby and tell her a big, fat lie; try Karen Burns again; my reservation at the Renaissance Grand near Laclede's Landing was already made. But did I want a taxi, or did I want to rent a car?*

Tapping my foot, I thought about it. I didn't know my way around St. Louis, so I'd need a car with GPS. And by chauffeuring myself around, it might be easier to track down the elusive Karen Burns.

Okay, next step—rent a car.

A sudden hand on my shoulder made my heart jump. *They've found me* ricocheted in my head.

And they had—I whirled around to face my lovely grandmother with a steely light shining in her green eyes.

"You didn't think you could go off without me, did you?"

I didn't need to rent a car. Abby had beaten me to St. Louis by driving instead of flying. We picked up my bags and headed toward the hotel.

Buckled in, I rubbed my palms nervously on my thighs. I couldn't make myself look at Abby. "I wasn't trying to shut you out," I blurted.

Her eyes darted toward me. "I don't like lies and secrets, Ophelia."

Shamefaced, I hung my head. "I know . . . I just wanted to keep you safe."

Out of the corner of my eye I caught Abby's sardonic grin. "May I remind you I've managed to do just fine for over seventy years?"

"I know . . . " I hesitated, lifting my head and studying

her. "But it appears I'm a target, and I don't want you caught in the cross fire, be exposed to danger."

Abby snickered. "My darling girl, I had a life before you were born. I grew up in the mountains. Poverty, moonshiners, revenuers . . . " Her voice faded and her eyes took on a faraway look. "I've seen my fair share of violence."

Surprised, I shifted sideways in my seat. Abby had always talked as if life in the mountains had been idyllic. I'd never considered that there might have been a darker side. "Really? Like what?"

Her head snapped toward me and back. "Never mind." Subject closed.

"How did you find me?" I asked, studying her profile.

"Your password," she replied with a smirk. "It took me about five minutes to figure it out, by the way. Once I'd done that, I checked your e-mails and saw your flight reservation."

Okay, so maybe I didn't love the Internet.

I slumped in my seat. "Don't you think that's an invasion of my privacy?"

"Drastic times . . . drastic measures," she said simply.

"What were you doing at my house in the first place?"

"I brought you lunch. I knew how upset you were with Tink gone, and I was afraid you wouldn't eat. I stopped by Stumpy's and Arthur made your favorite sandwich."

"Hot sausage?" My stomach rumbled. I had forgotten to eat. I'd even missed out on the peanuts.

She heard the gurgling. "Yes," she said with a quick "serves you right" glance.

"Shoot." I pressed on my stomach as I twisted in my seat. "Let's eat after we check in, okay?"

"Fine, but no food until you tell me exactly what you're doing," she replied, her voice determined.

"You're going to starve me?" I asked, arching an eyebrow.

She grinned. "If you're near starvation, then I suggest you start talking."

In the time it took us to drive to the hotel, I spilled everything—the instant connection I'd felt with Stephen, the dreams, leaving out the more titillating parts, of course.

Finished, I watched her, trying to judge her reaction. "What do you think?"

"Oh my," she whispered.

My forehead wrinkled. "That's it . . . 'oh, my'?" I groused. "That's not very helpful."

Abby pursed her lips. "I've never come across something like this before. I need to contemplate all the implications."

"Do you know what happens in the mind when someone's in a coma?" I snapped my fingers. "Of course you do—you were out of it for a couple of days when Charles Thornton conked you on the head. What was it like?"

"Dreams—" she faltered. "Lots of dreams that never end."

I thought back to that time when Abby lay in the hospital and we were so afraid she might never wake up. "Remember when I almost unleashed the Elements, but your voice stopped me at the last minute?"

"Yes, and it's a good thing it did," she said stridently.

"I agree," I answered with a wave of my hand, "but that's not what I meant. Were you aware of what I was doing?"

She tapped a finger on the steering wheel. "I can't answer that. My memory of that time is rather jumbled. I do remember feeling your need for vengeance."

"But you don't remember reaching out to me?"

"Not really," she said with a shake of her head.

"I need to know if that might be what Stephen is doing—contacting me with his mind. And the Paris stuff is some kind of symbolism."

"Maybe." She looked thoughtful. "You said you felt an immediate and strong link with him?"

Recalling the first set of dreams, the erotic ones, I blushed. "Yes."

"It was as if you'd always known him?"

"Yes." I shot her a perplexed look.

"Hmm." She fell silent.

"What?"

Still not answering me, Abby parked the car, got out, and handed the keys to the valet. We removed our luggage and headed toward the entrance.

I scrambled after her, hurrying to catch up. When I did, I tugged on her jacket.

"What do you think?"

"Well, when someone feels such a strong tie to a person they've just met, it could mean . . . " Her voice trailed away as she looked at me with a question in her eyes. "Have we ever discussed reincarnation?"

# *Eighteen*

The hotel lobby was elegant. Muted light reflected off soft neutral walls, and pots of large green plants placed around the room offered a sharp contrast. After entering, we turned left to the reception desk. Abby handled the desk clerk, while I stood silent, still turning over the reincarnation thing in my head.

What I knew about it would fill one page in a very small notebook. I did understand the concept that we all had lessons to learn, and according to some, we kept going around lifetime after lifetime until those lessons were mastered.

A nudge to my side brought my thoughts back to the present, and I followed Abby over to the gorgeous Art Deco elevator. Once inside, I watched the floors zip by. The bell dinged and the doors slid smoothly open. Exiting, we got our bearings and proceeded down the carpeted hall to our adjoining rooms.

Abby glanced over her shoulder. "You're very quiet. Did I upset you?"

"No," I muttered, pulling my small suitcase behind me. "If you're right about reincarnation, it's just one more thread leading nowhere."

At the door to my room, Abby released her suitcase and placed her hands on my shoulders. "We'll talk later, but let's eat first. I'll call Arthur, then we'll find a restaurant. Okay?"

"Fine," I mumbled, giving her a peck on the cheek.

My room matched the elegance of the lobby. A king-size bed, piled with pillows, sat along one wall; on the other wall, a large TV armoire with drawers, and a small desk next to the armoire. All the furniture was made of a dark, rich wood. A comfy chair, with a small table nearby, was placed by the long window.

After stowing my suitcase in the closet and my carry-on in the tiled bathroom, I crossed the room to the window. Holding back the sheer curtain, I stared out over the city.

The sky held no stars, their twinkle blocked by the lights of the city. I found it hard to imagine living in a place with no stars. Looking down, I watched the busy city street and pondered Abby's theory.

A person coming back again and again? My first reaction was: *How crazy is that?*

*Wait a second—how crazy is believing in magick, premonitions, runes, even fairies? Scratch the fairies—the jury's still out on that one.*

I shifted my weight uncomfortably. My reaction to reincarnation was disturbingly similar to that of the skeptics I'd been dealing with all of my life. My former fiancé, who dumped me when he learned of my peculiar heritage; Henry Comacho, a cop and my onetime nemesis who later became a friend; Bill.

My lips twisted in a wry grin. Ethan. He'd accepted my gift from the start. Funny, considering ninety percent of our conversations ended in an argument, that he'd never questioned my gift. Maybe that was why his lack of confidence now bothered me. I wondered where he was. He hadn't called since our heated discussion on Monday—not unusual—but since he seemed to stay in contact with Bill, he surely knew about the potshots in my backyard. He hadn't called to lecture me.

Hearing Abby's knock, I dropped the curtain and moved away from the window.

"How's Arthur?" I asked, swinging the door wide.

"Fine." Her lips lifted in a shy smile. "He has my keys, so he stopped by your house and checked on things."

"The animals were okay, weren't they?"

"Yes, they came scampering through the doggy door when they heard Arthur in the house." She chuckled. "He wondered if you knew you'd left your TV on."

"Did you explain I do that for Lady, Queenie, and T.P.? He didn't turn it off, did he?"

"Yes, I explained, and no, he left it on." She chuckled again, crossing to the chair and sitting. "He said he never knew animals enjoyed watching TV."

"They like watching Animal Planet, and *Orangutan Island* is their favorite show," I replied defensively. "Where would you like to eat?"

Abby tilted her head and studied me. "You look a little worn-out, dear. What about room service?"

"Hmm." I tapped my chin thoughtfully. "Hot food and the beverage of my choice delivered to my door? Requiring no effort on my part?" I gave her a cheeky grin. "Duh—yeah."

With a smile, Abby reached for the menu and skimmed it. "What would you like?"

I walked to the closet, opened the door, and unzipped my suitcase. "Just a hamburger and fries would be good," I said, kicking off my loafers, then pulling out my University of Iowa T-shirt and a pair of sweatpants. Entering the tiled bathroom, I stripped off my jeans and shirt while Abby placed our order.

"What else did Arthur have to say?" I called out, making small talk as I wiggled into my T-shirt.

"Not much. He mentioned the fund-raiser again," she replied nonchalantly.

I stuck my head out the bathroom door. "What fund-raiser?"

"The one for Chuck Krause . . . at the winery."

"Monday night?" I asked, pulling on my sweatpants.

"Yes." I heard the disapproval in Abby's voice. "I think it was in poor taste to hold it there after what happened the day before."

"Did Krause mention the shooting?"

"Of course," she commented sarcastically. "Arthur said he used it to segue into his policies on crime."

After folding my jeans and shirt, I combed my hair into a ponytail with my fingers and held it in place with a contraband scrunchie, one I'd saved from Darci's purge. "Did you meet Krause Sunday?"

"Briefly. Arthur was impressed with what Krause had to say about small business development, which is why he went to the fund-raiser."

Turning on the water, I washed my face. "Did Krause mention undocumented workers Monday night?" I called out over the running water.

"Undocumented workers?"

"Yeah, illegal immigrants."

"Arthur didn't mention it. Why?"

Turning off the water, I left the bathroom and joined Abby. I plopped on the bed, stretched out on my stomach and propped myself up on my elbows. "The other day on the phone, Claire went off on a tear about his policies. In her opinion, he's way too conservative."

Abby gave her head a little shake. "Ahh, that's Claire for you. It's a difficult situation and passions run high on both sides."

"What do you think?" I asked, cupping my face with my hand.

"I don't know . . . " She paused. "These people are escaping deplorable conditions in their own countries with the hope of a better life here." Her eyes traveled to the window and she stared at the lights of the city. "When I was a child, times were hard, but I never went to bed hungry, I never worried about death squads knocking on our door in the middle of the night. We had food and we were safe." She sat back in the chair. "But to answer your question—I think this is a very complicated situation and that there are no easy answers."

Rolling onto my back, I scooted up in the bed and fluffed the pillows behind me. Leaning back, I twisted the hem of my T-shirt. "Abby, about this reincarnation? You really think I might have known Stephen in a past life?"

My mind leapt ahead. *What if she says yes, and what if Stephen wound up being the reincarnation of the colonel?* In my dreams, the colonel was the only man Madeleine had a connection with so far. There was the missing lover, but he hadn't popped up yet. *Maybe Madeleine sold out and became Vogel's mistress? Yuck.* The thought gave me the creepy-crawlies.

"The idea of reincarnation troubles you, doesn't it?" Abby asked, noticing my expression.

"Yeah . . . it does. It seems to me this lifetime is complicated enough without worrying about what happened in a past life." I released the hem of my shirt.

Abby crossed her legs and leaned forward. "But you see, some of the problems we have now have their roots in our past lives." She sat back and steepled her fingers. "Maybe you and Stephen have some unfinished business that's carried over into this life, and now's the time to resolve it."

"Darci thinks he's my soul mate and that's why I've had the dreams."

"Maybe, or it could be, in the end, he's not good for you and your challenge is to walk away from him in this lifetime. Something you might not have done in your last one."

*Ugh, maybe Stephen was Vogel.*

I tapped the back of my head against the headboard. "This is frustrating. The dreams aren't exactly forthcoming with a lot of information. How am I going to know what to do? How do I make sure I meet the challenge?"

Abby rose and crossed the small space between the bed and the chair. Sitting next to me, she took my hand in both of hers. "I'm afraid it's going to require something that's always been hard for you—surrender control and trust that your gift will lead you to your answers." Rubbing my hand, she looked thoughtful. "In the end, child, maybe that's the real lesson."

Stretching, I lifted my arms over my head. I'd slept deeply that night, and for a second I didn't remember where I was.

*Oh, yeah—St. Louis—tracking down Karen Burns.*

I felt rested—the dreams hadn't troubled me last night. Could talking about them with Abby have ended them? Was it really that simple? That all I needed to do was trust myself and have faith? Wouldn't that be a relief? I could concentrate on learning why Stephen had been shot.

Throwing back the covers, I jumped out of bed. In the bathroom, I quickly showered, dressed, and threw on some makeup. Forty-five minutes later I stood knocking at Abby's door, ready to hunt down Karen.

"Ready?" I asked when Abby opened her door.

She was dressed in tan linen slacks and a light tunic. A floral scarf was held in place around the neckline by one of her favorite brooches. Today, she wore her hair coiled in a neat bun at the nape of her neck. She looked cool and elegant.

I glanced down at my red knit top, jeans, and loafers. Next to her, I felt sloppy. *Maybe I should pay more attention to Darci?*

"You look nice, dear," Abby said, as if reading my mind. "Are you ready for breakfast?"

I shifted my weight on one foot. "If you don't mind, I'd like to drive to Karen Burns's apartment first. If we arrive early enough, we might catch her."

Digging out her keys, Abby closed the door and linked her arm with mine. "Whatever you want, dear. Let's go."

Once in the car, Abby punched the address I'd given her for Karen's apartment into the GPS, and we were on our way. A short time later we pulled into the parking lot of Karen's apartment building, not far from Laclede's Landing.

The building was obviously old, but had been restored. Birds chirped in the large maple trees shading the entrance, while hydrangea bushes bloomed on each side. The atmosphere was peaceful and quiet this early in the morning.

Abby and I entered the cool foyer, where I found the buzzer to Karen's apartment and pushed it.

No answer.

I pressed the button again, leaving my finger on it a little longer this time.

Still no answer.

Fisting a hand on my hip, I hit the button again and again.

Abby finally reached out and touched my wrist. "I don't think she's home."

Great—as Nancy Drew, I was bombing out.

"Now what?" Abby asked as a woman, dressed in a jogging suit, leading a large boxer on a leash, entered the foyer.

"Maybe Karen is working at Stephen's condo?" I said hopefully.

The woman with the boxer paused and glanced at me over her shoulder. "I'm sorry . . . I don't mean to be eavesdropping, but are you looking for Karen Burns?"

I know my face lit up. "Yes," I replied excitedly. "Do you know her?"

"Yes, I live in the apartment across the hall. Are you a friend of hers?"

Time to tell another lie. "Yes, I'm an old classmate from out of town—"

Abby gave me a poke in my side.

Ignoring her, I continued. "I've been trying to reach her."

The women's face reflected her alarm. "Oh, dear," she said softly. "You don't know, then?"

I felt my excitement fade, and a sense of dread replaced it. "Know what?"

"Karen was mugged last night. She's in Lasalle Medical Plaza."

# Nineteen

"What do you think?" I asked Abby as we drove to the hospital.

"Muggings happen all the time in the city."

I inhaled sharply. "Her boss is shot less than a week ago, and now she's mugged." Watching Abby smoothly maneuver into the heavy traffic, I pursed my lips before I spoke again. "Too much of a coincidence, if you ask me. Wonder if Bill knows."

"The mugging occurred last night, so he might not have been contacted yet." She honked her horn as a car whipped over in front of her. "And who knows . . . law enforcement agencies don't always communicate with each other."

"Yeah, but as Ethan said, Bill's a good cop, I bet he contacted the St. Louis police after the shooting. You'd think they'd return the favor."

"It's a big city. Maybe the information concerning the mugging hasn't reached the right ears yet." Abby glanced my way. "You sound as if you want Bill to know."

I picked at the armrest. "I do—if it helps him solve the case—but I'm a little worried he'll come charging down here once he hears about it. And—"

"Find out you're here instead of in Summerset," she said, finishing my sentence for me. "Hmm," she went on, her tone teasing, "I've heard the jail's serving the prisoners meals from one of the restaurants now, so at least you'll eat well."

"Not funny." I shot her a dirty look. "Bill's always threatening to put me in the slammer, and one of these days he's going to carry through with the threat."

She reached out and patted my knee. "Don't worry, dear, I'll post bail."

We left the car in the parking garage and rode the elevator down to the first floor. Praying it wouldn't be a repeat of my experience at the Regional Medical Center, I marched up to the information desk.

"Karen Burns, please."

Without a glance, the receptionist ran her finger down the patient list. "She's in Room 224."

Walking away from the desk, I gave Abby a big smile. "That was easy."

"Don't count your chickens—we haven't talked to Karen Burns yet."

Peeking in the half-open door to Room 224, we saw a dark-haired woman in the bed in a half sitting position, facing the overhead TV. An IV pole with a large bag full of clear liquid sat next to the bed—its tubes running from the bag to her arm.

From where I stood in the doorway, she didn't look that injured. No bandages, no medical equipment other than the IV. To me, she just looked bored. Then her head rolled on the pillow to face me and our eyes met across the small room.

The entire right side of her face was one massive bruise. Her right eye was swollen shut and the corner of her mouth appeared to be cut.

Shocked at her injuries, I took one step back, bumping into Abby.

Moving me out of her way, Abby took control, crossing the room to the bed. "Hello, Karen. I'm Abigail McDonald, and this," she said with a wave toward me, "is my granddaughter, Ophelia Jensen."

Karen's good eye widened. "You're the one who's been leaving all the messages," she mumbled through puffy lips. "I don't want to talk to you." She turned her head away.

"Karen," I said gently, "do you know about Stephen?"

A tear trickled down her left cheek. "Yes," she whispered.

"The sheriff investigating the shooting thinks I might have been the target," I said, joining Abby. "But I wasn't, was I?"

"Don't know anything," she muttered.

The conversation was getting me nowhere.

"Karen," I said trying again. "Someone tried to kill me Monday night."

With a soft moan, she shifted her head on the pillow and said nothing.

What had Abby said? Drastic times, drastic measures? My eyes flew to Abby's face. She blinked once and gave me a slight nod.

"Karen." I kept my voice mild as I laid my hand on her arm and opened my mind.

Immediately I saw, felt, and heard what she had the night before. The smell of the river; pools of light from the street lamps; the sound of footsteps behind her; the sudden grasp of hands on her shoulders; the feeling of being spun around; a man, his face hidden in the shadows; the fist to her face again and again; the taste of blood sour on her tongue.

But most of all I felt the terror—black, all-consuming terror. *I'm going to die*, was her last thought before she mercifully lost consciousness.

With sweaty palms, and shaken to my core, I broke the connection.

Disoriented, Karen looked first at Abby, then me. "Who *are* you, really?"

"I told you, Ophelia Jensen. I'm so sorry that man hurt you," I said with compassion, "and I want to help you and Stephen."

The uninjured side of her mouth twisted down. "You can't. Stephen always told me if anything ever happened to him, to run. I didn't run fast enough, and next time they'll kill me—" Her voice faltered. "I'm going away where they can't find me."

"If whoever's behind these attacks isn't brought to justice, you'll spend your life looking over your shoulder."

"No, I won't. Once Stephen is out of the hospital, he'll take care of it."

"Stephen's in a coma and can't help anyone," I said brusquely.

Abby gave me a little nudge to the side and stepped closer to the bed. "Here, child, have a sip of water," she said, picking up a glass near the bed and holding the straw to Karen's lips. "Poor thing." She gently stroked Karen's hair.

Karen seemed to relax under Abby's soothing touch and took a long drink through the straw. "Thanks." Her tongue licked at her bottom lip, and she winced when it touched the cut.

Grabbing the railing on the bed, I gazed at her. "Karen, do you know why someone wanted to hurt you and Stephen?"

With a sigh, she closed her left eye. "The book."

"Which book?"

"The one he's working on now. He came back from the East Coast obsessed with this new project." She opened her eye and watched me. "Said he got the idea while in Boston."

*What idea would lead him from Massachusetts to Iowa to Texas?*

"Why would they attack you last night?" I asked.

"The disks."

"What disks?" My hands tightened on the railing with excitement.

"Stephen is paranoid when he's working on a book. Everyone knows about his quirk—he jokes about it on his website." Her fingers fidgeted with the blanket. "He puts everything—

notes, manuscript—on disks. He doesn't leave anything on his hard drive. I know they were after the disks."

"Have you looked at them?"

"No, I never read the ones that deal with his nonfiction until he's finished. I go through the notes at the same time as the manuscript and check for accuracy."

"Did you have any disks last night when you were mugged?" I asked.

"Yes. When he's out of town, he sends them to me at a post office box—registered mail. I sign for the package, then put the disks in his fireproof box." She swallowed with effort. "I was taking the latest disks to his condo."

Abby held the straw to Karen's lips again, and she took another long drink.

"Did they take them?" I asked.

"Yes. The police said my purse was stolen. They were in it."

I felt my excitement come crashing down. *So close.* "Everything's lost?"

"No, just the ones he mailed from Iowa. The rest are in the box."

"Karen . . . " I tried to keep the anticipation out of my voice. "May we borrow them?"

Her eyes traveled to the window, and the war going on inside her was apparent in her features. Loyalty to Stephen, fear, hesitation, all flitted across her damaged face. The last expression was resignation.

She lifted a hand as if it took great effort and pointed toward the closet. "The keys to Stephen's condo and the box are on a small key ring in the pocket of my slacks." She paused. "At least they were."

Almost holding my breath, I rushed to the closet and grabbed the pants. I fished around in the pocket until my fingers found a metal ring. With a sigh of relief, I held them up to her. "These?"

"Yes," she replied in a weak voice.

Crossing to the bed, I took her hand gently in mine. "Thank you, Karen. I know this is going to help catch the man who hurt you."

Another tear leaked from the corner of her eye. "I hope so."

Abby leaned close to her. "Do you have anyone to care for you after you're released?"

She nodded slightly. "A friend. The doctor said I can leave as soon as she gets here." Karen twisted her hands. "She's taking me away from the city."

Ripping a corner off the menu on the stand, I picked up a pen and scribbled on it. "Here's my cell phone number," I said, tucking it in her hand. "Stay in touch, okay?"

She glanced down at the paper. "Thanks, but like I said, I'm going away . . . far, far away."

Abby and I grabbed a quick sandwich and ate in the car on the way to Stephen's condo. It was located a short distance from Karen's apartment, in an old industrial building that had been converted to housing. It sat squarely on a corner, and across the cobblestone street, bars, bookstores, and antique shops lined the block. An outdoor café was within easy walking distance. Brightly striped awnings covered the doorway, and tables with tall umbrellas littered the brick sidewalk. Next to the café, at the end of the street, the Gateway Arch rose in the bright sunshine, towering above the brick buildings.

Pausing at the entrance of the condo, I could see what Stephen had meant when he talked about the energy of this place. People jammed the sidewalks—tourists, with cameras hanging around their necks, loaded with shopping bags; businessmen sitting at wrought-iron tables at the outdoor café, enjoying their lunch; couples strolling hand in hand, stopping now and again to browse the window displays. The air sizzled with an excitement that seemed to say, *Life's good, let's party.*

We walked into the building and headed straight for the elevator.

"Wait," the concierge called out, rushing out from behind his desk. "May I help you?"

Pivoting, we both stared at him. "Ah . . . ah . . . " I stumbled. I hadn't expected the gates to be guarded.

Abby stepped forward and extended her hand. "Hello, I'm Abigail McDonald, and this is my granddaughter, Ophelia Jensen. We're friends of Miss Burns." She gave him a gracious smile. "You know Miss Burns, don't you?"

"Yes," he replied with hesitation.

Abby's smile slipped away. "Did you hear of her misfortune?"

His eyes popped wide. "No, what happened?"

"She was mugged last night."

"No." His brows knitted together. "Is she going to be okay?"

"Yes, they're releasing her from the hospital today. In fact, we've just come from there." She smiled again. "Karen asked us to stop by Mr. Larsen's and pick up some important papers for her." She motioned to me. "We have her keys."

On cue, I removed the small key ring from my pocket and dangled them in the air.

His eyes narrowed in suspicion as he looked first at me, then Abby.

Abby met his gaze with an innocent one of her own.

Sizing us up, his face relaxed. "All right . . . you can't be too careful, you know. Our tenants don't like strangers wandering around the halls."

Abby gave him a small nod. "I'm sure they appreciate your diligence."

The concierge preened at her praise. "I do my best," he replied as he smoothed his tie.

"We'll just be a minute," she said, holding up one finger.

"Oh, take your time, ma'am."

In the elevator, I kept my eyes on the numbers as I rocked back and forth on my heels. "For someone who doesn't like lies, you sure spin a good one."

I caught her smirk from the corner of my eye.

"It wasn't a lie—I simply took the truth and bent it a bit."

"Uh-huh," I answered with a nod. "I'll remember that one."

As I stepped from the elevator, I heard Abby's chuckle.

Crossing to Stephen's door, I inserted the key, unlocking it, and carefully pushed it open. I stepped inside. A musty, not-lived-in smell greeted me. With a soft click, Abby closed the door.

Curtains covered a bank of windows along the far wall of the large room. Brick walls rose to a vaulted ceiling. A fireplace, flanked by rich burgundy leather couches, took up space on the wall to my left. A long table with a glass top, ringed by eight padded, wrought-iron chairs, sat adjacent to the kitchen. From where I stood, I could see a fine layer of dust covering the table's surface.

"This is kind of a lonely place, isn't it?" Abby said in a quiet voice. "It's beautiful, but it somehow lacks spirit."

I understood what she meant as my eyes roamed the carefully decorated room. Lovely, but it said nothing of the man who lived here. Is that why Stephen spent so much time on the road, so much time writing? Was he trying to escape the loneliness by creating a different world in his mind?

My gaze landed on a hallway jutting back from the kitchen.

"Come on," I said, striding across the room. "Stephen's office must be down the hall."

Abby followed me as I passed a bathroom and two bedrooms. Double doors marked the end of the hallway. Opening them, I stepped inside Stephen's office.

The atmosphere in this room was definitely different. This was where Stephen spent his life.

Framed covers of his books hung on the walls, along with photographs of Stephen at various book signings. A large desk faced a window with a magnificent view of the river. His computer screen sat on top of the desk along with his keyboard. A Nerf football was placed next to it, and I imagined Stephen playing with it as he studied his notes. Louvered doors covered the wall to my right.

The closet—I would have bet the fire box was in there.

Turning sharply, I pulled the doors wide, and there it was, on the closet floor. I squatted down and, using the key, opened the lid. It was crammed with rows and rows of disks.

*Great, I hope Karen had labeled them.*

I picked up a handful and shuffled through them. There was one marked TERROR ON THE SEINE. Another set had just the word MOB written on the top case—notes for the book Darci had mentioned. *Boy, I bet they contained some juicy information.*

I felt the sudden sensation of someone standing close. Whipping my head around, I noticed Abby wandering around the room, a distance away. I shook the feeling off, but rifled the disks faster. Finally, I saw a set of disks labeled BOSTON. Karen had said the inspiration for his new book had come to him there. These had to be the right ones.

I shoved them into my purse, got to my feet and turned toward Abby. "Come on, let's get out of here."

Perplexed by my sudden haste, she said nothing, but without comment followed me down the hall and out of the condo. In the hallway, I spun around and quickly locked the door. I almost fled to the elevator.

"Why are you in such a hurry?" Abby asked in a puzzled voice.

"I don't know," I replied, punching the Down button a couple of times, "I just am."

Shifting my weight back and forth on my feet, my eyes were glued to the numbers above the elevator. I watched as each floor slowly lit up as the elevator rose. And as they did, the tension I felt seemed to build. Finally the doors opened, at the same time as the one next to us did. Hustling Abby into the elevator, I glanced over my shoulder and caught a glimpse of a dark-haired man exiting the other elevator.

The doors slid smoothly shut, and with them, my nervousness slowly ebbed away.

As we crossed the lobby floor, I noticed that the concierge was gone.

# Twenty

As Abby and I left the building, I saw the concierge down the street, arguing with a cab driver. Whatever the argument was about, it looked heated. Abby gave him a little wave, but he was too busy with the driver to notice.

On the way to the hotel, we made the decision not to drive back to Iowa today. It was approaching four o'clock, and Abby didn't relish driving six hours at night. I reluctantly agreed, mentally cursing myself for leaving my laptop at home. I was dying to read what was on the disks snuggled safely in my purse.

*Hmm, maybe there's an Internet café nearby? Or I could use the hotel's business center?* Patience was never my strong suit, and I was eager to peruse those disks. *Nope, better not.* The runes had stressed caution, and maybe now would be a good time to put that into practice. I could wait twenty-four hours.

In my room again, I called Tink for a quick update. Yes, she was having a good time. Yes, Great-Aunt Mary was making her do her lessons—but she was a hard taskmaster.

That comment caused me to smirk. I'd told Tink that Great-Aunt Mary wasn't a pushover, but she hadn't believed me.

But then Tink spoiled my moment by informing me that Great-Aunt Mary wasn't nearly as ghastly as I'd said. She was actually kind of nice in her own way.

Her reaction didn't stack up to my memories of the woman, but then again, maybe Great-Aunt Mary just didn't like *me*.

Tink concluded the conversation by grousing about getting up early with Aunt Dot to commune with the fairies. No, she hadn't seen them, and no, Aunt Dot hadn't been tippling the elderberry wine that early in the morning.

After my phone call to Tink, I felt antsy. I missed her, I missed my pets, and I missed my cottage. Suddenly, I regretted our decision to wait until morning to go home. Maybe a walk would help? I'd never been in St. Louis before and it seemed a shame to return home without at least getting a closer look at the Gateway Arch. I picked up the brochure on the nightstand and read it.

The arch was less than a mile away. A short distance for someone who'd grown up roaming the woods around Abby's farm.

I rapped sharply on the connecting door to Abby's room. When she opened it, I saw she was on the phone.

"Just a minute," she said into the receiver, then mouthed *Arthur* to me.

"Sorry to interrupt, but I'm feeling cooped up. I'm going for a walk. Want to come?"

"Thank you, dear, but I'm rather tired. I think I'll rest a bit before dinner."

"Okay, I'm going to walk down to the Gateway Arch. I'll be back soon."

"Be careful."

"I will," I replied, shutting the door. Grabbing my purse, I checked to make sure I had my key card and removed the disks.

"Hmm," I said to myself as I slapped the case on the palm of my hand, wondering where to put them.

My suitcase—it locked.

Confident the disks were safe, I left the hotel and began walking east toward the Mississippi River. I passed office buildings and a couple of restaurants before turning to my right and heading south.

The tall buildings along this stretch cast deep shadows on the sidewalk. The air seemed close, and I felt hemmed in. As I got closer to the arch, the office buildings were replaced by a parking ramp. On the next block sat the Old Courthouse, taking up the entire space. I stopped and admired the fine old building.

In the background, the arch rose above the green dome of the Old Courthouse like a silver rainbow. And atop the white building, a tall flagpole extended high into the cloudless sky. An American flag fluttered from its pinnacle.

Pulling the brochure out of my back pocket, I read about the building.

The Dred Scott trials began in there, and now, two of the historic courtrooms had been restored to hold mock trials. It also contained a museum with artifacts and a theater showing a film about the history of St. Louis. *That would be interesting—a nice break from all the mayhem.* I scanned the brochure for the hours. *Dang, it closed at four-thirty.*

Turning my head, I glanced across the street. A green park, with wide paths and a pool with sprays of water shooting up around a statue of a runner, took up the other block. I switched my gaze to the Old Courthouse—the arch was on the other side, to the east. Did I want to continue walking, or plant myself on one of the benches in the park?

The cool greenness and the sound of splashing water coming from the pool called to me. I voted for the park.

I meandered to the center of it, passing tourists in T-shirts snapping pictures of the Old Courthouse, mothers pushing babies in their strollers, and teenagers just hanging out. Near the pool with the statue, I sat on one of the benches and tried to relax.

It was less than a week since Stephen's shooting—and so much had happened. My head felt crowded with bits and pieces of information that lacked any kind of a connection. I didn't know how I would ever make sense of it all. I rolled my shoulders, trying to loosen some of the tension. Closing my eyes, I lifted my face to the sun as a breeze from the river stirred the air around me.

My peace lasted only a moment—I jumped when the cell phone in my pocket began to vibrate.

*Damn.* I flipped the phone open and answered.

"Where the hell are you?" asked a gruff voice in my ear. Bill.

"Um, you see . . . " I hedged.

*Oh, get it over with, Jensen.*

"I had to come to St. Louis," I blurted out.

"You've pushed me too far this time, Ophelia," Bill yelled in my ear.

Frowning, I held the phone away as he continued.

"I'm going to throw your butt in jail. I'm going to charge you—"

"Hey," I yelled back as I moved the phone back to my ear, "you didn't tell me not to leave town."

"I didn't think it was necessary." His tone sounded scathing. "I thought you had more sense than to go traipsing off somewhere. I don't have the time to chase you down."

I watched a mother carrying an infant walk by. "I'm safe," I replied with a smug smile. "And I have some information for you."

"What?" he barked.

"Karen Burns? Remember her? Stephen's assistant—"

"Yeah, what about her?" he growled, not letting me finish.

"She was mugged and the disks to Stephen's new book were stolen."

"Were the disks in her purse?"

"Yes," I said with hesitation.

"What do most muggers take, Ophelia?" He questioned me as if I were a child.

"The purse." I spit the answer out.

"Ms. Burns lives in a city, and I take it the attack happened at night?"

"Okay, you don't have to draw me a picture," I replied, my voice grudging. "You're trying to tell me they weren't after the disks, aren't you?"

"Give the lady a free prize."

"No need to get snarky, Bill," I objected forcefully. "I think it's a big coincidence that she was mugged right after her boss was shot."

His tone softened. "Coincidences do happen."

"How's Stephen?" I asked abruptly.

"He's still in a coma."

"No change at all?"

"The doctors are a little more optimistic, but he's still in intensive care. I hear you met his mother."

"Yes, I did . . . a very nice lady. She believes he was the victim—someone from his past with a grudge."

"I know. I spoke with her briefly . . . " He paused before continuing. "There's another theory—"

"I know, I know," I cut him off. "I was the intended victim."

"No, you were right about that one," he said guardedly.

I almost dropped my phone. "What?"

"There's been a new development."

He stopped abruptly, and I could envision the debate going on inside him.

"What the hell—you're going to hear about it when you get back," he said, making his decision. "Someone tried to assassinate Chuck Krause Thursday night. His aide was killed."

I sat forward on the bench. "Where?"

"As they were leaving campaign headquarters. A witness saw a motorcycle peel away."

"I don't get it—three shootings and no connection."

"It's not up to you to 'get it.' You're not the investigating police officer . . . " His voice faded. "But then again, neither am I."

"Huh?"

"Since Krause is running for office, the DCI has taken over the investigation. I guess they don't think a country sheriff is smart enough."

What a blow to his ego—getting pulled off his investigation. Now I felt guilty for all the problems I'd caused him. "You're a good cop, Bill. Even Ethan thinks so, and he's with the feds."

"Thanks, but it's not important who catches the shooter, as long as he's caught."

"So why do they think Stephen was shot?"

"I probably shouldn't tell you this, but . . . they think the shooter mistook him for Krause."

"How?"

"They're both blond, they were dressed similarly—"

"Oh, come on, give me a break," I huffed. "They think the assailant was just lurking in the trees, waiting for the off chance that Krause might come strolling along?"

"Stranger things have happened."

"Okay," I said, switching gears, "forget that dumb idea for a second. Why did someone shoot at me?"

"You were a witness . . . a loose end."

"Humph, I don't buy that at all," I exclaimed.

"I doubt the DCI's going to care whether or not you agree with them."

"Bill, I know they're wrong," I insisted.

"Well, Ophelia, unless you have proof, I'd keep my mouth shut if I were you. These boys don't strike me as the type to believe in your hocus-pocus."

"Great." My jaw clenched. "While they're pursuing their bogus theories, someone could get killed."

*Like me?*

"Listen, the DCI has a lot more resources than I do, and they don't make many mistakes." He sounded disgruntled. "I was told to let the big guns handle it, and I suggest you do the same." With that, he hung up on me.

I snapped my phone shut while I fought the urge to beat my head on the bench. The DCI was wrong, wrong, wrong, and I had less of a chance getting them to listen to me than I did Bill.

This development was *not* good.

Looking to my left, I noticed that the sun had slipped lower in the sky. I decided to get back to the hotel before Abby became worried. Rising, I made my way out of the park and turned to go back the way I'd come.

Since the sun had sunk so low, the shadows between the buildings were deeper now. And no breeze penetrated the concrete canyon as I walked. Lights were coming on in the office buildings and the doors were opening as office workers left for the day. Ties askew and briefcases swinging, they looked anxious to start their weekend. Their steps were hurried and their attention was focused straight ahead as they marched by, headed in the opposite direction, toward a parking garage.

My steps slowed as I thought about my conversation with Bill. Part of me was sorry I'd ever gotten involved. I noticed a woman wearing a suit and tennis shoes rush past me, carrying her high heels and clutching a folder.

*I bet she isn't worrying about someone shooting at her.* No, I imagined all she cared about was having fun over the weekend. Wouldn't that be nice?

I gave my shoulders a little shake. *Stop the pity party!* I'd made a choice, and I needed to see it through.

People had thinned out in this section of the city, and I found myself virtually alone on the street. Anxious for food and suddenly feeling sweaty, I increased my pace. Right now all I wanted was food and a hot shower.

I thought about my plans as I walked. What would I do

when I arrived home? First—read Stephen's notes. A thought popped into my head. Would the DCI want to follow up with Bill's investigation and talk to me? I hoped not—I'd answer their questions but wouldn't volunteer any information.

Craning my head back, I peeked at the strip of sky overhead, and a sense of being closed in hit me. I took longer steps.

I heard the sound of heels clicking on the sidewalk behind me. Another office worker anxious to get home? But the parking ramp was in the other direction. I snuck a look over my shoulder, and as I did, the man behind me did a little side step, as if he didn't want me to spot him.

Strange. I upped my pace.

So did the steps in back of me.

I whirled around, and recognition slammed me. It was the man from Stephen's condo. The one I'd glimpsed leaving the elevator.

I took off at a dead run and didn't look back. From the sounds echoing off the building, I knew he followed. Suddenly, a man popped out of a doorway. I dodged him and kept running. From behind me, I heard an angry "Hey" and the sounds of scuffling, but I didn't turn.

At the end of the block, I made a sharp turn to my left. *More people now, thank God.* I caught their surprised looks as I sprinted past them. My side hurt and my breath came in short pants, but I was almost there.

I finally slowed my steps as I approached the hotel and peeked over my shoulder.

The man had disappeared.

# Twenty-One

With my head down, I quickly crossed the hotel lobby and entered the elevator. I felt relieved that no other guests joined me. Right now I couldn't stand the idea of a crowded elevator. I needed space—and to get the hell out of there.

Once inside my room, I hurried to the connecting door and pounded. "Abby, Abby," I hollered.

The door abruptly swung as I was about to pound on it again.

Her eyes wide, Abby's hands shot out and gripped my arms. "Ophelia, what's wrong?" she asked, alarmed.

I shook off her hands and spun around. "Come on," I said, heading toward the bathroom. "They've found us. We're getting out of here."

"Who's found us?" she called after me.

"The guy from Stephen's condo," I replied over my shoulder.

Abby followed. "Wait a minute . . . what man?" She sounded baffled.

"There was a man getting off the elevator on Stephen's floor as we were leaving." My words poured out. "I only caught a glimpse, but I know he's followed us here."

Yanking my carry-on out from underneath the sink, I be-

gan cramming my stuff into the deep pockets. As I did, I
caught my reflection in the mirror—hair straggling around
my face, my brown eyes holding a half-crazed look. I appeared afraid.

I was.

My gaze slid to Abby's reflection. She stood leaning
against the door frame, frowning at me.

"Ophelia, slow down. Tell me what happened? I thought
you went for a walk?"

"I did . . . to a park." I tossed my toothbrush in the bag. "A
man followed me. Chased me."

She pushed away from the door frame. "You're positive it
was the same man from the condo?"

Whirling around, I leaned against the sink. "Yes, I'm
positive. And I'm positive he chased me. I ran . . . he ran.
That's being chased, isn't it?" I asked with sarcasm.

She crossed her arms and gave me a chilly look. "Don't
get in a snit. You're not making much sense, you know."

"Well, *excuse me* for rambling." I spun around and pitched
my toothpaste in the bag. "I just did a ten block sprint trying
to get away from some stranger."

Abby crossed the tiled floor and placed a hand on my
arm. "Should we call the police?"

"And tell them what? I didn't get a good enough look at
the guy to give a description." Taking a deep breath, I laid
my palms on the counter and exhaled slowly. "Abby, it's fight
or flight . . . and if I'm going to fight, I'd rather it be on my
own turf, not in some strange city."

Silently, she nodded and left the bathroom to go pack.

Twenty minutes later we were barreling north out of St.
Louis. Knots of stress tightened my shoulder, and I gripped
the wheel so hard my knuckles were white.

*What if they follow us?* I tried to recall the roads we'd be
driving. Did Highway 61 turn into a two-lane road at any
spot along the way? A deserted stretch of highway . . . in the
middle of the night . . . two women alone.

The knots in my shoulders pinched. Maybe fleeing St. Louis hadn't been such a hot idea after all?

"Ophelia," Abby said in a calm voice. "You need to simmer down . . . you're speeding."

Glancing down, I saw the needle of the speedometer quivering at 75 mph. Letting my foot up on the gas pedal, it slowly inched its way back to 60.

"I know they're after the disks," I muttered, focusing on the road. My mind leapt backward to that afternoon at Stephen's condo, and I tried to put the pieces together. "I bet the man on the elevator, the one who chased me, broke into Stephen's condo."

"But the concierge? He—"

"Was outside arguing with that cab driver," I said, finishing for her. "The guy I saw slipped in and out while the cab driver kept the concierge busy."

"That's a pretty big assumption."

"It makes sense, though."

Out of the corner of my eye I saw her shrug. "I suppose. But if that's the case, it would indicate that there's more than one person involved."

"There is—I haven't had a chance to tell you this—I got a call from Bill. Someone tried to kill Chuck Krause Thursday night and got his aide instead."

"Oh dear!" she exclaimed, and shifted toward me. "Ophelia, turn those disks over to Bill when we get home . . . please?"

"It won't do any good," I said shortly, then quickly filled her in on the rest of the conversation.

" . . . the DCI won't listen to me. They'll think I'm just another crackpot."

"If you tell them about the man chasing you?"

I pushed myself back against the seat. "I don't have anything to tell them—I can't give a description. All I remember is dark hair and jeans."

"Datolite," she said firmly.

"What?" I wasn't sure I heard her correctly.

"Datolite," she repeated. "Do you have any?"

I gave my head a quick shake. "What in the devil is datolite?"

"It's a crystal that helps with memory and recalling details." Her voice sounded confident. "Hold the datolite and concentrate on the man you saw. It will come to you."

She sounded so sure of herself. "Abby," I slid a glance her way, "is there anything a crystal won't fix?"

"Yes, that which can't be remedied, but anything else . . . " Her voice faded as she lifted a hand.

"Okay, I'll give it a shot. Where can I find this datolite?"

"Obviously, we don't have time to go shopping, so I'll lend you mine—" She cut herself off and wagged a finger at me. "But you'll need to cleanse it first."

"Got it."

"And while you're meditating, I'm laying a spell around your house."

I groaned. "Abby—"

"Shh." She held up her finger again. "I'll not have any nonsense from you, Ophelia. You need all the protection you can get."

Abby settled back in her seat and fell silent. Soon I heard her even breathing.

She had such faith, such confidence in her magick—and although I wouldn't admit it to her, I envied her. Maybe if I felt that same assurance, all these loose threads would miraculously connect? Had she always been so certain of her gift? Had she ever felt as lost as I sometimes did? I didn't know—she never spoke much about the training she'd received as a girl.

At Hannibal, I pulled in for gas while Abby went inside the station. With one eye on passing cars, I filled the tank, then entered the building. I met her coming out of the restroom.

"Next," she said with a grin.

I found her again, wandering up and down the aisles
She handed me a cup. "Here."

I waved it away with a wince. "Nah, I'm jittery enough—
the last thing I need is coffee."

"You need something to eat." She turned and perused the
junk food on the shelves. "Take this," she said, grabbing a
bag of trail mix. "Not the best, but it will have to do until we
get back to Summerset."

At the counter, I paid for the coffee, gas, and trail mix.
Steeling myself for another four hours on the road, we
crossed the parking lot to the car. We were almost there
when Abby stretched out her hand.

"I'll drive."

I made a fist around the keys. "No, you won't."

She stopped short. "Yes, I will. My little nap did wonders,
now you need to relax and get some rest."

*Man, she's stubborn. No sense arguing in the middle of
the night, in the parking lot of a gas station.*

With reluctance, I handed her the keys. "Keep an eye
out, okay? And if you see anything suspicious, wake me
up."

Once in the car, I buckled up and tipped the seat back.
Staring out the window, I watched the lights of Hannibal fly
by as sleep claimed me.

I pedaled my bicycle down the shady side streets of Paris,
sticking to those areas not frequented by the Germans. Taking a cab or the Metro would have been easier, faster, and my
legs wouldn't be shaking with exertion as they were now, but
I needed to be anonymous.

I wore pants and one of Henrick's shirts bloused out
around my waist. A vest hid the shirt's bagginess. With a cap
low on my forehead and covering my auburn hair, I believed
I resembled every other Parisian on the street this summer's
day. Nothing about me that would make anyone take a second glance. Or so I hoped.

Turning northwest, I headed toward Parc des Buttes Chaumont, and to a small apartment on Place de Danube. Once there, I pulled my cap lower and scanned the street in both directions. Only children playing catch at the end of the street. Good.

After leaning my bicycle against a lamp post and entering the building, I walked swiftly to the apartment located at the rear. Walls, once bright with colored wallpaper, were now faded and dusty. The air smelled like a mixture of boiled potatoes and cabbages. I knocked twice followed by one short rap. The door opened a crack, and a tired woman with sad brown eyes peered at me.

"Phoenix," I whispered softly.

She nodded, and without speaking, handed me a small package wrapped in string. With a furtive look toward the entrance of the building, I opened my shirt at the waist and tucked the parcel safely against my body, then rebuttoned the shirt.

The door closed softly.

Out of the building, I headed my bicycle away from the children and pedaled out onto the busy street. My destination was a quay located on Canal Saint Martin near the Hospital Saint Louis.

I rode past cafés where soldiers sat sipping wine and enjoying the Parisian sunshine, butcher shops closed for lack of meat, and empty vegetable stands. At the corner of Boulevard de la Villette, I stopped to wait for a German truck to lumber by.

A large black car pulled up alongside as I waited.

"Madeleine? Is that you?" someone called from the car.

Glancing over my left shoulder, I saw Colonel Vogel motioning me over from the back seat. Blood pounded in my ears and I instinctively tugged at the vest covering the illegal package. Schooling my face to show nothing, I walked my bicycle closer to Vogel.

"Hello," I said, trying to keep my voice even.

"You're a long way from home."

"Oh, it's such a beautiful day and I wanted to enjoy it." I gave a little giggle. "And, Colonel, after the excellent meal you served at your dinner party, I needed the exercise. I've already been scolded for gaining weight."

Vogel's eyes roamed my body and I tensed. A slow smile spread across his face. "You have nothing to fear—your figure is lovely, my dear," he said condescendingly. "Is Henrick still in Sweden?"

Relieved at the change in subject, I made myself relax as I bobbed my head. "Yes, but he's back tonight."

The colonel raised an eyebrow. "Ahh, but when I saw you here, I had hoped I could persuade you to have a glass of wine with me at a nearby café?"

"Oh, Colonel, I'm so sorry." I tried to look crest-fallen at the thought of not being able to join him. "I haven't seen Henrick in weeks, and I've a reunion planned for us." I looked down at my watch. "In fact, I really must be going."

The colonel reached out and wrapped his hand around mine, startling me. "I understand your haste. I consider Henrick a friend, but I want you to know I don't agree with him leaving you alone for such long periods. A woman like you deserves better treatment."

Squirming out of his grasp, I pasted a bright smile on my face. "But I love him, Colonel. Our time apart only makes our time together that much sweeter."

His jaw muscle twitched as he forced the corners of his mouth up in a parody of a grin. "Henrick is a lucky man." Leaning forward, he tapped his driver on the shoulder, and the car slowly drove away.

# Twenty-Two

I watched the car turn right and debated what to do. After the conversation with Vogel, did I dare proceed to the drop point at Quai de Valmy? So close—only a few more blocks—but what if Colonel Vogel decided to double back and follow me? If he caught me, it would be certain death not only for me, but the woman with the sad brown eyes, Brother Sebastian, and God knew who else. No, the drop would have to wait until tomorrow. Turning right, I pedaled down the Boulevard to Rue de Menilmontant and my apartment.

Storing my bicycle in a shed located in the small garden at the rear, I ran through the back door and up the stairs to my second floor apartment. Recalling the building at Place de Danube, I thought about how lucky I was to live here. I still faced the same shortages as my countrymen, but I didn't live in poverty. My apartment was light and airy. No sour smell of cooked cabbage in my building.

I inserted my key in the door to my apartment, but it was unlocked. I knew I'd locked it before leaving this afternoon. A moment of uncertainty rippled through my mind. Would Vogel have had the audacity to not only show up at my apartment, but convince the landlord to let him in? I cautiously turned the knob with one hand, and with the other pushed the door open a crack. Peering through the slit, I saw him.

He stood on the other side of the room with his back to the door. His blond hair caught the light of the late afternoon sun pouring in the tall windows and making it look like spun gold—soft and fine.

With a shriek, I flung the door wide and ran to him. "Henrick!"

His arms grabbed me as I threw myself at him. Laughing, he lifted me off my feet and whirled me around. My hat flew off my head while I buried my face in his neck, just to inhale the scent of him. *Pine—Henrick always smelled like fresh pine needles—cool and crisp.*

Still laughing, he set me on my feet, and taking my face in his hands, gave me a kiss that seemed to last forever.

Lost in him, I was vaguely aware of his hands moving over my shoulders, down my back, and finally settling on my waist. Abruptly the kiss ended.

"What's this?" he asked, patting my side.

*Damn, the package had shifted.*

"It's nothing," I said as I stepped out of his embrace. I crossed to the kitchen and removed the bottle of wine I'd been saving for his homecoming. "Let's toast your return, my love."

Henrick leaned carelessly against the counter. "Madeleine, what are you up to?"

"Nothing," I replied with an innocent smile as I uncorked the wine. "I went out for a bit, that's all." Pulling out the cork, I poured Henrick a glass of the pale pink wine and handed it to him. Laying my palm on his cheek, I gazed into his blue eyes. "I have such plans for us tonight," I murmured softly.

His fingers curled around my wrist. "What is underneath that shirt . . . I believe it's one of mine, isn't it?"

"Yes." I gave a little tug and pulled away from him. Pouring a glass for myself, I flounced into the living room and flopped down on my old couch. "I haven't seen you for weeks and weeks, and all you want to do is ask questions," I pouted.

"No, Madeleine, just one question," he said, placing his wine on a small table and sitting next to me. "What's under the shirt?"

"Oh, all right," I said with a frown. I loosened the vest, unbuttoned the shirt, then removed the package and laid it on the couch.

Henrick picked it up and sniffed it. His eyes rounded in horror. "Madeleine, these are explosives!" he hissed. "You were riding around Paris with explosives! What if—"

I jumped to my feet and grabbed the package. Holding it loosely in my hands, I stomped into the bedroom with Henrick at my heels.

"Madeleine, talk to me," he commanded.

I put the package on the floor and moved a chair away from the window, where the fabric skirting it had hidden that part of the floor. "I'm not going to talk to you if you're going to scold me," I said indignantly.

Henrick marched toward me and grabbed my arm. His fingers dug into my soft flesh. "Are you insane? This isn't a game—"

"I know it isn't a game—people are starving, and my city is in the hands of invaders," I interrupted in a hushed, angry voice as I twisted away from him and squatted on the floor. Removing a loose board, I stowed the package in a small hole, then replaced the board. Standing, I shoved the chair back over the board and dusted my hands. "There, the package is gone and you never saw it." Pushing past him, I left the room.

Henrick followed me, shaking his head.

"And," I rasped at him over my shoulder, "you're a fine one to talk about games—what of the game you play with the Germans? You not only hate them as much as I do, you're cheating them." Picking up my glass of wine, I drained it in one gulp. "At the same time, you pretend to be their friend."

With a scowl, I tromped into the kitchen and grabbed the bottle of wine. Returning to the living room, I smacked it down on the small table by the couch. "Here," I said with a jerk of my hand. Spinning on my heel, I put my back to him.

"You know Sweden is neutral," he reasoned, "and if we want to stay neutral, we have to give the Germans what they want."

"Iron ore from your father's mine," I said, my mouth twisting. "But if they learn you're padding the accounts?"

"I'm a Swedish citizen, plus . . . " He paused. "My father will protect me."

Turning my head, I shot him a skeptical look. "You're cheating your father, too."

"I'm his only son," he said, as if it justified his actions. "I'm doing this for us. With the money, we can make a life together after the war."

"It's blood money, Henrick."

"It's our future, my love." Coming up behind me, he rested his hands gently on my waist and pressed his cheek to mine. "I can handle the Germans and my father, but I fear for you. You're taking a great risk by helping the saboteurs."

I felt my anger at him soften. "Many people are," I replied quietly. "In exchange, they're giving me counterfeit food tickets. I can use those tickets to feed one more family of refugees." I crossed my arms. "And you needn't worry—I *know* I'm not going to be caught."

He rubbed my cheek with his, and I felt his smile. "I hope you're not counting on your 'talent' to keep you safe."

"Humph," I snorted. "I know you doubt me, but my cards don't lie to me."

Turning me around, he gazed into my eyes. "A deck of playing cards can't tell the future."

"Mine do," I insisted stubbornly.

"Ah, Madeleine." He shook his head, looking up toward

the ceiling. "Telling fortunes with piquet cards is a charming parlor trick, but no more—"

I stamped my foot. "I don't care if you believe or not. I know what I know. Didn't the reading for Giselle show Andre was lying to her?"

"My love, everyone *except* Giselle knew Andre lied."

"But the cards proved it to her, and she left him."

"One can't let a deck of cards steer one's life." He brushed a lock of hair from my cheek.

"My grandmother did. And everyone in our village. They all came to her for advice." I narrowed my eyes and stared at him defiantly, daring him to doubt my words. "She saved many a farmer from ruin."

"They are superstitious country folk." He cupped my face with his hands. "And you're no longer a wide-eyed child living among them in a southern province. You've seen more than they could ever dream."

"Henrick, the truth is the same no matter where you live."

"You *will* persist in clinging to these antiquated beliefs, won't you?"

"Yes," I replied with a lift of my chin.

He dropped his hand and crossed to the couch. "Don't rely on your cards to protect you from Colonel Vogel."

"Vogel suspects nothing. I ran into him today and—"

Lowering his head, he pulled his fingers through his hair. "You what?"

"I saw Vogel at the corner of the Boulevard de la Villette."

"Did he recognize you?"

"Of course." I poured more wine in both glasses. "In fact, he wanted me to join him at a café. I declined and he went on his way." Setting the bottle down, I ran a finger around the rim of my glass. "He's becoming too friendly—I think it would be wise if I avoided him."

He sank to the couch. "Madeleine—"

"Come, I don't want to fight anymore." I placed my glass on the table and curled up on his lap. Leaning back against the arm of the couch, I let my hand steal up his chest. "You've been away so long."

I felt his heart beat faster against my palm as he lowered his head to nuzzle my neck.

"What am I going to do with you?" he murmured into my ear.

With a little laugh, I stroked his soft blond hair. "I can think of many things." Suddenly an idea occurred to me. "If you're so worried about my safety," I whispered, "one of those things would be to marry—"

He abruptly stopped nibbling and reared back his head. "We've been through this," he said in a curt voice.

I scooted off his lap and sat on my legs. Leaning forward, my eyes searched his face. "I don't understand—your father will look the other way while you cheat him, yet wouldn't accept me as your wife?"

"You're not Swedish," he said simply. "That's why I need the Germans' money. With it, I can escape my father and have a life with you."

"But if we married now, your country's neutrality would protect me, too."

"Madeleine," he said slowly, "no country in the world can save you if the Nazis catch you blowing up their railways."

# Twenty-Three

I felt Abby's hand gently shaking me. "Ophelia, we're home."

"Huh? What?" I shot upright in my seat, my hand grabbing the dashboard.

"We're home," she said again.

As I looked at my cottage, my front yard, my familiar neighborhood, my brain felt like mush. I tried to shake the muddle from my mind.

"Let's get you inside."

With stiff legs, I hobbled out of the car, opened the back door, pulled out my suitcase and carry-on. Hoisting the carry-on, I crossed to Abby and gave her a hug. "Talk to you tomorrow," I mumbled.

"Oh, no," she said with a chuckle. "I'm staying here."

"Abby—"

Touching my lips softly with a fingertip, she silenced me. "No argument—I'm spending the night."

Too tired to put up a fight, I grabbed her bag along with mine and trudged to the house. Unlocking the door, we stepped inside to a flurry of yips and yaps.

After sniffing at me and then Abby, T.P. darted toward the front door. I lunged at him as he ran by, but missed. He headed out the door and to Abby's car. Running around in circles, he sniffed all the tires at least twice. Not finding what he was looking for, he padded back into the house and sat at my feet with a hopeful expression.

I glanced at Abby with a wry smile. "He's looking for Tink, isn't he?"

"Yes," she replied, squatting down beside him and rubbing his ears.

T.P. looked sad, and I felt my own spot of emptiness again. "I miss her, too, boy."

Abby rose and threw an arm around my shoulder. "You get to bed. We'll talk in the morning."

Agreeing with her suggestion, I hauled my stuff up the stairs and into my room. Lady and Queenie followed me, while T.P. pranced after Abby. I guess he figured if he couldn't have Tink, Abby was the next best thing.

Once inside my bedroom, I heard my bed calling to me. *My own room, my own bed, my own pillows.* Changing in a rush, I threw back the covers and flopped onto the mattress on my stomach and wiggled down under the sheets. With a deep sigh, I crossed my arms under my pillow and nestled my cheek against it. *Home at last.* My eyes slowly closed.

One eye popped open. *I really didn't like Henrick.* During the dream, I'd felt Madeleine's passion for him, but I thought he led a selfish life. He seemed more worried about himself than the suffering of millions.

*Drop it, Jensen, it's one in the morning—go to sleep.*

I turned my head to the left. *Was Henrick Stephen?*

Rolling onto my back, I listened to the night sounds— Lady softly moaning in her sleep as she dreamed of chasing a squirrel, the low rumble of Queenie's purr coming from the other side of the bed, a fly buzzing against the window.

I forced my eyes closed.

Even though I didn't like Henrick all that much, he was still better than Vogel. That guy was a creep.

I turned on my side and punched up my pillow.

*I'm acting as if I agree with Abby—my dream could be*

*of a past life.* That was the burning question: Did Madeleine and Henrick ever exist? Or did they live and love only in my imagination? Did meeting Stephen somehow trigger this elaborate dream? Or could it be that I was picking up energy from something that had happened over sixty years ago and thousands of miles away? I'd dreamed of the past before, but never one so long dead, or of a location that far away. And in those dreams, I'd been a spectator, not a participant.

*Just forget about the dreams,* I told myself. If I wanted to stew about something, my time would be better spent focusing on now and the future—or I might not *have* a future.

But the last dream—Madeleine was on her way to drop off the explosives. Where? Oh, yeah, Canal Saint Martin, near Hospital Saint Louis.

I pushed up in bed. Hospital Saint Louis? Was it a real place? Or had my subconscious picked that name because I was in the *city* of St. Louis? I'd check it out tomorrow on the Internet. If such a hospital did exist, and if it were near a Canal Saint Martin, then I'd know my dreams were one of two things—Abby was right and they were memories of a past life, or for some reason I was reading energy from events long ago and maybe, somehow, they played into what was happening now.

*What did I know of Madeleine? Were there other facts I could check on the Internet? Were there similarities between her and me?*

Reaching over, I turned on my lamp and removed a pen and pad from the nightstand drawer. Drawing my knees up, I balanced the pad and began to make notes.

Madeleine was a Parisian model born in the south of France. Well, we both had grown up in rural areas—something in common there. But we differed on fashion—I had none.

In the last dream, it was apparent Madeleine had a gift for *reading* cards—some psychic ability. And it was a family talent—inherited from her grandmother. That was a no

brainer with one huge difference. Madeleine was supremely
confident, but I'd never felt that way about my gift.

I chewed on the end of my pen. What else? She was madly
in love with Henrick. I gave a sharp snort. We parted ways
there.

She was involved in something dangerous. Gee, another
thing in common?

Scanning my notes, I saw the parallels between myself
and Madeleine. But what else? The key—we'd both received
keys. I didn't know what her key was for, but mine led to the
disks. I wished I knew more about Madeleine's key.

I felt a stir of excitement. What if I tried forcing the
dreams? Tossing the pen and pad on the nightstand, I shut
off the light and scooted down in bed. Folding my hands on
my chest, I waited . . . and waited . . . and waited.

After twenty minutes of laying like a corpse, hoping for
sleep to come, and with it, the dreams, I gave up. If I wanted
answers, the disks were my best hope.

Throwing back the sheet, I climbed out of bed and unzipped my suitcase. I tiptoed down the hallway then the
stairs with the disks clutched in my hot little hand. Crossing
the living room, I stole into my office and softly shut the
door. I lit a candle and booted up the computer.

The screen came on, casting a faint blue light into the
room. As I hunched forward, I watched impatiently as each
of the icons clicked on. Finally it was ready. Clicking on MY
COMPUTER, I opened the D drive and slid in the first disk.

Loading . . .

A box popped onto the screen.

*Enter password.*

The garbled sound of voices coming from downstairs woke
me. I rolled over and looked at the alarm clock: 9:00. I'd finally crept up to bed at three after trying to break Stephen's
password. I'd used every combination of words I could think
of. Stephen's name, where he lived, the color of his eyes, his

hair—nothing worked. I'd even held the disk between my palms and tried to sense some sort of image, but my mind stayed blank. All I felt was the cool, plastic disk resting in my hands.

Abby was better at sensing things from objects, I thought as I tumbled out of bed.

Anxious to talk to her, I dressed quickly in shorts and a T-shirt. Slipping my feet into an old pair of flip-flops, I hurried to the bathroom, brushed my teeth, and splashed cold water on my face. I twisted my hair up, holding it in place with a clip, as I rushed out of the bathroom, but then I stopped.

I figured one of the voices belonged to Abby, but whose was the other voice? What if it were Bill and the DCI? It wouldn't look good if I suddenly came tearing into the kitchen. I continued at a slower pace down the stairs.

Rounding the corner of the kitchen, I pulled up short. Abby stood at the stove frying eggs and bacon, while the owner of the second voice sat at the kitchen table.

Darci. She took one look at me and leaned back in her chair, crossing her arms. "You lied to me," she said, her eyes narrow. "You told me you were staying out of the investigation."

I felt a sheepish expression steal across my face. "Ah, I take it Abby filled you in?"

"Yeah." Her red lips puckered in a pout. "What's the big idea leaving me out?"

With a shake of my head, I crossed the kitchen and poured myself a cup of coffee. "As I recall, you encouraged me not to get involved."

"Maybe, but that was before I found out you're reincarnated."

I shot Abby a dirty look over my shoulder. "You told her about that?"

She waved the spatula in my direction. "She already knew you'd been dreaming . . . I simply gave her my theory."

Snagging a piece of bacon, I munched on it thoughtfully.

"Seems to me there's too many theories. And right now they don't mean squat."

Abby flipped an egg in the skillet. "Would you make the toast, dear?" She opened the refrigerator door and grabbed the orange juice. "I heard you roaming around last night— did you read Stephen's notes?"

"No." I shoved down hard on the lever of the toaster. "They've got a password."

Leaning against the counter, St. Louis, Karen Burns, and the man chasing me seemed far away from my bright kitchen. Darci sipping coffee at my table . . . Abby cooking . . . the animals curled up in a spot of sunlight, waiting for a handout. It all seemed so normal.

Darci broke the spell. "Forget about the password for now, tell me about being reincarnated." Turning in her chair, she watched me with anticipation. "Was I right? Stephen's your long-lost love, isn't he? You had a tragic affair, didn't you?" she asked, peppering me with questions.

A grin flicked across my face. *So much for normal.* The bread popping out of the toaster saved me from answering right away. Buttering it and placing it on a plate, I tried to frame my answer. At this point, I wasn't sure if Stephen was Vogel or Henrick. As Ophelia, I didn't care for either one of them.

Crossing to the table, I placed the plate in the center. "I don't know," I replied truthfully. "And before you get too wrapped up in the reincarnation idea, I have another thought. What if I'm just picking up energy from events that took place long ago?"

Darci tossed her head. "Why would you do that?"

"Who knows?" I glanced at Abby. "Any thoughts?"

"Not really." She set the eggs and bacon on the table, and pulling at a chair, sat. "You need more information. Is there any way you can learn if Madeleine really did exist?"

"Oooh." Darci squirmed in her chair like a little kid. "Me, me, let me . . . "

I half expected her hand to shoot up in the air.

" . . . I can do an Internet search."

Abby's eyes sparked with amusement. "I think that's an excellent idea, don't you, Ophelia?"

"Yeah, I do," I replied, dipping my toast in the center of my egg. "Madeleine was a Parisian model and—"

Darci's eyebrows shot up and she giggled. "You? A model? In a past life?"

"Hey, what's so funny about that?" I chomped down on my slice of toast.

She cocked her head and gave me a long stare. "Shall we go through your closet again?"

"Okay, okay. I've already caught the irony of living a life as a model," I groused. "You don't need to hit me over the head with it."

"Well, I think—" she began.

"Girls," Abby said, cutting Darci off. "It's my understanding that if something brought us unhappiness in a past life, we avoid it in this lifetime."

"I get it—she loved fashion, but it didn't make her happy, so now she hates it . . . " Darci picked at her egg.

"Exactly," Abby answered.

They were talking as if I were invisible. "Hey," I said, waving a hand. "I'm sitting right here."

They ignored me.

"Humph, that would certainly explain all the polyester," Darci said in a voice tinged with sarcasm.

"I don't have *that* much polyester," I interjected indignantly.

"Thanks to me," Darci shot back.

I covered my face with my hands and shook my head in frustration. "Don't you think we have more important things to discuss other than my wardrobe?" I asked, lowering my hands and glaring at them.

Abby reached out and gave me a sympathetic pat on the arm. "You're right, dear." Focusing on Darci, she said,

"You're going to try and find references to Madeleine on the Internet." She turned to me, her green eyes bright. "What can I do?"

"Well," I said, giving her a knowing look, "since you seem to be so good at cracking passwords, how about giving Stephen's a try?"

A cagey smile lit my grandmother's face.

# Twenty-Four

After we finished breakfast, Abby and Darci joined me in my office. Abby took a seat in the office chair next to my desk. I handed her the disk, and after she took it, her eyelids drifted shut. She took several deep breaths as she rubbed her open palm over the case.

Darci and I waited.

"This is so cool," Darci said, her voice vibrating with excitement. "I don't get to see you guys do your mojo very often."

"Shh," I hissed, laying a finger on my lips.

Her voice dropped. "Does she go into some kind of a trance, or what? Does she know we're here?"

"Yes, she knows we're here, and no, she doesn't go into a trance," I replied with a sneer and a roll of my eyes. "Her head doesn't spin around either. But she does need to concentrate."

Darci shifted from one foot to the other. "Okay, I'll be quiet . . . not another word . . . promise." She made an X over her heart.

Standing at the corner of the desk, I watched Abby. Her breathing was slow and even, and her body relaxed. She turned the case over and over in her hand while a slight frown darted across her face. Slowly, she opened her eyes and handed me the case.

"Well?" I said anxiously.

"Flames and ashes." She leaned back in the chair and folded her hands.

"That's all?" I groused, looking down at the case in my hand. "What kind of password is that?"

"I don't know—I saw flames erupt, leaving a pile of ash."

I gave her a scowl. "I hate to tell you, Abby, but that doesn't help me a whole lot."

She met my expression with a smile. "What did you expect? That I'd envision Stephen's password in big red letters?"

"It would be nice," I declared, tapping the case on the desk.

Hopping up, I moved around to the computer. Abby stood, and I took her place at the desk. She watched over my shoulder as I inserted the disk. Darci moved to my other side.

"Okay, let's try 'flames.'" I typed in the word.

Nothing. I entered *fire*.

*Invalid password.*

Placing her hand on the desk, Darci leaned in. "Try 'flames and ashes.'"

"Okay," I said, swiftly typing the words.

No go.

Darci nudged me with her hip. "Let me try."

"Whatever," I said, switching places with her.

Her fingers flew over the keyboard as she typed every synonym for "flames and ashes" she could think of. She tried uppercase, lowercase, and still couldn't break the code.

With a sigh of exasperation, she sat back in the chair and chewed on her lip. "I need to think about this." She tore her gaze away from the computer and glanced up at me. "Karen Burns didn't mention a password?"

"Jeez, Darci." I leaned against the desk and glared at her. "Don't you think if she did, I would've tried it?"

Her eyes focused back on the computer screen as if staring at it long enough would make the password magically appear. "All right, so that was a dumb question."

"It might be she didn't know Stephen used a password," Abby commented in a reasonable voice. "She said she didn't look at the disks until he'd finished the manuscript."

"Well," I said, pushing away from the desk, "I'm going to call her and find out. Oh, while you're at it, Darci . . . would you go online and type 'Hospital Saint Louis, Paris, France' in the search bar. My password is"—I shot a look at Abby—' "magick.' "

Placing my hand on Darci's shoulder, I leaned down to watch the screen as she logged in then typed the words in the search bar. She hit Enter.

My fingers squeezed into her shoulder.

"Ouch," she said with a squirm.

"Oh," I mumbled, my eyes never leaving the screen, "sorry."

There it was—Hospital Saint Louis. It was a real place. Did it mean Madeleine was real, too?

After Abby left, I tried to reach Karen Burns, but failed. At a loss what to do then, I wandered back to the office where Darci had commandeered my computer and refused to budge. She was determined to discover Stephen's password. Slouching in one of the armchairs, I watched as her fingers continually tapped the keyboard. The clacking sound of her long nails hitting the keys made me jumpy.

"Have you tried 'conflagration'?" I asked.

"Uh-huh." She typed faster.

"How about 'flare'?" I drummed my fingers on the arm of the chair, keeping time with Darci's typing.

"Yeah."

' "Inferno'?"

Her fingers paused. "Yes."

' "Pyre'?"

"Will you stop?" she asked, leaning back in the chair and glaring at me. "You're making me nervous."

I popped to my feet. "What about you?" I wiggled my fingers at her. "All that clacking and clicking's bugging me."

"Then go find something to do." She turned her attention to the screen and resumed typing. "Go do some psychic stuff," she said, dismissing me.

Frustrated, I paced out of the office. "Do some psychic stuff," I grumbled to myself. *Right, like it was that easy.* It wasn't a switch I could flip on and off. I wished it were; then maybe I'd have my answers.

I wandered into the kitchen, and grabbing my cell phone off the kitchen counter, tried Karen Burns again. Nothing. I was beginning to think the woman didn't want to talk to me. I hoped that was the case, and not that she *couldn't* talk to me. I was at an impasse without the password, without any more information about Madeleine.

I picked up the paper and glanced at the front page. The main story was about Chuck Krause and his aide's murder.

The young man, Benjamin Jessup, had been leaving Krause's campaign headquarters with Krause when a man on a motorcycle speeding by opened fire. The DCI were investigating and had "no comment." The article went on to quote Krause. He was shocked, appalled, at Jessup's death, and saw the situation as one more reason to push harsher penalties for lawbreakers.

Disgusted, I threw the newspaper down. A young man was dead and Krause was using it to promote his own political agenda.

Shoving my hands in my back pockets, I stared off into space. What next? I snapped my fingers—Stephen's date book. Maybe I'd missed something.

I ran upstairs to my bedroom and pulled the copy out

of my nightstand drawer. Sitting cross-legged on the bed, I thumbed through it. Nothing new hit me until I noticed the phone number entered next to *The Bookworm*. A 515 area code. I'd been so focused on finding Karen Burns that I hadn't tried calling that number. I picked up the phone and dialed.

It rang twice. A young woman's voice came on the line.

"Krause for representative."

I swiftly covered the receiver to hide my gasp.

"Hello? Anyone there?" she asked.

"Ah, hi . . . " I stuttered, stumbling to my feet.

"May I help you?" Her voice sounded strained.

"Umm, this may sound odd, but I found this number listed in a friend's date book . . . and, well . . . "

"Who is this? Is this a crank call?"

"No, honest . . . a friend of mine, Stephen Larsen—"

"The author who was shot?"

"Yes—"

"We've already talked to the police," she cut me off curtly. "Good—"

"No, wait," I said in a rush, "don't hang up. I'm, I'm . . . "

*I'm what? Think, Jensen, think.*

"His mother, Louise Larsen, asked me to call." The lie rolled out of my mouth quickly, but I didn't think Louise would mind. "We're trying to retrace Stephen's activities before the shooting, and he had this number listed—"

"Look," she said, cutting me off again, "I'll tell you what I told the police. I refer—referred—calls like that," her voice cracked, "to Ben."

"So you did talk to Stephen?" I felt a rush of excitement.

"I don't remember." Her voice sounded sullen.

"But the call would've been transferred to Ben—why?"

"Ben handles—" She caught herself. "—handled, all

requests for information, interviews, anything to do with the press. If this guy identified himself as a writer, I automatically would have bucked the call to Ben. So would everyone else on staff."

"I see . . . " I paused for a moment. "Do you know if Ben did talk to Stephen?"

"No."

"Does anyone know?"

"Maybe his girlfriend, Gina Torreli."

"Do you know how I can contact her?"

"Lady," she huffed, "I don't know who you are, but her boyfriend just got killed. You should leave her alone!"

The crash of the phone slamming down sounded in my ear.

That went well, I thought sarcastically. I definitely needed to work on my people skills.

Rushing downstairs, I whipped out the Des Moines phone book and looked up the name Torreli. There was one listing: Torreli, G. The address was at an apartment complex in West Des Moines, about thirty minutes from here. Since I'd muffed it with the young woman working for Krause, I decided not to call. I'd show up at her apartment.

Going back upstairs, I quickly put on makeup and changed into capris, a decent shirt, and a pair of sandals. I hurried down the stairs and to my office. Sticking my head in the door, I saw Darci still typing away.

Her blond hair tumbled around her face as if she'd pulled her hands through it again and again. A pencil was clutched tightly in her teeth while she muttered to herself.

"Hey, I've got an errand to run. I'll be back in a couple of hours," I said.

She nodded, her eyes never leaving the computer screen.

"If I'm not back before you leave, lock up, okay?"

No response.

"Okay?" I asked again.

She paused her typing and waved a hand in my direction.

I guess that meant she would. As I crossed the living room, I heard the sound of her sweet voice coming from my office.

Gee, I didn't know Darci knew *those* words.

# *Twenty-Five*

The apartment complex sat on the west side of Des Moines, right off Interstate 80. I knew exactly where it was located due to their numerous TV ads, which showed young professionals living there.

The tan buildings were all the same: two levels with decks off the back of each apartment in long rows, forming a square around a huge parking lot. Locating Gina's apartment, I parked the car and walked up to the door.

I rang the bell and waited.

The door opened with the security chain still in place. I saw half of a young woman's face peeping at me through the gap in the door.

"Are you Gina Torreli?"

"Are you with the police?" she asked, her voice heavy.

Her sudden question surprised me. "No."

The door started to close. I pressed my hand against it. "No, wait. I'm a friend of Stephen Larsen."

"Who?"

If she didn't know Stephen's name, it didn't bode well for her having any other information for me.

"Stephen Larsen—the author who was shot last Sunday?"

"Leave me alone." The door began to close again.

"Wait—I want to talk to you about Ben."

The eye peering at me through the crack flared. "Ben?"

"I'm sorry to bother you. I know this is a difficult time—"

"You have no idea," she snorted.

"I have ID." I rummaged around in my purse and grabbed the first one I laid my fingers on. "Here." I handed it through the crack in the door.

Her eye narrowed as she read it. "This is a library card."

"Whoops." I felt my face grow warm. "I am the librarian in Summerset, but I have a driver's license, too," I babbled, taking the library card back and handing her my license.

"Why do you want to talk to me?"

"Ben." I glanced over my shoulder. "May I come in?"

"I guess—how dangerous can a librarian be?" She shut the door, and I heard her removing the security chain. Seconds later the door opened, revealing a small apartment.

The living room and dining area were all one room. A bar, with tall stools lined up on one side, separated the kitchen from the rest of the apartment. A plaid couch faced a big screen TV. On both sides of the TV there were huge stereo speakers.

I felt something at my ankle, and looking down, saw a large, yellow cat rubbing against my bare leg. I leaned over and scratched his ears. "Nice cat . . . what's his name?" I asked as the cat rolled over on his back for a tummy rub.

"Brody."

Straightening, I took my first good look at Gina. She looked like hell. She wore a man's sleeveless undershirt, apparently without a bra, and running shorts. A white tag stuck out on one leg. She had them on inside out. Her brown hair hung around her face in limp locks, and hollow eyes so dark they were almost black stared at me from a blotchy, red face.

"You wanted to talk to me about Ben?" she asked, turning her back to me and wandering over to the kitchen.

"Yes," I replied, following her. "I'm sorry to bother you at a time like this, but I'm trying to track Stephen's activities the week before the shooting." Pulling out a bar stool, I sat as Gina meandered around the kitchen. "The number for Krause's campaign headquarters was listed in Stephen's date book, so I called it—"

"Would you like a Mountain Dew?" Gina opened the refrigerator door and stared inside, not moving.

"No, thank you," I said with a slight shake of my head. "A young woman told me all inquiries were handled by Ben. Do you know if he ever met or talked to Stephen?"

"I don't know." She bent at the waist and reached into the refrigerator. Withdrawing a can of Mountain Dew and a can of Diet Coke, she popped the tabs. She placed the Mountain Dew on the counter and set the Coke in front of me.

"Ah, thanks," I mumbled, glancing down at the can.

Gina crossed to the cupboard. "Ben's been distant for the last couple of weeks, and we fought about it." She swung the door of one cabinet wide and grabbed a small amber bottle. "I thought he was cheating on me." Pressing her palm down on the white cap, she unscrewed it. "What time is it?" she asked with a tilt of her head and a vague expression.

"Umm . . . " My eyes flew to the clock above the stove. "One."

"Okay."

I watched her mouth move as she counted silently on her fingers up to four. Removing the cap, she shook a tiny pill into the center of her palm, and with one smooth move tossed it in her mouth. She washed it down with a long swig of Mountain Dew. She tottered over to the bar and placing her elbows on the bar, leaned toward me.

I studied her carefully. The reason her eyes appeared black? Her pupils were dilated to the max. *Gina's doped to the gills.* "Are you okay?"

"Yeah." Her voice sounded a little slurred. "It was hard

going through Ben's apartment this morning, so a friend gave me some of her tranquilizers."

"You shouldn't take medication that's not prescribed for you," I commented sternly.

"I know." She tried focusing on my face. "But I couldn't stop crying."

In her current condition, I worried she might overdose. "Is anyone coming to stay with you?"

"My mom—" Her voice faded. "She's supposed to be here at two."

"That's good." A paper lying on the counter caught my attention. It was some kind of list.

Gina noticed. "That's why I thought you were with the police."

"The paper?"

"Yeah, it's a list of everything missing from Ben's apartment."

I gripped the edge of the bar. "His apartment was burglarized?"

"Last night. Dumb reporter," she muttered, "putting Ben's address in the news article."

Perplexed, I stared down at the paper. This girl wasn't making much sense.

"Don't you get it?"

"Ah, no."

"Thieves check news articles, obituaries, for people who recently died, and get their addresses. If the house is empty . . . they rob it." She blinked her bleary eyes. "I heard the cop say they had two other burglaries last night . . . same deal . . . people had passed away in the last couple of days."

"What did they take?"

"I don't know—I didn't know the people who died."

"No, I mean Ben—what did they take from his apartment?"

"Oh," she said with a wave of her hand, "mostly electronics." Her head drooped. "I'm sorry, but I'm really tired."

"Gina," I said, getting up and going around the bar, "why don't you lie down until your mother gets here. I'll stay if you want."

"Gee, that's nice," she mumbled as I helped her to her feet and led her to the couch.

She lay down, and I tucked the afghan on the arm of the couch around her.

"I'm sorry." She watched me with wide eyes. "But I'm not myself. One more week and this wouldn't have happened."

I crossed over to an armchair left of the couch and sat. "What wouldn't have happened?"

"Ben—next week, he wouldn't have been with Krause," she said, curling a hand under her chin.

"What do you mean, Gina?"

"Ben didn't like Krause anymore," she said, her voice faint.

"Ben was going to quit the campaign?" I asked, sitting forward in the chair.

"Yeah," she replied, her eyelids drifting shut, "quitting. He was going back to his old job at the winery."

I waited at Gina's apartment until her mother arrived. She seemed surprised to see a stranger with her daughter, but her main focus was on Gina's condition. I was able to gloss over any details and was out the door within fifteen minutes.

When I arrived home, Darci had left and locked up as I'd asked. Walking back to the office, I found a note in her swirly handwriting, taped to the screen, *I give up—call me*, followed by lots of exclamation points.

Smiling, I threw the note away and, accompanied by Lady and T.P., went to change from the capris into shorts and a T-shirt.

As I dressed, T.P. would *not* leave me alone. He tugged on the shoestrings of my tennis shoes, jumped on the bed, and balanced on his back feet while his front paws rested on my leg.

"You're bored, aren't you?" I asked, giving him a scratch behind the ears. "Okay, come on, let's go."

He and Lady went scampering from the room, and by the time I made it down the stairs, they were both waiting expectantly by the front door. Grabbing their leashes, I hooked them up and off we went for a walk.

Mid-afternoon on a summer's day—the air hummed with the sound of lawn mowers, and the smell of fresh mown grass drifted on the slight breeze. The rain last week had given the flowers much needed moisture, and they now bloomed in riots of color. Spicy tea roses, candy cane gladiolas, bright orange California poppies, and golden marigolds had the bees flitting from flower to flower in a frenzy.

Lady and T.P. pranced along next to me with heads held high, sniffing the air. As we passed by, squirrels in the top branches of the maple trees chattered down at the dogs. A couple of cars going by tooted their horns, their drivers giving me a quick wave. Approaching the city park, I heard the sound of children laughing.

The violence, the dreams, all seemed out of place as I walked along with the dogs.

At the city park, I chose a picnic table under a big elm to sit and watch the children play on the swings and teeter-totters. Across the park, one table had yellow, red, and orange helium balloons fastened at the end. They bounced gaily in the air above the bright tablecloth, announcing HAPPY BIRTHDAY.

Lady and T.P. picked a spot at my feet where they could check out all the kids. I noticed their bodies tense with anticipation whenever a child ran by. They wanted to join the fun, but I didn't dare let them off their leashes.

T.P. suddenly scrambled to his feet and his tail whipped from side to side. Following his eyes, I saw a child break away from a group of children by the slides and come running toward us, her brown curls bobbing.

Evita.

"Miss Jensen," she said, falling to her knees in front of Lady and T.P. "Are they yours?"

T.P. immediately scrambled onto Evita's lap and began licking her face with his long pink tongue.

Grabbing his collar, I tugged him off her. "Sorry, he needs a little work on his manners."

"That's okay," she replied with a little giggle, and rubbed his face. "He's nice. So is this one," Evita said as Lady sidled up to her.

"He's a puppy and a little rambunctious. And to answer your question . . . Lady's my dog, but T.P. is my daughter's."

She paused, petting both dogs and cocked her head, looking up at me. "Do they smile?"

I laughed. "Kind of, I guess." I patted Lady's head. "They're very good at letting me know if they're happy or not."

"Brandon's having a birthday party," she said, pointing toward the balloons, "and he invited *me*."

"That's terrific, sweetie. Have you been to the library lately?" I asked as Evita stood and scooted next to me on the bench.

She dipped her head. "No, Papa won't let me."

I felt a flicker of annoyance. Just because I'd upset Mr. Vargas wasn't a reason to deny Evita the joy of reading.

"That's too bad," I murmured, and bit my tongue to keep from saying more. Not your place to interfere, I thought.

She leaned close to me and held her hand up to her mouth. "I wasn't supposed to say anything about my aunt," she whispered.

"Oh, Evita, I'm sorry if my visit landed you in trouble."

"It's okay," she replied with a toss of her brown curls. "Mama says Papa will get over it once my aunt's here."

"Will she be here soon?"

"I don't know—she's in Phoenix right now, I think." Evita's mouth formed a little pout. "They never tell me anything, but I overheard them talking about why it's taking her so long to come from Mexico."

"Your aunt lived in Mexico?"

"Yes, she's Papa's little sister. He had to leave her when he came to this country. All these years he's been working to pay for her to join him—" She hesitated. "But I'm not supposed to know that either."

"Evita, you shouldn't eavesdrop."

She gave a little wiggle. "I wouldn't have to if they'd tell me what's going on—like that man on the motorcycle. I don't know why Papa got so mad at him."

I turned to face her. "Evita, what man on the motorcycle?"

She wrinkled her nose, thinking. "I forget when, but a man came to the house after I went to bed. I heard him arguing with Papa out in the front yard, so I peeked out the window. And—" She stopped when a little girl called out.

"Hey, Evita, come on," she yelled, waving her arm. "Let's teeter-totter."

Evita hopped to her feet. "That's my best friend, Jenny," she said with a big smile. " 'Bye, Miss Jensen. I'll be back at the library soon for a piece of candy."

"I'll make sure the jar's full, sweetie," I called after her.

As I watched Evita run across the park, I felt sick at my stomach. Man on a motorcycle? Antonio Vargas had talked to Stephen and probably known Ben Jessup when he worked at the winery. Now a mysterious man on a motorcycle was showing up at his house late at night. Was Vargas somehow involved in Stephen's shooting and Ben Jessup's murder?

# *Twenty-Six*

I walked back to the house with heavy steps, and somehow the world didn't seem so peaceful anymore. Should I tell Bill about my conversation with Evita? That she'd seen a man on a motorcycle arguing with her father? Motorcycles were common this time of year—it didn't necessarily mean Antonio Vargas was mixed up in anything illegal. But if he were? That poor child's world would come crashing down around her.

I couldn't do it—go running to Bill with only the ramblings of a ten-year-old. I needed more information. Abby could help me. She'd recommended using the datolite, but I had a better idea. I'd ask her to do a "reading" on me instead. The thought made me a little uncomfortable—my grandmother tiptoeing around in my mind, ferreting out information. When we'd done readings before, it always left me feeling a little rattled.

But Abby was good, and I had more faith in her achieving results with a reading than me trying to use the datolite.

She was in the greenhouse when I arrived. Getting out of the car, I turned the dogs loose to let them run while I searched for Abby.

She'd arranged baskets of bright fall mums near the ancient cash register. Shelves, holding potting soil, gardening gloves, and grass seed, lined one wall. From the back of the greenhouse I heard the noise of running water. *Ahh, she's watering the plants.*

Heading toward the sound, I took a deep breath—the smell of damp earth, fertilizer, and flowers hit me—the smells of my childhood when I helped Abby, as Tink did now. I paused and took another deep breath, savoring the memory of those days.

Life was sure easier back then, I thought with a sigh.

I found Abby in the back. Noticing me, she shut off the hose and studied me.

"You look like you just lost your best friend," she commented, curling the hose around her arm. "Is everything okay with Tink?"

"Yes, she's fine . . . I talked to her this afternoon." My lips tightened. "She's taking to the mountains just swell. In fact, she's starting to sound as if she'd been raised there."

A small grin played at the corner of her mouth. "I knew Tink would adapt well."

"That's not why I'm here," I stated, then told her about my day—meeting Gina and my talk with Evita.

"I don't know what to do next," I said, following her up and down the rows of plants as she pinched off dead leaves.

"I told you—use the datolite. Use your insight to get a description of the man in St. Louis."

Leaning against one of the tables, I crossed one leg over the other. "I've been thinking about that. It would be better if you just did a reading on me."

Her eyes darted my way. "You hate that."

"I know, but I'm desperate."

She picked off a dead blossom. "No."

"What? No?" I exclaimed, pushing away from the table. "You won't help me?"

"I'll lend you a piece of datolite," she replied calmly.

"That's it?" I snapped a dead flower off the nearest mum and began shredding the petals.

Abby continued down the row of tables. "Yes."

I threw the petals on the table and hurried after her. "Wait a minute," I said, grabbing her sleeve. "My back's against the wall and I can't figure a way out. All I have are a bunch of loose ends."

"Use your gift."

"I'm not as good as you are," I pleaded.

"Yes, you are," she answered in a firm voice as she gently pulled away from me. "You just don't believe it."

She meant it—she wasn't going to help me. My shoulders slumped, and my shock was replaced by a sense of defeat.

Abby eyed me over her shoulder. "Oh, don't look so forlorn." Picking up a potted mum, she turned toward me.

The plant was heavy with bronze flowers, and even standing a few feet away, I could smell its tangy fragrance.

"See this plant? Remember what it looked like last spring?" she asked.

"Yeah . . . two little leaves on a skinny stalk. So?" I groused.

"Right. I watered it, gave it fertilizer, protected it from extreme temperatures, and look at it now."

"All right, I agree it's gorgeous. But what does that have to do with anything?"

"Well, I've given this plant a good start," she said, fingering the soft petals, "and its roots are strong. If I planted this in the earth, it would not only survive, but thrive."

I scuffed the concrete floor with the toe of my tennis shoe. "Are you trying to tell me I have my own root system now?"

Abby gave a little chuckle. "Yes." She came to me, her face glowing as she laid a hand on my arm. "You are one of the chosen, my dear. What you need is buried inside of you. All you have to do is reach down and take it."

Later that night, armed with my piece of datolite, I prepared my space. Taking a purple candle, I dipped the tip of my finger in patchouli oil and traced the runes, Laguz and Pertho, on the side of the candle. Laguz, to add energy to my psychic powers; Pertho, the rune of mystery, of things hidden, with the hope that it would help me to find what I couldn't see.

Holding the datolite lightly in my left hand, I tried to relax, but tension gripped me like a vice. Anxiety bit into me. *I can't do this.*

*Yes, you can,* said a voice in my head.

I stretched my neck, rolled my shoulders, and concentrated on taking steady breaths. In, out—in, out. I lit the candle and picked up a pen and notebook, ready to write down my impressions.

I imagined I was back in St. Louis, at Stephen's condo. I remembered feeling the need to hurry, the sudden sense of panic as we were leaving. The elevator opened, and at the last second I glanced at the man stepping into the hallway from the other elevator.

Height—medium, less than six feet, with a slight build. His ethnic background appeared to be Latin. Thick black hair, short in front, longer in back, brushing the neck of his shirt. He wore jeans, motorcycle boots with heavy heels, and a dark T-shirt. A chain was attached to his belt, with whatever was on the end shoved in his pocket.

Scribbling down the description, I noticed I'd failed to see his eyes. I needed to see the eyes.

My memory flashed forward to the park—the sound of splashing water, the peacefulness I'd felt sitting there. I imagined what I'd seen, heard, and felt as I left the park—the dead air, the tall buildings, the shadows, and finally the footsteps behind me.

In my head I saw myself whipping around.

Black eyes stared at me. Greedy eyes . . . greedy with a hunger not satisfied. A thin scar ran from the corner of one eye down the side of his cheek. His tongue darted out and licked thin lips. A gold medallion around his neck flashed.

Shutting my eyes, I burned the man's image into my brain. Slowly, I opened them. Yes, my impressions lingered, and I'd recognize him again.

No name, nothing else had filtered through, but now my pursuer had a face.

# *Twenty-Seven*

Later, curled up in bed, I felt tired, but my spirit was light. Abby had been right—I did it. The knowledge gained might not tie up all the loose threads, but knowing who hunted me was one more piece of the puzzle.

"All a matter of faith," I murmured to myself as I floated off to sleep.

The shadows were lengthening—I had to hurry. I pumped the pedals of my bicycle faster as I turned the corner. *Good— the church of Saint Flora was up ahead.*

I touched the package tucked in the pocket of my slacks. Precious food tickets—my payment for acting as courier for the saboteurs. The tickets had been waiting, locked in a shed near Quai de Valmy, when I made the drop. Using the key Brother Sebastian had given me, I'd unlocked the shed, left the explosives, and taken the counterfeit food tickets.

When I reached the alley next to the church, I made a sharp right turn and coasted to the rear of the building. Hopping off my bicycle, I left it propped against the side of the stone building and walked to a small wooden door. With a glance toward the end of the alley, I tapped twice. A second later the rasp of a bolt being thrown back sounded softly. The door opened, and Brother Sebastian silently drew me inside.

Touching a finger to his lips, he pivoted and strode down

a narrow hall—his cassock whispering faintly against his legs. I skipped behind, trying to keep up with him. At the end of the hall I saw another door. He stopped, took a key from his pocket and unlocked it. With a wave, he motioned me down a flight of wooden steps.

A single bare lightbulb hanging from the ceiling lit my way as I descended. The air became cooler, and a musty smell seemed to radiate from the damp walls. At the bottom of the stairs, I found myself standing in an ancient cellar.

The space was cluttered with old wooden chairs stacked haphazardly against one another, moldy books rotting on dusty shelves, and empty wine bottles. Brother Sebastian crossed the room to one of the shelves and slowly moved it away from the wall, revealing yet another door. It only measured four feet in height and had been completely invisible behind the shelf. He opened the door, and a small square of light appeared on the stone floor. Crouching, he went through the doorway.

I followed.

Straightening, I stood in a small room. Three pallets, laid side by side and covered with threadbare blankets, took up one wall. A single kerosene lamp, sitting on a square table in the center of the room, provided a small circle of light that didn't quite reach the murky corners of the room.

I jumped when a man suddenly stepped out of the shadows. In the dim light, I sensed his body tense. He wore peasant clothes—a homespun shirt, rough trousers, and heavy boots. An old slouched hat covered his head. Even though the brim of his hat cast a partial shadow over his face, I could see his complexion spoke of his Gitan heritage.

Brother Sebastian crossed the room and laid a hand on the man's arm. "It's all right, Jacques, this is Madeleine. She's here to help."

I reached in my pocket for the food tickets, but stopped abruptly when Jacques took a half step toward me.

A small hand appeared on his shoulder, and someone whispered, "Jacques."

His head whipped around as a woman holding a child stepped out from behind him.

"Come, Marie," Brother Sebastian said, taking the woman's arm and leading her to one of the chairs sitting by the table.

Marie sat, settling the child on her lap and wrapping her multicolored shawl tightly around the little girl. Jacques followed, and coming up behind her, put a hand protectively on Marie's shoulder while he stared at me with suspicion.

Marie was also Gitan—high broad cheekbones, with black eyes and hair. Those eyes watched me now with fear hiding in their depths.

I looked at the child—a girl. Although petite, I judged her to be around nine or ten. She had inherited the best of both her parents. Caramel skin from her father and her mother's black eyes. Her eyes didn't watch me in fear like her mother, or with suspicion like her father. Her eyes held nothing but bright curiosity.

"Jacques, Madeleine has brought the food tickets." Brother Sebastian nodded in my direction.

I took a step forward and placed them on the table by the lamp.

"Madeleine, this is Jacques and Marie Gaspard. And this," he said, chucking the little girl under her chin, "is Rosa."

I squatted in front of the child. "Hello, Rosa."

"Hello, mademoiselle," she replied shyly.

My eyes traveled up to Marie. "May I give her something?"

Marie relaxed against the back of the chair and nodded.

"Do you like candy?" I asked, and withdrew a peppermint stick from my pocket.

"Oh, yes!" Rosa exclaimed, her eyes dancing.

Handing her the candy, I smiled as her tongue darted out and licked the red and white stripes.

Marie bent her head down and whispered something in Rosa's ear.

The child paused for a moment and gave me a wide smile. "Thank you."

"You're most welcome," I said, smiling back at her.

She leaned her head back against her mother and continued eating her candy. As she did, a medallion around her neck glimmered in the soft light. It was a circle of gold surrounding four petals.

"Your necklace is lovely, Rosa," I commented.

Marie smiled and laid a hand over the gleaming gold. "It's very old." She kissed the top of Rosa's head. "It protects her from harm."

As I talked to Marie, Brother Sebastian had drawn Jacques to the other side of the small room, and they stood talking in low voices.

He turned to me. "Madeleine," he called abruptly.

Standing, I patted Rosa on the head, then joined them.

"I didn't want to frighten Marie and Rosa," Brother Sebastian said quietly, "but I want you to hear this. Go ahead, Jacques."

Jacques removed his hat and wrung the brim with his hands. "When the Germans came, one of the village priests helped us escape. Keeping to the woods, he took us to the next village and to the church that was there. The priest from that village moved us to the next, and so it went, until we reached Paris and Brother Sebastian."

"It must have been a long journey for you," I said.

"Yes," he said, lowering his eyes. "And we've a longer journey ahead."

"Tell Madeleine what you learned at the last church," Brother Sebastian prodded.

"To the east," he said, his eyes darting to Brother Sebastian before settling on me, "saboteurs had blown up a bridge. Someone reported to the Germans that those responsible for the bridge were hiding in a small village nearby. The Germans came to the village—" His voice faltered.

"Go on," Brother Sebastian urged.

Jacques's complexion paled. "Without asking questions, they massacred the entire village. One woman survived by hiding in the bushes—everyone else—every man, woman, and child—dead."

Bile rising in my throat threatened to choke me. I swallowed twice. "How many?" I croaked.

"Over six hundred."

I gripped Brother Sebastian's sleeve. "What does this mean?"

"For your safety, Madeleine, stay away from the saboteurs—"

"But how will we obtain the food tickets?"

"The black market—I know of a man selling them."

"But that's dangerous, too," I pointed out.

Placing a hand on my arm, Brother Sebastian gave me a grim look. "These are dangerous times—all we can do is trust that Providence will protect us . . . " He paused. " . . . and be smarter than the Germans." His eyes traveled around the small room. "We've used this place too many times. We're moving Jacques, Marie, and Rosa to a new hiding place until we can transport them north."

"Where?" I asked.

"The Catacombs," he replied.

A chill shook me. The Catacombs—a series of tunnels dating back to the old Roman mines. A place of death—a place where millions of bones had been moved after many of the old cemeteries became overcrowded and had to be closed.

The thought of that sweet child being forced to exist among the dead had the bile rising again.

"You don't want to frighten them?" I asked with a jerk of my head. "What do you think seeing a wall made of bones and skulls will do?"

"Madeleine, not all the tunnels are used as ossuaries. There's one near Rue de Menilmontant."

"When are you going to move them?"

"Tomorrow," Brother Sebastian replied.

I glanced over at Marie and Rosa, still enjoying her peppermint stick, and shook my head. "Brother Sebastian, the Germans will take one look at them and know they're refugees . . . they'll ask questions." Looking back at Marie, I sized her up. "We're close to the same build. I'll bring a suit, hat, and shoes for her. She'll look like a Parisian when I'm finished. And Jacques? I'll borrow some of Henrick's clothes—" I hesitated. "But as for Rosa—I don't have any children's clothes."

Brother Sebastian's lips lifted in a small smile. "I hadn't thought of their appearance. You're very clever, Madeleine," he commented. "Don't worry about Rosa, I'll find clothes for her."

"They have to be stylish," I said, shaking a finger at him, "not castoffs. Otherwise the Germans will know."

"I'll take care of it."

"How long will they have to stay in the Catacombs?"

"Not long. I'm arranging safe houses to the north. There's a man with a fishing boat who will take them to Sweden."

"Sweden?"

"Yes, Jacques knows a family there."

I gripped Brother Sebastian's sleeve. "Henrick is Swedish—maybe he can help them. I'll—"

"No." Brother Sebastian's voice echoed in the small room, startling Marie and Rosa. "That wouldn't be wise."

I lifted my chin. "Henrick would never betray me," I insisted.

Rushing up the stairs to my apartment, I couldn't wait to talk to Henrick. I didn't care what Brother Sebastian said . . . I loved Henrick and trusted him. I knew he'd help me if I asked.

Flinging the door open, I burst into the room, only to pull up short, my greeting dying on my lips.

Henrick sat on the couch, a glass of wine in his hand, talking like a long-lost friend to . . . Vogel.

# *Twenty-Eight*

"You forced me to play hostess to that man for two hours," I shrieked as I stomped into the bedroom and flung myself on the bed. Enraged, I pummeled my pillow.

"Madeleine, don't be this way," Henrick pleaded, following me into the bedroom. "I'm sorry . . . I had no choice. I ran into him at Place de la Republique and he rather invited himself to the apartment."

I felt the bed dip, and rolling over, I sat up. Scooting into the corner, I glared at Henrick. "I don't want him here. I feel violated." My head whipped around as my eyes scanned the room. "I want to open all the windows, I want to fumigate."

"You're being overdramatic, my love," he replied, stretching out his hand to me. "You know I had to do what I did. For your sake and mine, Vogel must continue to think we're his friends."

I flounced deeper into the corner. "You're a fool, Henrick, if you think Vogel just wants to be my friend. Didn't you see the way he watched me?"

Henrick's chin dropped. "Madeleine, Vogel may be a German, but he's not without honor. He wouldn't dare act inappropriately with you."

"*Pah,* he would dare much. Nazis have no honor." I got to my knees, and placing my hands on the bed, leaned forward. "Today I learned they slaughtered an entire village," I exclaimed. "Over six hundred people died."

"Where did you hear that?" he asked, lifting his head.

"Never mind," I answered, sitting back on my heels.

"Rumors—" He stopped and sighed. "Rumors and the propaganda of the communists. They want to incite the people of France, and they won't be happy until the streets of Paris run red with blood."

"You're wrong—it happened," I insisted.

Henrick laid a hand on my knee. "I know you hate them . . . I hate them, too . . . and right now things seem hopeless, but it won't last. Hitler's attacked the Soviet Union, and it's a battle he can't win any more than Napoleon could. Also, the Americans have entered into an agreement with the British. It's only a matter of time before they enter the war."

"How does that help France now?" I asked, clenching my fists.

"It doesn't, my love, but it means someday this will be over and we can have a life together. We just have to survive and do the best we can until then." Henrick lifted my fist to his mouth and placed a long kiss on the inside of my wrist. "Please, let's not fight. I'll think of a way to keep Vogel at bay. He won't be here again."

My eyes narrowed. "Do you promise?"

"Yes," he answered, tugging me toward him. "I would do anything for you." Wrapping his arms around me, he laid me back on the bed.

Anything but marry me, I thought to myself, but said nothing. Henrick was desperate to pacify my anger—that gave me the upper hand. And made it a good time to ask for favors.

I relaxed my body against his and laid an open palm against his face. "You would do anything for me?" I asked sweetly.

"Yes," he murmured as he placed a kiss on my forehead.

"Would you help me get a refugee family to Sweden?"

He jerked to a sitting position. "No."

Scrambling to the other side of the bed, I jumped to my feet. "Then you lie!"

Henrick shifted to where he could watch me. "We can't risk making the Germans suspicious. We could lose everything, and—"

"Not we," I said, cutting him off and jabbing a finger at him. "You. You could lose access to their money." I stamped my foot. "You're a selfish, selfish man, Henrick Sorenson, and you care nothing for others, not even me." Whirling, I strode to the bathroom, where I pivoted and grabbed the door. "Someday you'll learn what's really important," I cried, slamming the door in his face.

My cheeks were damp with tears—poor Madeleine. Her anger, her disappointment in Henrick, lingered in my mind. Believing in the man he could be, she was torn between her love for him and the man he was.

What did the dream mean? I didn't know. I'd fallen asleep confident that my gift would show me the way, but now that feeling was gone. Instead, I felt wrung out by the disturbing dream. I tossed and turned, dozing for a few minutes, only to wake up with a start, and then remaining awake for the rest of the night.

As I watched the sunrise lighten my bedroom, I resolved to put the dream behind me and concentrate on today. I needed to know if the man on the motorcycle, the one who'd gunned down Ben Jessup, and the man who chased me were one in the same. My meditation with the datolite had revealed the scar on his face, something I'd missed in St. Louis.

Only one person I could think of might know the answer to that—Antonio Vargas.

Though anxious to talk to him, I waited a decent amount of time before driving to his house. I didn't want to roust him out of bed.

When I arrived, I spied him around the side of the small

house, pruning a climbing rosebush with long-handled loppers. He wore old jeans, a work shirt, and long leather gloves. A wheelbarrow next to him was already half full of thorny spines.

Getting out of the car, I crossed the yard before calling out. "Hi, Mr. Vargas," I said in a cheerful voice.

He paused and glanced at me, but the slouched hat he wore made it hard to see the expression in his eyes. His lips, though, tightened in a thin line. Without speaking, he turned back to the rosebush and, with a swift snap of the lopper's handles, clipped another cane. It fell to his feet. Bending at the waist, he picked up the stick and threw it in the wheelbarrow with the rest of them.

"Isn't that a Seven Sister?" I asked, touching one of the canes.

He clipped another and tossed it toward me. I stepped to the side to avoid it hitting me.

*I'm not giving up.*

Clenching my fists, I tried to keep my voice pleasant. "My grandmother, Abigail McDonald, has one of those. Maybe you know her? She owns Abby's Greenhouse."

Vargas's only reply was to prune another branch off the bush.

*Jeez, if he keeps cutting instead of talking . . . there isn't going to be anything left of that bush.*

"The roses are beautiful when they bloom, aren't they? Oh, you have a trumpeter vine." I pointed to the woody vine, laden with orange trumpet-shaped flowers, twining up the light pole. "Abby has one of those, too. Has Evita ever picked the flowers and put them on her fingers, like fake fingernails? Abby always got so upset when I did that."

His mouth softened when I mentioned Evita, but an instant later settled back into a hard line.

"Ms. Jensen, I don't think you drove all the way out here to talk about gardening," he finally said in a curt voice. "What do you want?"

"I wasn't completely honest when I was here last week," I said, stepping back toward the wheelbarrow.

I saw his eyebrows lift as if to say *No kidding.*

"But I'm going to tell you the truth now," I continued. "I think someone shot Stephen Larsen to stop him from writing his next book."

Vargas quickly moved to the other side of the rosebush.

*Ahh, I'd hit a nerve there.*

I walked up to him. "And I think the same person, or someone working with him, killed Ben Jessup. You remember Ben, don't you? He worked at the winery?"

He whirled suddenly when I mentioned Ben.

I pressed my advantage. "They also mugged Karen Burns, Stephen's assistant, *and* tried to shoot me."

"I think you'd better leave."

I crossed my arms and drilled him with my eyes. "When whoever it was killed Jessup and took a shot me, he was riding a motorcycle."

"Many people ride motorcycles."

"You're right, but I think this man has a scar running from the corner of his eye down his face. Know anyone like that?"

Vargas turned his back to me as he cut off another rose cane. "No."

"The man who visited you last week, on *his* motorcycle, didn't have a scar?"

He waved his loppers in the direction on my car. "I think you'd better leave—"

I reached out and grabbed his sleeve, interrupting him. "Please, Mr. Vargas, these men are killers—"

A vein in the side of his neck twitched as he whirled and stared at me. "If it's as you say—they're killers—for the sake of my family, do you think—" He broke off and in rapid succession cut three more canes down. "I must protect Deloris and Evita."

"Mr. Vargas—" I pleaded, taking a step back.

I didn't finish—we both turned to see a sheriff's car roll to a stop in the driveway.

Vargas whirled on me. "If you've brought trouble to my home—" he said, jabbing the loppers in my direction.

"No," I said, holding up both hands. "Honest—"

"What's going on?" Bill called as he hoisted his pants and walked toward us.

"Nothing, Bill. I'm just paying a visit." I tried to look nonchalant.

Vargas threw the loppers on top of the rose canes and removed his long leather gloves. "Sheriff Wilson," he said, holding out his hand.

"Antonio, nice morning," Bill said in greeting as he shook Vargas's hand. "Looked like you folks were having an argument," he commented, watching me carefully.

"Oh, no, Bill," I said, meeting his eyes, "nothing like that. We were discussing overdue fines."

Bill removed his hat and rubbed his head a couple of times, then cleared his throat. "Antonio, you have a sister."

It was a statement, not a question, but Antonio didn't pick up on it. A sense of foreboding formed inside of me.

"Yes, in Mexico." His skin paled and his eyes darted my way in a silent plea.

I kept my mouth shut and tugged on my bottom lip.

"Is Deloris here?" Bill asked abruptly.

"No, no, they're at church." He removed a handkerchief from his pocket and mopped his face. "Why are you here, Sheriff?" He twisted the fabric in his hands. "Something hasn't happened to my wife and daughter?"

"No." Bill clapped a big hand on Antonio's shoulder. "I'm sorry, Antonio . . . I received a call from Yuma, Arizona, today. The body of a young woman was found in the desert—"

Antonio's knees wobbled, then he stiffened. "My sister," he said, his voice bleak. "What happened?"

"She was with a group of immigrants trying to cross the

border. The Yuma County sheriff didn't know if the smuggler they'd hired abandoned them or just failed to pick them up. They were found by some guys on ATVs." Bill's voice was soft and low. "Your sister was already gone by the time the group was discovered. I'm sorry."

Vargas seemed to shrink with each word, as if a terrible weight crushed him. The handkerchief slipped from his fingers. "She wouldn't listen . . . I've been working for years to get her a visa . . . she was growing impatient." He lifted haunted eyes to Bill's face. "She was only twenty."

Bill dropped his hand from Antonio's shoulder and reached in his pocket, withdrawing a piece of paper. "Here's the number for the Yuma County Sheriff's Department and the hospital where they took your sister, if you want to call them."

Antonio took the paper from Bill and stared at it as if he couldn't decipher the words. "Thank you," he whispered.

"Do you want me to go pick up Deloris and Evita and bring them home for you?" Bill asked.

Antonio shook his head. "No, that would only frighten them . . . they'll be home soon." His voice broke.

Taking my arm, Bill took a step toward the waiting cars. "Come on, Ophelia."

I shook his hand off and crossed to Antonio. "I'm so sorry for your loss, Antonio," I said with sympathy.

He stood there, not speaking, just staring at the paper in his hands.

"Let's go," Bill called out.

I joined Bill and together we walked to the waiting cars. Bill opened my door then clapped his hat on his head. "What were you doing here?"

Sliding into the car, I looked up at him. "It's a long story."

"I bet," he said with a snort. "You want to tell me?"

"No." I closed the car door and rolled down the window. "You wouldn't believe it."

Even if he did, my story would only bring more trouble to the Vargas family, and they had enough problems right now.

Bill leaned down and braced his forearm on the car door. "The next time I run into you, young lady, it better be at the library where you belong."

# Twenty-Nine

I drove home confused and depressed. Antonio Vargas knew that his sister had left Mexico, and I bet he knew who she'd hired to smuggle her into this country.

My knowledge about these smuggling rings was minimal. I'd heard a few rumors and stories of how "coyotes" made money off the desperate. And everyone in the state had heard of the immigrants who lost their lives after being shut in a railway car used to haul grain. His sister and the others had been locked in and then abandoned. The boxcar had sat, supposedly empty, in a railway yard in Texas for several months before being sent to Iowa to haul grain. The bodies were discovered when the car was finally opened.

Right now I had theories, but no proof. I needed to get into those disks.

At home, I threw my purse on the counter and went back to the office. I sat down and inserted the disks, determined to succeed where Darci had failed.

Four hours later it felt like my eyes were crossed and my mind was seeping away. I'd typed in so many combinations of "ashes and flames" that my fingers were cramped.

Stretching my arms above my head, a heaviness weighed on me, body and soul. I was tired. After my restless night, I needed a nap.

Once in bed, the last thing I remember was the heaviness enfolding me.

The sharp wrapping on a door wakened me, and I bolted upright. *Wait a minute, this isn't my room . . . got it . . . still asleep.* The "Ophelia" part of me surrendered to the dream.

I threw back covers still warm from Henrick. Shrugging into my robe, I jumped from the bed and hurried to the door.

A young priest stood in the hallway, shifting nervously from one foot to the other.

"Madeleine?"

I held my robe tight against my throat. "Yes?"

"Phoenix," he whispered.

Grabbing his sleeve, I pulled him into the apartment and shut the door. "What's wrong?"

"Brother Sebastian has been 'detained' by the Germans," he replied, wringing his hands.

I stumbled to the couch and sank down. "Oh no," I gasped. "When?"

"Last night . . . he was with a man who sells food on the black market." The young priest paced the floor in front of me. "We don't know if they were after the man or Brother Sebastian."

"It doesn't make a difference who was the target—they're interrogating Brother Sebastian now."

"We must move the Gaspards as soon as possible." He took a packet from his pocket and handed it to me. "Here are their papers and a map to a safe house in the north."

With eyes wide, I looked down at the envelope in my hands. "You want me to transport them?"

"There's no one else. We must move quickly—we don't know what they'll force out of Brother Sebastian." The young priest's Adam's apple bobbed as he swallowed twice. "The Nazis are very persuasive."

I closed my eyes, thinking of the horrors Brother Sebastian might be suffering.

"Did he have a plan to get them out of Paris?"

"I think so, but he didn't tell me. He said the less I know, the better." He hurried to the door, then turned. "Can you do this?"

I nodded.

"Good, I'm going underground for a while, until we learn Brother Sebastian's fate. I suggest you do the same."

I sat for a minute and tugged at my bottom lip. I couldn't stand the thought of the Gaspards falling into the hands of the Nazis. I rose, clinging tightly to the envelope. I needed guidance. Running to the bedroom, I tore open my dresser drawer and removed my deck of cards. I sat on the bed and, placing the envelope next to me, shuffled the cards quickly.

I drew nine cards, laid them facedown on the bed and flipped them over, one by one.

The eight of clubs, the seven of spades, the ace of spades, the jack of spades, the jack of clubs, the nine of spades, the seven of hearts, the ten of spades, the jack of hearts.

Clubs signified that I needed to take action against the enemy; hearts indicated I was emotionally vulnerable; and spades signaled a transformation.

Reading the cards, I understood immediately what they said. The ace, nine, and ten of spades indicated some kind of death. The jack of hearts spoke of a man unable to commit. The jack of spades meant a man capable of deception. The eight of clubs told me of a journey. The death would be my relationship with a man unable to commit, meaning it was time to move on. We had been deceiving ourselves by thinking there would ever be a future for us.

I looked down at the envelope. It would be so easy for Henrick to help the Gaspards. He could get them to Sweden safely. As a foreign businessman, he had a car provided by his father. It would be simple for him to drive them to the north. But no, if he couldn't commit to me, how could I expect him to commit risking his life for strangers?

Wait—the car.

I flew out of the bedroom to the kitchen window and looked out at the back alley. His car was there—he hadn't taken it that morning. *I'd* drive the Gaspards north and then disappear.

Rushing back to the bedroom, I looked in the cup where Henrick always placed his keys. Indeed, they were there. I tossed them on the bed. Henrick's gas rations from the bottom drawer joined the keys and the envelope. Next, I tossed in my cards.

I crossed to the closet and, flinging the doors wide, grabbed my battered suitcase. Cocking a hip, I studied my clothes hanging neatly from the closet rod. So many fancy things, I thought, shuffling through them. Some Henrick had purchased for me, and some were from the fashion house. *Had they brought me happiness?* I asked myself as I fingered the fine material? *No.*

Shoving them to the side, I grabbed simple clothes—skirts, blouses, pants—and threw them in the open suitcase. Sensible shoes and underthings followed.

I rushed to the bathroom and opened the medicine cabinet. Expensive creams, perfumes, and lotions lined the shelves. I didn't need them either. Grabbing only a few toiletries, I added them to my suitcase.

I closed the suitcase and moved to the chair by the window. I pushed it aside and opened my hidey hole. Deep in the recess of the floor was another envelope containing all the money I had in the world. A sizable amount—not as much as Henrick had stolen from the Germans, but enough to get me by for a while. It might also come in handy to pay bribes.

As I dressed, I thought once again of Henrick. I did love him, but I would never fit in his world. It was best for both of us to end it. My eyes swam with tears. Should I leave a note? And tell him what? Not about the Gaspards—the cards had warned of deception. No, just a simple good-bye.

I wrote the note, folded it, and propped it on the dresser where he would see it. Shoving both envelopes in the pockets of my slacks, I picked up my suitcase and walked out of my bedroom for the last time.

I drove to a quiet street and parked in front of an empty lot. Armed with a flashlight, I tramped through the high grass to the far corner. A wooden hatch hidden by weeds lay at my feet. Grasping the rusty iron ring, I pulled and the door creaked open. Cold, dank air wafted around me as I peered into the darkness below. After buttoning my wool coat, I turned on my flashlight and descended into the inky blackness. Pausing on the fourth step, I reached up and pulled the wooden hatch shut, closing off the square of sky above me. The only light was the faint beam of the flashlight.

Rung by rung I climbed down the metal ladder. Each one was damp with condensation, and the leather soles of my shoes kept slipping. I clung to the ladder tightly with one hand and to my flashlight with the other. I couldn't drop the flashlight. If it broke on the limestone floor I'd be alone, in the dark, in the kingdom of the dead.

With each step, the temperature dropped, and I was thankful for my heavy coat. I hoped the Gaspards had been given enough blankets to keep them warm in the cold, clammy tunnels. As I moved lower and lower into the Catacombs, I heard the faint echo of dripping water.

Finally, my right foot hit the stone floor. In with the Gaspards' papers, Brother Sebastian had included a map of the Catacombs and where the Gaspards were hiding. I withdrew the map now and studied it. The Catacombs extended over three hundred kilometers underneath the streets of Paris, and without the map, I could wander down the wrong tunnel, lost.

I would proceed straight ahead, past the ossuary, to where the tunnel split to the right and left. I'd stay to the left. According to the map, the Gaspards were in a small chamber off that passageway.

I pulled a knit hat from the pocket of my coat and put it on my head. With a sigh, I began walking down the tunnel.

My feet slopped through puddles while the beam of my flashlight bounced crazily off the walls, revealing graffiti over a hundred years old. My hand appeared to be shaking, but I didn't know if it was from the cold or from fright. All I wanted to do was find the Gaspards and return to the sunshine.

After going several meters, I stopped and checked the map again. The ossuary should be straight ahead. I shoved the map back in my pocket and marched on.

When I passed the ossuary, I tried to keep my eyes focused on the path in front of me, but they strayed to the macabre sight on my left.

A pile of bones, several feet high, marked the center of the room. Near the remains, a sign announced the name of the cemetery where the skeletons had originated. The walls of the ossuary were lined with femurs, one stacked on another, the knobby end facing out into the room. Among the femurs, as if watching over the ossuary, were hundreds of skulls.

The sight chilled my blood. I couldn't imagine what terror Rosa must've experienced as she walked by. Shaking off my fear, I took a step forward and sent something skittering down the passage.

Shining my light ahead, a jawless skull with hollow eyes grinned up at me. A scream fought its way up my throat, and I clenched my jaw tight to stop out. The sound came out as a whimper that reverberated off the walls.

Keeping my eyes averted from what lay at my feet, I hurried down the corridor and finally reached the section where the passage branched. Staying to the left, I peered down the tunnel, searching for the Gaspards. After walking a few meters, I called out softly. "Jacques? It's Madeleine."

Another light suddenly shone into the passage from a chamber farther down and to my right. I rushed toward the light.

Turning the corner to the chamber, I saw Jacques, Maria, and Rosa huddled in a corner. A loaf of bread and cheese lay half eaten on a blanket spread on the chalky floor.

Jacques rose and hurried over to me. "Where's Brother Sebastian?" he asked as he gripped my arm.

I didn't want to increase their fear, so I lied. "He sent me. I'm going to drive you out of the city, to the north."

I felt a deep chill as a voice seemed to prompt me, *Give him the envelopes.*

I took them, and the car keys, from my pocket, and forced them into his hands. "Here, take these. It's money and your papers. Do you know how to drive?"

He nodded, stuffing the envelopes in his pocket.

"Good, we can take turns." Looking at Maria and Rosa, I smiled as I walked toward them. Crouching down, I laid my palms on the child's cheeks. They were freezing. I ripped off my hat and settled it over her black curls. "This will help keep you warm." My eyes traveled around the grim place. "It's not very nice here, is it, Rosa?"

Her wide eyes stared into mine. "No," she said in a small voice.

"Then let's get you out of here and into the sunshine."

Standing, I helped Maria and Rosa to their feet while Jacques picked up their small bundles.

"Follow me," I said with a wave.

Silently, we crept back the way I'd come. I tried to keep my strides short for Rosa's sake, but I was so anxious to get out to the Catacombs, I kept pulling ahead.

Soon, soon, I thought as I approached the ossuary.

Then a light blinded me.

"Madeleine, you're a little far from the fashion salon, aren't you?"

*My God! Vogel.* "Run!" I shrieked.

# *Thirty*

The sound of running feet echoed off the wall, and in the beam on my flashlight, I saw Vogel holding his own flashlight and a gun in the other. Raising my light, I aimed the beam at his eyes. He raised an arm to block the light just as the gun fired. The shot went wild, and the noise of the bullet pinging off the stone walls went on forever. He aimed again and I rushed him, using my flashlight like a club. Swinging hard, I sent the gun flying from his hand, Then flicking off my light, I whirled and ran.

I'd only gone a few feet when my shoes hit a puddle. The slick leather soles gave me no purchase, and I fell on all fours, my flashlight rolling out of my hand.

Vogel grasped the back of my coat and hauled me to my feet. He spun me around, grabbed my throat with one hand and shook me like a dog shaking a rat.

In the dim light, I saw his face red with rage.

He stopped and loosened his grip. "They won't escape. The entrance is blocked." His lips stretched over his teeth in a snarl.

The flashlight he still held, pointing at the floor, cast his face in partial shadows. His eyes were hollow, and he looked like a death's head—like the skull that had grinned up at me.

Vogel released my throat and grabbed my wrist, spinning

me around again with my arm at an angle behind my back.
I heard a pop, and excruciating pain shot down my arm. My
knees buckled.

His other arm snaked around my waist and held me on
my feet. I felt his body press against mine as he whispered
in my ear.

"I can save you, sweet Madeleine." The hand at my waist
held the flashlight, casting light at our feet.

I spit on the toe of his shiny boot.

He whirled me around, releasing my arm, and struck me
hard across the face.

My knees gave out and I went down. I tried to break my
fall but my left arm dangled useless at my side. Hitting the
floor, I rolled to my right side.

Vogel stood over me, shining his flashlight in my eyes.
I was inching backward on my side to escape the beam
when the fingers of my right hand felt something smooth
and round. I crept my hand slowly toward it until my fingers
could curl around it.

Somewhere in my fogged brain it registered that I was
grasping the skull I'd kicked earlier.

Vogel squatted next to me, resting his hands on his knees
and shining the light toward my feet.

Picking up his revolver, he stroked the side of my face
with the barrel. "I don't think I'll turn you over to the
Gestapo right away. No, I'll keep you for myself until I tire
of you." He ran the gun along my chin. "Are you frightened,
Madeleine? Or do you think your beloved Henrick can save
you?" His laughter rang off the walls. "He can't. If he tried,
he would risk all the lovely money he's stealing from the
Third Reich."

My breath caught.

"Ah, you're surprised that I know." He moved the gun
away from my face. "I plan to talk to him about it one day,
and demand my share." He tilted his head back and looked up
at the ceiling. "You or the money? Which do you think—"

I slammed the skull against his temple, and he fell backward.

Scrambling to my feet, I ran into the dark passage, trailing my right hand along the cold wall to guide myself.

There was a flash as Vogel's gun barked, and I stumbled when the bullet hit my back, propelling me forward. My right hand suddenly touched nothing, and I pitched myself sideways to the floor in a small niche cut into the limestone. Scrambling back into it, I drew my legs up to my chest and waited.

Footsteps thundered down the passage while the ray from Vogel's flashlight careened off the walls.

They came closer and closer, then passed right by me. I strained to hear them as they echoed into the darkness.

I was alone and totally without light.

Hot tears warmed my cheeks. I felt the blood seeping down my back. I'd failed—I knew what fate awaited the Gaspards, first at Drancy then at Auschwitz. I leaned to my side and vomited. After wiping my mouth with the back of my hand, I tried to stand, but my legs wouldn't hold me.

Feeling the metallic taste of blood on the back of my tongue, I rolled onto my knees. I would die here, alone, in the dark.

*No,* my mind screamed, *I would die, but not in darkness.*

Slowly, I raised myself to my knees and, using my right arm, inched my way out of the niche. I edged my body toward the ossuary, stopping to pat the cold floor as I searched for my lost light. At long last my fingers touched a cold cylinder. With a cry, I clutched the light and flicked the switch. Cuddling the light close to me, I curled on my side. My legs grew numb. Maybe from lying on the cold stone? Maybe not. I didn't care—I wasn't in the dark anymore.

From a distance, my ears picked up the sound of whispers. Did I hear my grandmother's voice?

Abruptly, hands grasped my shoulders and lifted me off the cold stone floor.

"Please," I whispered, "don't let it be Vogel."

Looking up, Henrick's face swam into focus. "Ah, Madeleine, I found you."

"How?"

"Brother Sebastian."

My eyes closed. "Good. He lives." I coughed and tasted blood again. "Family . . . Gitan . . . Vogel . . . save them."

Henrick lowered his face and pressed a kiss to the top of my head. My vision dimmed, and the last thing I saw was a golden circle surrounding four petals.

My sobbing woke me. My throat ached and I had my wet pillow pressed tight against my cheek. *Madeleine died, she died.* Her cards hadn't lied—only it wasn't just the death of a relationship—it was her death she saw. Rolling over, I curled into a ball of misery and pulled my other pillow to my chest. And not only Madeleine, but Rosa, that sweet little girl who loved peppermint sticks; Marie, with her beautiful black eyes; Jacques, so protective of his family—they perished along with the millions.

*Can heartache kill you?* I didn't think so, but I felt like it would. *Stop it!* I had to get ahold of myself, but the more I tried, the harder I cried. My nose clogged and I couldn't breathe. I stumbled to the bathroom and, grabbing a tissue, blew my nose. Glancing up, I saw myself in the mirror.

Swollen eyes above a bright red nose stared back at me. My hair tumbled around my face and looked like it had been combed with an egg beater. I hiccuped.

Turning on the faucet, I picked up a washcloth and soaked it with cold water. Without wringing it, I held it to my eyes and let the rivulets of cold run down my chin and onto my shirt.

*Think about it, Jensen, if Abby was right and the dreams were of a past life, it meant Madeleine had to have died. Otherwise, right now I'd be older than Abby.*

That thought boggled my mind and only added to my confusion.

And Rosa and her parents?

I lowered the washcloth and wiped my face and neck with a towel.

It had happened over sixty years ago and couldn't be changed. All I could do was carry their memories with me. I had to deal with what was happening now, and dreaming of Rosa made me long for Tink. I needed to wrap my arms around her and keep her safe forever . . . so unless I wanted her to live in the mountains permanently, I knew I'd better find my answers. Then I could bring her home and hug her as much as she'd let me.

I went back to the bedroom. It was still dark outside, and I looked at the clock: 5:00 A.M. I'd slept eleven hours. It would be sunrise soon. Stepping over to the window, I held the curtain back and stared into the night.

What to do now? I hadn't a clue what tonight's dream meant, and all I had were some theories, but no proof.

Dropping the curtain, I turned away from the window. What had Abby said in St. Louis about lessons? That maybe my lesson was to learn to surrender control and trust my gift? I thought I'd done that when I used the datolite, but maybe not. How did I get in touch with my inner spirit?

It hit me. I knew exactly what to do.

Crossing to the closet, I grabbed my white cowled robe.

# Thirty-One

My robe slapped against my legs as I climbed the hill behind Abby's house. In the east, the sky was beginning to lighten, and the world was quiet.

I'd been to this place of magick before, where the energy of the earth ran close to the surface. Then, I'd sought to use magick in the wrong way. Today, I wasn't looking for revenge—today, I sought enlightenment.

While the horizon became tinged with rose, I made my circle of salt. I faced the north and thought of the rich black earth beneath my bare feet. I made a quarter turn and faced the brightening horizon to the east. Taking a deep breath, I let sweet, clean air fill my lungs. Turning again, I faced the south and pictured in my mind the safety and warmth of the hearth, of fire contained. And last to the west, and saw water giving life to all living things.

Finished, I spread the mat I carried on the dew-soaked grass and sat. The air around me throbbed with repressed energy, as if only waiting to slip its bounds. Sitting there, I tried to let the silence fill me and my mind to still. No thoughts of Madeleine and the Gaspards, Stephen, or the Vargas family. It was hard. My mind was like a radio tower picking up twenty stations at once, all containing nothing but static.

*This is wrong. My mind should be empty, not jumping from thought to thought in random order.*

I couldn't control it. I felt my brow wrinkle in concentration as I struggled with the images flitting through my head. Madeleine, the Gaspards skeletal bodies piled in heaps, a golden necklace. Other images, other faces, flashed by . . . a Romany woman holding a china cup close to her face as she studied the tea leaves gathered in the bottom; a tall blond man wearing a funny hat, casting bits of bone on a skin rug in a smoky longhouse made of logs; a warrior monk standing guard in the snow at a temple gate high in the mountains.

A heavy weight crushed down on me as if I were being buried alive. A hot wind blew through my soul, bringing with it the fire and the flame. My skin burned, and I felt consumed by heat. Panting, I struggled to fill my lungs, but the parching wind seared my throat. I burned from the inside out. I saw myself crumbling, piece by piece, until nothing remained of me but a pile of ash. Destroyed, the fiery wind would blow what was left of me to the four corners.

And when I thought I couldn't stand anymore, I felt a drop of water touch my spirit. The flame within me sizzled and the wind stilled. The drop was followed by another, then another, and another, until a torrent of water poured over me, washing away the ash and leaving me clean and new.

The cascading water slowed to a gentle rain, and with the rain came the deepest sense of peace I'd ever know. A warm glow spread through my mind, my body, my spirit—to the tips of my fingers, to the tips of my toes. I felt at one with the world.

I opened my eyes expecting to see scorched, muddy earth. The world around me had changed—the woods below the hill were filled with birdsong under a sky shot with streaks of pink and gold.

Sitting quiet and still, I savored the importance of this moment. Part of me had been stripped away, and in its place was a confidence I'd never experienced. Nourished by the earth, strengthened by the wind, tempered by the fire, and quenched by the water, my sense of self, who I was, what I was, spread its roots like a growing thing.

Rising smoothly to my feet, I closed my circle—grateful for the understanding I'd been given. Abby had always said we were conduits, but I never quite got what she meant. Now I did. The vessel must be empty before it can be filled. I had to surrender before I could receive.

And I did receive. In the process of giving up control, I saw that the answers I'd sought were there all along . . . in my dreams, in my conversations, in Abby's vision of flames and ash. Stephen's password—a mythical bird rising from its own ashes.

Phoenix.

Abby answered her back door at my second knock. Dressed to work in the greenhouse, she wore a chambray shirt over a light top, jeans, and clogs. Her silver hair snaked down her back in a braid.

Holding the screen door open and drawing me inside, her eyes scanned me from tip to toe. "All you all right?"

"Yeah," I croaked, my voice sounding funny to my ears. "I think so."

Abby wrapped her arms around me in a tight hug. "Of course you are." She kissed my cheek. "I'm so proud of you," she whispered in my ear. "Come on," she said, ushering me into the kitchen and guiding me to a chair. "You need to eat." Her eyes traveled down to the bottom of my robe. "The hem's wet. Do you have clothes with you?"

I shook my head. "I'm wearing shorts and a T-shirt underneath."

"Well, then, let's get that robe off of you," she said, helping me to my feet and stripping off the robe as if I were a child. She draped it over the back of one of the chairs, spreading the sleeves wide.

It looked like a second guest sitting at the table.

Pushing me back down in the chair, she busied herself making breakfast. "First you need tea." She stoked the fire in the wood cook stove, and soon the teakettle whistled merrily. Pouring the hot water over the silver tea ball in a mug, she carried it to the table and placed it in front of me. "Put plenty of sugar in it—you need to replenish your energy."

I watched her, puzzled, as I waited for my tea to steep. "Abby, do you know what happened?"

"Not the details, but I know you went through your trial." Her voice was calm, like what I'd experienced was an everyday occurrence. "The change is written on your face."

My hand flew to my face. "I have marks?"

"No," she said, and laughed, "but your eyes are different. There's a light in them now that was lacking."

Shaking my head, I sipped my tea and fell silent.

Lost in our thoughts, Abby and I didn't speak for several minutes. The only sound in her kitchen was the sizzle of sausage and the click of the wire whisk against a stoneware bowl as she scrambled the eggs. When she removed the toaster from the cupboard, I stood to help her. She waved me back into my chair.

"Drink your tea," she said, popping two slices of homemade bread into the toaster. "You need to replenish your fluids. After breakfast, you can have a nice nap in your old bedroom."

"I feel fine. Kind of euphoric." I sat back in my chair and smiled at her. "And I'm not tired—I slept eleven hours last night."

She poured the eggs in the skillet, making it crackle. "It just hasn't caught up with you yet . . . it will," she said, whirling the eggs in the skillet.

When the toaster snapped, Abby quickly buttered the slices and brought them to the table on a small plate. "Here," she said, setting the plate in front of me, "go on and eat your toast."

"Why didn't you ever tell me how to get in touch with my abilities?"

She patted my head before returning to the stove. "It's not something one can explain. I could only try and guide you in that direction."

I picked at a piece of the toast. "That's what all the lecturing about letting go, the empty vessel, etcetera, was about?"

She tossed me a grin over her shoulder. "Yes, but you had to reach the point in your journey where you could accept that on your own."

Crumbling a bit of crust with my fingers, I thought about her words. "Abby, it's taken me so long . . . does this mean I'm a late bloomer?"

Her laughter rang out. "No—it means you're a little more stubborn than most." She frowned as she flipped the sausage. "I think the guilt you felt over Brian's death, the feeling that you should've been able to save him, slowed your progress."

"Now that I get it, everything will be easier, right?" I asked, and bit into the toast.

Scooping the eggs into a bowl, she arched an eyebrow. "Whatever gave you that idea?"

My head jerked in surprise. "But isn't that the point? To achieve a sense of peace, an understanding of my gift, and to accept?"

"Yes," she replied in an even voice, "but that doesn't mean you'll never again face a challenge, or that life will roll along without problems. It means you now have the ability to deal with them." Taking up the sausage, she carried both the crisp brown links and the bowl of eggs to the table and placed them in the center. She returned to the cupboards and quickly took out plates and silverware. Handing me mine, she sat in the chair across the table from me.

"Life's about lessons, my dear, and we never quit learning," she said, and handed me the platter of sausage. "It's different for everyone, but I think all the garbage you've carried for so long had to be burned away . . ."

I paused as I forked a link onto my plate. "I thought you said you didn't know the details?"

"I don't, but I know you. You needed to find your core, but you've never been able to do that. Your center was too full of past hurts and resentments to allow anything else in."

"I guess," I said, cutting the meat into tiny pieces.

Abby smiled at me from across the table. "Now that you've rid yourself of all of that, you have a place of peace inside of you. Getting in touch with that will help you whenever you're feeling troubled."

"I'll find my answers within?"

"Something like that," she commented, filling her plate. "But that doesn't mean you'll always like those answers."

My fork clattered to my plate as I jumped out of my chair. "Answers . . . the disks. I don't have time to eat. I know Stephen's password now." I took a step away from the table. "I have to go."

She pointed her knife at the chair I'd just vacated. "You sit right back down. You've waited this long to read his notes—you need food and rest before you tackle the next problem."

I sank back into the chair as I realized that the elation I'd felt earlier had slowly ebbed away. My muscles now quivered with a deep tiredness. Propping my head in my hands, memories of my dream stole over me.

I raised my head and looked at Abby with weary eyes.

"I saw Madeleine's death," I told her.

# *Thirty-Two*

Abby rose from her chair and came to stand behind me. Bending down, she wrapped her arms around my shoulders and laid her cheek next to mine.

"I'm sure it was hard for you to witness that," she murmured.

"It was," I said, squeezing her hand. "If Madeleine really did live, she died trying to save a Romany family from the Nazis." My voice caught in my throat. "She failed." I released her hand and picked at a piece of toast. "If my dreams *were* true, it happened so long ago and I can't change it . . . but their deaths still haunt me."

Letting go and standing straight, Abby laid a hand on the top of my head as if in a blessing. "What's gone before is always with us, my dear. And whether your dreams were about real events doesn't matter. They showed you something and they had a purpose. If nothing else, they led you to this morning and becoming one with your gift."

She moved back around the table and sat in her chair.

I frowned. "One thing that isn't clear . . . If I did truly live as Madeleine, do you think Stephen was Henrick Sorenson?" I played with the food still on my plate. "Henrick was kind of a jerk."

"I don't know. They do seem to have different approaches to life."

I snorted. "No kidding. Louise, Stephen's mom, told me that all of his life, Stephen has always fought for the under-dog. In my dreams, all Henrick seemed to care about was money."

Abby moved her plate away and crossed her arms on the table. "Maybe he's making amends in this lifetime for being selfish in his last life."

"Who's making amends?"

Jerking around in my chair, I saw Darci standing in the kitchen doorway.

"Sorry to bust in. I did knock," she said, pointing to the doorway, "but no one answered."

"That's fine," Abby replied with a smile as she stood. "Would you like to join us for breakfast?"

"Oh, gee, thanks," she said, and slid into the chair next to mine. After eyeing the robe still draped on the other chair, she looked at me, then Abby, and gave us a bright smile. "So what's up?"

Finally, after answering Darci's endless questions and tak-ing a nap, I was home and in front of my computer. The disk drive hummed as it scanned Stephen's disk. The familiar ENTER YOUR PASSWORD box popped up, and with trembling fingers I typed in *Phoenix*.

Closing my eyes, I clasped my hands in my lap and prayed, "Please, please be right."

The computer stopped buzzing, and I peeked at the screen. A page of notes appeared in front of me. I had to stop myself from jumping to my feet and doing a happy dance around my desk. Quickly, I became engrossed in Stephen's notes.

They told of his meeting with a young Latino from El Salvador while Stephen was in Boston. Stephen had won the young man's confidence, and the man had related his jour-ney to the United States to him.

It was terrible. It took him over three months traveling by bus, train, trucks, on foot, and his journey was filled with hardships. Preyed on along the way by bandits, smugglers, and gangs, when he reached California, he was kidnapped from a safe house by a gang and actually held for ransom. The gang contacted his family in Boston and demanded money to ensure his release. When he finally made it to Boston, the trip had cost him over three thousand dollars.

The young man had come into this country with seventeen other immigrants. Reading down through the notes, I saw that Stephen had done rough calculations. This one smuggling ring had made over $51,000 on a single trip bringing these people in. He multiplied that by the over 200,000 immigrants sneaking into the U.S. every year and came up with some major bucks. No wonder it was so hard to stop—too much money was changing hands.

His notes went on to mention how the largest source of foreign income for Mexico is the money sent home to families still living there, so it wasn't in their best interest to discourage migration across the border. He talked of young women being sexually abused and the hundreds of people that died every year in the deserts along the border.

He listed the money the United States spent on guarding the borders, apprehending undocumented workers, and deporting them. It was astronomical.

And caught in the maelstrom of political opinion for and against immigrant workers were people like this young man from El Salvador, just looking for a better life.

"What a mess," I muttered to myself.

It was obvious to me why Stephen had wanted to talk to Vargas. He somehow had found out about Antonio's sister. Had he talked to Ben Jessup about undocumented workers, too? What would Ben have known about the situation?

I counted up the number of people either hurt or dead: Stephen, Ben Jessup, Antonio's sister. Three lives. But what's three lives when you're trying to protect your share of millions? I needed to call Bill and turn these disks over to him.

While dialing, I drummed my fingers on the desk.

"Hi, this is Ophelia Jensen, but this isn't an emergency," I blurted out when the dispatcher answered. "May I speak to Bill Wilson, please?"

"I'm sorry, he's not in," she replied.

"Is there any way I could reach him?"

"Would you like to speak with a deputy?" she asked, not answering my question.

"No, could I have his cell phone number?"

"No. We're not allowed to provide that information."

"Can you tell me how I can find him?"

"He's at the scene of an accident."

"Where?"

"We're not allowed to provide that information."

I thought about asking if there was any information she *could* give me, but decided the remark might come out kind of snippy.

"Okay, thanks," I said with a sigh, and hung up.

Leaning back, I locked my fingers behind my head and swiveled my chair in a slow circle. *Now what?*

I remembered my notes from the rune reading and pulled them out.

Scanning through them, it was obvious the reading hadn't been about me at all. It had been about Madeleine. Her present in Paris 1941 had indicated a psychic talent. That was true—my dreams had revealed her talent at telling the future using cards. Her past was in the hands of an official.

My mouth twisted with bitterness. Vogel.

Her future had shown that she'd receive no assistance. Again, that was true. Henrick could have helped her save the Gaspards, but refused. As a result, she died.

The doorbell rang then, startling me, and I shoved the notes back in my desk drawer. When I reached the front door, I saw Darci standing on the front porch, literally bouncing up and down.

As I opened the door, she rushed past me, waving a sheaf of papers in her hand.

"I've got it," she cried with excitement.

"Got what?" I asked, shutting the door and following her into the living room. "Don't you have a class today?"

"Nah," she replied, plopping down on the couch, then spreading the papers across the coffee table. She stopped and studied me. "Have you done something different to your hair?"

Instinctively, I reached for my head. "No. Why?"

She tapped a finger to her chin as she looked me over. "I don't know . . . there's just something different about you."

I hadn't shared my experience on the hilltop with Darci, and didn't want to try and explain it now. It was too new, too personal, to share with even my best friend. Maybe later, once I felt more comfortable, I could.

Instead, I sat down beside her on the couch and changed the subject. "What's this?" I asked, pointing at the papers scattered on the table.

"Well, the only names you gave me were the Gaspards, Madeleine, and Henrick Sorenson," she said with a wiggle, "First I tried looking up Jacques Gaspard on the Internet, but didn't find anything."

I felt a wrench of sadness. "I don't imagine you did. If they did exist, they would have disappeared in the Holocaust, like so many others."

"And," she picked up where she left off, "with just 'Madeleine,' I tried looking up French resistance fighters, but the search came up empty. If you do this again, try and get the last name, too," she chided.

I arched an eyebrow and stared at her. "Darce, I don't plan on doing this again," I said vehemently. Picking up the papers, I rattled them at her. "So if you couldn't find anything out, what's this?"

She gave me a sly look. "I didn't say I couldn't find *any* information." Her lips formed a smug smile. "Henrick Sorenson."

I glanced at the papers in my hand in disbelief. "You found Henrick? He really did live?"

"Umm-hmm," she said with a self satisfied nod. "And he was honored by Sweden for his work in helping refugees escape the Nazis."

"But . . . but in the dreams," I stuttered, "all he cared about was ripping them off."

"Not between 1941 and 1944. He used his father's company to smuggle them into Sweden."

"Really?" I was amazed. "What happened after 1944?"

"Well, the honor was given posthumously—"

"He died?"

"Yup." Taking the papers from my hand, she thumbed through them quickly. "Here it is," she said, giving me a page. "The war was turning against Germany. The Soviet Union had driven them back, and the Allies were getting ready to launch the invasion of Normandy." She pointed to a paragraph. "Henrick went back to Paris for the last time. There, he lured a German colonel . . . umm . . . what was his name?" she asked, peering at the paper my hand.

"Vogel," I said without looking.

"Right," she commented with a snap of her fingers, "Vogel. Henrick persuaded Vogel to meet him in the Catacombs, near—"

"Menilmontant," I provided for her.

She cocked her head and stared at me. "Hey, did you already know this?"

"No," I said softly.

"Once he had Vogel in the Catacombs, he executed him using a garrote."

"He strangled him to death."

"Yeah, slowly, I guess. One source quoted Sorenson as saying during his interrogation that he didn't want Vogel to die an easy death."

"I take it Henrick was arrested?"

"Yeah. After he killed Vogel, he calmly turned himself in. He faced a firing squad the next day."

# *Thirty-Three*

My experience on Monday must have drained me—I'd slept a dreamless sleep. But I hadn't expected the dreams to come. They didn't have anything else to tell me. I'd witnessed Madeleine's death, and thanks to Darci, I knew Henrick's fate. The only unanswered question was what happened to the Gaspards. I never expected to find that answer—there had been too many deaths for one little family to be remembered. My heart felt heavy as I thought about them.

I tried Bill again and talked to the same dispatcher. He still wasn't in, and she was just as unhelpful as she'd been the day before. Now that I knew what Stephen had written on the disks, I wanted them out of my house and in Bill's hands. Once he had them, maybe this whole thing would be over and I'd feel safe about bringing Tink home.

She'd pressed me last night during our daily conversation as to when I thought that event would happen. It wasn't that she wasn't having a swell time and learning a lot from Great-Aunt Mary—I didn't question her about that claim—but she missed her friends, me, Abby, T.P., Lady, and Queenie. I noticed she had mentioned her friends first, but let it go.

I spent the entire morning wandering around the house in my jammies as the animals followed me from room to room.

Giving up on trying to accomplish anything productive, I showered and changed into jeans and a T-shirt. I decided to go to Abby's and bug her, thinking I might get a free meal out of the deal.

Downstairs, I was ready to slip on my tennis shoes and head out the door when the phone rang.

"Ophelia . . . ?" said a bright voice in my ear.

"Yes . . . ?"

"Louise Larsen. I wanted to call you with some good news." She paused and took a deep breath. "Stephen's opened his eyes."

"Oh, Louise," I exclaimed, "you must be so relieved."

"I am. He has a long road to recovery. He's still on the ventilator and has to be gradually weaned off, and he drifts in and out quite a bit, but the prognosis is much improved."

"Is he able to communicate?"

"Not really. With the ventilator, he can't speak. And he's not with it enough to hold a pencil." Her voice caught. "But he does squeeze my hand when I talk to him."

"I'm sorry I haven't been to the hospital—" I broke off. I didn't want to tell her about Karen's mugging. "I've been out of town. Is there anything I can do for you?"

"No, I'm fine, especially now that Stephen's better. Well, I must go—I just wanted to give you the news."

"Thank you. I'll slip down to the hospital tomorrow."

"That will be fine. I'll look forward to seeing you again."

After Louise hung up, I pumped my fists in the air. Good, good. I'd turn the disks over to Bill, and Stephen was not only going to live, but could explain how he thought this whole mess started.

But my excitement quickly faded. Eventually he could talk to Bill, but from what Louise had said, Stephen wasn't in any condition to be questioned. A thought occurred to me then. Since Stephen was semiconscious now, did it put him at a greater risk? Was he more vulnerable to an attack? Unconscious, he hadn't been a threat, but now it seemed he was. Would the killer show up at the hospital and try to silence him once and for all?

*Nah.* I shook my head. Surely Bill would have a deputy on guard.

But he wasn't in charge of the investigation . . . the DCI was handling it, and they didn't believe Stephen had been a target.

I had to do something, but what?

The doorbell ringing broke into my thoughts. Darci, I thought. She'd probably been up all night surfing the Web, trying to dig up more information.

I was wrong. Claire Canyon waited on my porch. Opening the door, I bent to pick up the daily paper. "Hi, Claire," I said, adding it to the growing pile of unread newspapers lying on the table near the door. "Come on in."

"No," she said with a quick glance at her watch. "I can't stay. I'm on my way to a meeting at the town hall. I stopped by to give you this." She handed me several papers.

"What's this?"

"The guest list . . . remember you wanted to write thank-you notes?"

Dang. I'd forgotten about my lie, and now I was stuck writing a bunch of notes.

From her spot by the front door, Claire eyed the stack of newspapers. "Have you read about the accident?"

"What accident? I've been kind of busy and haven't been paying attention to the news."

She lowered her glasses and peered at me over the rims.

I squirmed, shifting my weight back and forth.

"Really, Ophelia," she said as she settled her glasses back on the bridge of her nose. "You ought to make more of an effort to stay informed. The interstate between here and Aiken has been closed for the last twenty-four hours. The driver of a van fell asleep at the wheel and the van crossed the median, hitting a semi head-on."

"How awful," I said in a shocked voice. "And they closed the interstate?"

"Yes. The van was carrying several immigrants. They were all thrown out into oncoming traffic, and—"

My stomach rolled. I held up a hand, cutting her off. "That's okay . . . I don't need the details. I can imagine what the accident must've been like if they shut down the highway."

She leaned in. "I heard the driver was one of those coyotes. You know, someone who—"

I nodded quickly. "Yeah, Claire, I know all about them." More than I wanted to, but I didn't share that with her.

"I think they're using some abandoned farmhouse around here as a base," she said, wiggling her glasses and peering at her watch. "My goodness, look at the time." She spun on her heel and skipped down the steps. "Send those out soon, will you?" she called over her shoulder.

I stood in the doorway, thinking, as I watched her whip out of my driveway.

I didn't doubt Claire was right about the smugglers using a nearby house. Too many events dealing with undocumented workers had popped up recently. Were these the same men responsible for trying to smuggle Antonio Vargas's sister across the border? And who then left her to die? If so, Antonio knew more than even I had expected. Was he a threat to them now, like Stephen had been?

I tugged on my lip. Why Ben Jessup? Were they really aiming at Krause? Then why had Ben's apartment been burglarized? What had they taken? Oh yeah, electronics—as in computers. Suddenly, I got the connection between Stephen, Vargas, and Ben, and it felt right.

I whirled around and slammed the door. I knew where they were hiding the immigrants, but I needed proof. I couldn't reach Bill, so I'd have to go to the DCI. And I knew I'd better have something more than dreams and premonitions to tell them.

Sliding down to the floor, I grabbed my tennis shoes and shoved my feet into them. As I was tying them in a rush, I hit my elbow on the leg of the table and sent the newspapers cascading into my lap.

"Ouch." I scooped up the pile and, scrambling to my feet, shoved them back on the table. That day's paper happened to land facedown.

Staring up at me from below the fold was the article about the accident on the interstate. Accompanying the story was a picture of the driver. Even though the black and white picture was grainy, I recognized the photo.

The man in the picture had a scar running down the side of his face.

While driving to the winery, I made my plans. If the man who chased me in St. Louis was the killer, as I suspected, I should be safe. He was beyond hurting anyone else now. And the old church should be abandoned. All I had to do was slip out there and find the proof I needed. Once I did, I'd beat it back to my car and call Bill on my cell phone. If I couldn't reach him, I'd talk to a deputy.

Piece of cake.

There was a chance the trash had been left by construction workers, but I doubted it. I was convinced they were using the old church as a hiding place. Did that mean Ron Mark was involved, or were they passing off the new faces as workers? And what construction company was handling the renovations?

I'd worry about that one later. And whether or not Ron was involved, I didn't think that after the last incident, he'd welcome me back to the winery with open arms. I'd have to make sure he didn't spot me.

Glancing in my rearview mirror, I noticed one of Tink's baseball caps on the backseat. I'd wear that, and sunglasses. Not much of a disguise, but it would have to do.

When I drove down the gravel road to the winery, I saw a

big silver bus pulled over to the side. *Great, a tour.* I'd blend in with the group and wait for my chance to slip away.

I parked behind the bus and slipped on my sunglasses. Getting out, I reached in the back and picked up Tink's hat. I pulled the hat on, settling the brim low on my forehead and tucking my hair underneath.

Walking around the corner of the bus, I caught sight of the tour group and groaned.

Hair, ranging from flat black to odd shades of silver, shone in the sunlight. The group was dressed in almost identical outfits—textured polyester shorts, knit polo shirts tucked into elastic waistbands, and white tennis shoes with anklets folded neatly below varicose-veined calves.

From the back, I guessed the average age to be about eighty. How in the devil would I blend in?

In front of the group I saw the young woman from the gift shop. Her voiced carried across the heads of the little old ladies as she explained the art of grape cultivation.

Pulling my hat even lower, I edged my way to the back of the group, trying to fit in with the group of seniors. I'd mosey along with them until I could make a break for the woods. The gravel crunched as I stepped behind a lady with flat black hair wearing mint green shorts and a yellow polo shirt.

She turned at the sound, and from behind her glasses shrewd blue eyes appraised me.

"Hi," she said pleasantly. "Are you with us?"

"Um, sort of," I stammered.

"Good," she said, moving back and linking her arm with mine. "It's so nice to have young people join us. I'm Lucy and this is Mabel." She pointed at the woman on the other side of her, wearing a bright purple sun hat, lavender shorts, and a pink shirt.

*Gee, this was working out better than I thought. As long as I didn't run into Ron Mark, I'd be okay.*

I waved at Mabel.

Lucy gave me a friendly smile. "We're from Sunset Retirement Homes—"

A soft snort came from Mabel, cutting Lucy off. "What a stupid name—Sunset. They might as well call it 'End of the Trail.'"

"Now, Mabel," Lucy admonished, "you have to give us a chance." Lucy turned to me. "Mabel's children talked her into selling her house and moving to Sunset. She's not happy about it," Lucy whispered loud enough for Mabel to hear her.

"Well," I said, scanning the backs of the ladies in front. "You look like a pretty lively bunch."

"Oh, we are." Lucy's eyes flashed. "We come here every year for a tour and a dinner with all the wine we can drink."

I chuckled. This Lucy reminded me of Aunt Dot.

"But," she lowered her voice again, "we've got to keep an eye on Phoebe over there. She can't hold her liquor and she gets a little crazy."

I didn't want to know what was considered crazy for an eighty-year-old, so I let the remark slide.

"Do you know if the old church is on the tour?" I asked.

Mabel whipped her head around so fast that I swore I heard her neck pop. "Is it haunted?"

It was to me, but I wasn't going to explain that one. "No, I've never heard that it was."

"Does it have an old graveyard?" Mabel was getting excited.

"I suppose," I replied with a small frown.

Mabel straightened her shoulders and stood tall. "I'm psychic, you know. I can sense spirits."

I suppressed a smile. "Really?"

Lucy waved a wrinkled hand in Mabel's direction. "Oh, don't get her started."

Mabel's face fell. "Well, I am, and—"

"Oh look, there's Ron," Lucy exclaimed, and dropped my arm.

I watched as both she and Mabel raced up to the front of the group, crowding the crazy Phoebe out of the way. Each took his arm. His chuckle drifted back to me as I ducked my head and fell a few steps behind the rest of the group.

The gang followed Ron, Lucy, and Mabel toward the winery while I stayed as far back as I could. We neared the path and I saw my chance. Quickly, I dodged to my left and ducked behind a tree. Holding my breath, I waited until the voices became fainter.

Then I whirled and took off down the path at a dead run.

# *Thirty-Four*

Wise now to the old memories lurking in the clearing around the old church, I stopped for a moment before I approached. Taking a deep breath, I thought of my experience on the hilltop and imagined the warm glow I'd felt within. It ran through me, around me, making a fierce shield. With a long sigh, I felt prepared, ready to face any challenge.

Instead of entering the clearing directly in front of the old church, I made a half circle through the woods to the back. Mabel had been right, the old cemetery was directly behind the church. The building had blocked my view when I was there last week.

Pine trees cupped the graveyard, and not only cast the ground in deep shade, but the wind sighing through the boughs sounded like the whispers of the dead. The weathered stones either stood or lay tumbled on the ground in precise rows. Some tilted at crazy angles, their bases having sunk partially into the black soil.

The breeze tugged at a strand of hair that had escaped the baseball cap, but when I stepped into the graveyard, the air calmed. Nothing moved—not the deep grass, not a butterfly, not a bird—the only motion was mine as I walked through the tall grass. A heavy stillness seemed to weigh down on this place. While crossing the graveyard, I noticed that many of the headstones had an angel or a lamb carved deep into the pitted surface. I didn't need to pause to read the dates— those were the markers of children gone too soon.

I reached a single door located on the side, at the rear of the church, and stopped. To my left were two large doors extending out from the building at a downward slope. Cut into the foundation next to them was a boarded-up square. The cellar doors and the old coal chute.

I extended my hand and was about to touch the doorknob when I dropped the hand to my side. Did I really want to do this? I could leave now, run back to my car, and leave this place for good. I could dump it all in Bill's lap and let him figure out what was happening.

A sudden buzzing in my ears urged me to finish what I'd started, and I reached for the doorknob again and slowly turned it. The door opened with a creak that reverberated through the quiet glade. I glanced quickly over my shoulder. Why—I had no idea—it was only me and the spirits of the long dead here now. Stepping inside, I softly closed the door.

Dim light shone through grimy windows placed high in the wall to my right. I stood in a hallway leading to the front of the church, and ahead of me spied a door to my left. Creeping up the hallway, I grasped the tarnished knob and turned it slowly. Then, with a hard push, I flung it open.

Nothing—the room was empty save for some mildewed boxes and an old kerosene lantern sitting on a decrepit end table. Crossing to the boxes, I flipped one open, sending a fine cloud of dust into the air. I sneezed. Again nothing— old newspapers that had been shredded into a mouse's nest. Yuck. I quickly closed the lid.

I wiped a grimy hand across my forehead and scanned the room. No one had been there for a long time. Looking down at the dirty wooden floor, I saw that the only footprints tracked through the dust were mine.

I left the room and proceeded to the main part of the

church. A shaft of late afternoon sun shone down through the hole in the ceiling, and dust motes danced in its beam. The room was as it had been last week, except the pile of trash and the moth-eaten blanket had vanished.

I stuck my hands in the back pockets of my jeans and did a slow 360 while I searched the room for any sign of life. *How could this be?* I'd been so sure I was right. For once, I'd believed in my gift, and thinking over the last week and a half, every clue, every step I made had led me back to the old church. The smugglers *had* been using this building. I was sure of it.

I snapped my fingers. *The cellar!*

Hurrying back down the hallway, I went out the back, and after another glance over my shoulder, studied the cellar doors. They appeared newer than the other doors leading into the church. The hinges were a bright and shiny silver, not rusted like all the others. Grasping one of the rings, I heaved the door open. Its top edge fell back against the side of the building with a thump. I did the same thing with the second door.

At my feet, stone stair steps led down into the gloomy cellar.

*Dang, I didn't have a flashlight. How could I snoop around without any light?*

*The kerosene lantern.*

I ran back into the church and to the small room. Picking up the lantern, I shook it and heard a satisfying slosh. *Yes . . . it still had kerosene.*

My bubble burst, and I placed the lantern back on the table. How did I intend to light it without matches? Then I thought, If there was a lantern, there had to be matches somewhere. I opened one of the old boxes and with a wince stuck my hand in the shredded paper. No matches.

I tapped my foot in frustration. The sun would be setting soon, and the idea of prowling around these old grounds at night gave me the creeps. I didn't have time to run home and grab a flashlight. I noticed a drawer in the old table and yanked it open, and saw a box of farmer's matches.

Excited, I slid the box open. There were three matches inside. I had three chances—it had better work.

Setting the precious matches on the table, I lifted the latch at the top of the lantern and raised the glass globe, exposing the wick. I stuck the first match and the smell of sulfur rose. The match spluttered and died. I scraped the second one. The flame flickered twice and suddenly caught. Shielding the burning match from drafts with one hand, I carefully touched the fire to the wick. It crackled once, then a thin blue line of flame shot across its frayed edges.

I slid the globe down and locked it into place. I didn't know how much kerosene the lantern held so I had to hurry. Grabbing it by its metal handle, I rushed back the way I'd come and to the cellar steps.

Reining in my excitement, I took each step carefully. Dead leaves crunched beneath the soles of my tennis shoes as I descended one step at a time. The first few steps were illuminated by the fading sun, but the lower steps were shrouded in shadows. I held the lantern higher, making its circle of light wider.

At the bottom of the steps, a chill hit me, and I rubbed the arm holding the lantern. The walls were of rough limestone above a dirt floor. Above me, the fine strands of spiderwebs crisscrossed the floor joists. The atmosphere was dank and dreary, and along with the musty odor, the scent of stale cigarettes and the sour smell of too many bodies in too small a space lingered.

Old mattresses covered with grungy blankets littered the floor. A heap of plastic bottles, empty styrene coffee cups, tin cans, and food wrappers sat in one corner.

Yup, I thought with a sense of exhilaration, people had definitely been living down there. But how did I prove they were undocumented workers smuggled in by the coyotes? I needed something concrete that I could take to Bill.

Crossing to the pile of trash, I placed the lantern on the floor, squatted down, and began to rummage through it. If I could find a piece of paper with a name, a bus ticket, anything to show who had been camped out down there. I held each piece of paper next to the lantern and skimmed it quickly before discarding it. My pile grew bigger, and still I found nothing.

Suddenly, a hand on my arm yanked me to my feet and spun me around.

Antonio Vargas . . . and in his hand he held a snubbed nose revolver.

I stepped back, holding my hands in front of me. "Antonio, don't do this . . . think about Deloris and Evita," I pleaded. "What will happen to them if you kill me and go to prison?"

In the light of the kerosene lantern, I saw a perplexed look run across Antonio's face. "I'm not going to kill you," he protested. "I want to shoot the men who left my sister to die in the desert."

I dropped my hands. "You *do* know them."

"Yes, they contacted me. The man on the motorcycle—he lied. He said they were holding my sister in Phoenix for ransom. If I paid them more money, they'd let her go." His voice broke. "All the time, she was dead."

"Tell the sheriff what you know—Bill will arrest them—"

"No." His voiced bounced off the limestone walls. "They'll just deport them."

"No, they won't. They'll be punished," I insisted.

*"Basta ya!"* someone yelled from halfway down the stone steps.

Antonio whirled around as I peaked over his shoulder.

A man holding a gun came down the steps as he yelled at Antonio in rapid Spanish. Antonio yelled back and waved his gun.

I didn't comprehend what they were saying, but it looked like a standoff. Both had guns, and it was only a question of who would fire first.

The man stood at the bottom of the stairs now, blocking any hope of escape. I had to do something. My eyes flew around the room looking for a weapon, but all that lay at my feet was trash. I could kick over the lantern and start a fire. Maybe that would create enough of a diversion for us to make a run for it.

I began to inch my foot toward the lantern when I caught the word *familia* and saw Antonio's shoulders sag. The gun in his hand thudded to the floor, and he kicked it toward the stranger.

The man's eyes never left us as he stepped over to the gun, bent, and picked it up. With an evil grin, he stuck it in the waistband of his jeans.

Great, we were trapped. But for some reason, I didn't feel afraid. I felt calm and in control. It seemed the warm glow of my shield hardened around me. I wasn't foolish enough to think it would stop a bullet, but it gave me courage that I hadn't known I possessed.

I stepped out from behind Antonio. "Hey," I said, calling attention to myself, "you speak English?"

The man looked me up and down. "*Poco* . . . a little," he replied.

I darted a look at Antonio. "What's 'witch' in Spanish?"

"*Bruja.*"

This had worked once before when I was in a jam. It was worth a try now. Squaring my shoulders, I glared at the stranger. "I'm a *bruja,*" I said as I tapped my chest.

"Yes?" The man looked amused.

"Yes . . . and if you don't release us, I'll curse not only you," I replied, jabbing my finger in his direction, "but your entire family."

He glanced at Antonio. "*Que?*"

Antonio translated my words.

The stranger laughed in my face, then said something to Antonio.

"He said he doesn't believe in witches."

*So much for that idea.*

From where I was standing, I saw a shadow fall across the top step. I prayed it meant rescue as I tried to keep the hope out of my face.

Two feet wearing wing tips appeared on the top step, then a body dressed in a gray suit. Then Chuck Krause emerged from the shadows at the bottom of the steps.

My knees felt weak with relief, and I opened my mouth to cry out a warning, but before I could, Chuck spoke.

"Enrico, what in the hell are you doing?"

*Oh, great.*

Enrico answered him in Spanish, and Chuck argued back in Spanish, too. Then with a shake of his head, Chuck turned and climbed back up the stairs. Moments later he was back with two ropes.

# *Thirty-Five*

Hours later we were still being held in the basement. Antonio and I sat with out backs to the wall. A rope led from our hands, tied behind our backs, to our necks. I'd squirmed at first, when Chuck and Enrico tied us up, but any movement seemed to tighten the noose. I stopped struggling after a couple of tugs on the rope around my throat.

So I sat, trussed up, on the hard-packed floor and watched the light shining down the steps fade to nothing. The kerosene in the old lantern had long ago run out, and the only light now came from Enrico's flashlight. I still wasn't afraid yet—I'd come too far, learned too much, to have it all end now in some dark, smelly cellar. And after my dreams of Madeleine, there was a certain amount of peace in knowing death wasn't the end. But that knowledge didn't mean I intended to face death today.

I wanted to ask Antonio if he had known of Chuck Krause's involvement with the smuggling ring, but speaking made the rope chafe against my skin. Right now all I could do was wait.

Finally, we heard Chuck call out from the top of the stairs in Spanish. Enrico answered him, then motioned for Antonio and me to stand. I inched my way up the wall to my feet, trying to keep as much slack in the rope as I could. Rattling off something else at Antonio, Enrico jerked his head at me.

"He wants us to turn around," Antonio said.

Facing the wall, I didn't want to anticipate what might be coming next, but part of me expected to feel the cold steel of a gun barrel pressed up against the back of my skull at any second.

*Now I was scared.*

Instead of feeling the gun, however, I felt the bindings around my wrists fall away. The noose around my neck tightened as my hands were freed, and I twisted away from the wall, choking.

Enrico stood in front of us, his gun in one hand and his other holding our ropes taut. With a wave of the gun, he indicated we were to climb the stairs.

Antonio and I trudged up the stone steps into the night air, away from the dank cellar. Chuck Krause waited for us, holding a gun of his own.

The moon had set, but the stars strewn across the sky winked and blinked as Enrico led us like a couple of dogs past the tombstones. The beam from his flashlight caused the writing on the headstones to appear then disappear while we walked by. He stopped abruptly at the far corner of the cemetery, his light reflecting off two shovels propped up against the trunk of one of the pine trees. Stepping away from us, he let the rope play out of his hands as he joined Chuck. He pointed his light at the shovels, then moved it to the ground at our feet.

"You've got to be kidding me," I croaked. "We're supposed to dig our own graves?"

"Just one, Ms. Jensen. Two would take too much time," Chuck said. "Now please pick up your shovel, and don't try anything or we will shoot you."

Antonio and I grabbed the shovels and started digging. Or made an attempt to—every time I shoved the point into the hard ground, the rope around my neck got in the way.

I let the shovel fall to the ground. "Look, I can't dig with this around my neck. Take it off. You have guns . . . we're not going anywhere."

Chuck and Enrico exchanged a look, and Chuck nodded. Reaching up, I loosened the slip knot and tore the thing over my head. Antonio did the same. Rubbing my chapped skin, I thought about making a break for it. We were close to the trees, we might make it, but recalling what happened to Madeleine when she ran from Vogel, I thought better of it.

All of a sudden Chuck felt chatty. "I'm curious, Ophelia, how much did you figure out?"

Picking up the shovel, I rammed the tip into the ground and stepped on the top with my foot. "It's pretty obvious . . . you were using the church as a place to stash the immigrants you were transporting across the country." I threw the dirt to the side. "But the last group were killed in that car accident." I paused, resting my arms on top of the handle. "Stephen Larsen and Ben Jessup knew, so you shot them."

"*Cavar*," Enrico hissed, waving his gun at me.

"He wants you to keep digging," Chuck translated.

The blade of my shovel hit the ground again, and picking up a scoop of dirt, I calculated how far I could fling it. Nope, they weren't standing close enough for me to hit them. *If I could lure them closer . . .*

"I thought you were just a smarmy politician." I tossed the dirt to my other side and inched a step closer to Chuck and Enrico. "I didn't know you were running the show."

"I'm not," he declared hotly, and stepped forward. "I'm just as much as a victim as you are."

I stopped digging and stared at him. "I doubt that, Chuck. You're not the one holding the shovel."

He took another step. "They're blackmailing me."

"Why?"

"My father's landscaping business in California—"

"Let me guess, he uses undocumented workers."

In the glow of his flashlight, I saw him sneer. "No need to be politically correct, let's call them what they are." He pointed his beam in Antonio's face.

Antonio raised his arm to shield his eyes, and I sensed Chuck's intolerance and hatred swell to pour out of him like a fury.

"They're illegal immigrants," he jeered. "And I never hired them—my father did fifteen years ago."

"If it wasn't you and it happened that long ago, why worry about it now?"

"Don't you know the past has a way to come back and haunt you?"

Boy, did I!

"If the party found out, they'd drop me like a stone, my career would be ruined. I had no choice," he declared in a vehement voice, and took a half step forward.

Abruptly, Enrico reached out and pulled Chuck back toward him. Enrico was quiet, but he wasn't stupid. He had no intention of letting Chuck get close to me. I glanced at Antonio. His hole was a lot bigger than mine. He needed to slow down—*we* needed to take as much time as possible.

"Please, just show me a way out of this," I muttered to myself.

"What did you say?" Chuck leaned forward.

"Nothing." I pressed the blade of the shovel into the ground and felt it strike something. "You could've admitted you were wrong."

"I couldn't do that—"

"A better choice is to have your aide killed and Stephen shot?"

"I had nothing to do with that," he answered sanctimoniously. "When I told Enrico that Ben had learned about the blackmail, I had no idea they'd kill him."

"So you're not responsible for anything, are you, Chuck?" My temper shot up as I wiggled the blade into the dirt to pry out whatever lay beneath the topsoil. Suddenly, the thing I'd been digging at burst out of the ground and landed on the other side of me.

"What's that?" Chuck asked, trying to hit it with his light.

"Nothing, just a root," I lied.

It wasn't a root. Grinning up at me in the shadow of Chuck's flashlight was a human skull. I nudged it back into the darkness with the toe of my tennis shoe. Glancing over my shoulder at Chuck, I stared past him into the cemetery.

Around the headstones a mist seemed to be gathering. Wispy at first, but before my eyes it coalesced into a heavy vapor that began to roll and tumble across the ground. Even at this distance, I felt the energy as the fog shimmered with a ghostly blue light. In my head once again, I heard women crying and could smell the smoke.

The cloud headed right for Enrico and Chuck.

Enrico must have read the expression on my face. He whirled around to face the fog. *"Dios mio!"* he cried out.

Antonio seized the moment and launched himself toward Enrico, swinging his shovel high above his head. He struck Enrico in the center of his back, and Enrico tumbled forward.

Chuck looked at the fog then at me and seemed to freeze for an instant. I grabbed the skull, its teeth cutting into the palm of my hand, and hurled it with all my strength, aiming straight for his head.

My aim was true. The skull caught him in the chin and snapped his head back.

As his gun went off harmlessly in the air, I heard a voice cry out from the other side of the old graveyard.

"See, Lucy, I told you this place was haunted!"

# Thirty-Six

Four days later I sat at Stephen's bedside telling him the rest of the story. He'd lost weight and his eyes had a hollow look around them, but he was off the respirator and in a private room.

"Wow, you threw a skull at Krause?" he said with surprise.

"No, she didn't," Bill said as he walked into the room. "It was a rock. We found it lying near the hole she dug." He paused long enough to give me a hard look.

I simply shrugged. I knew what I'd picked up, and it wasn't a rock. Rocks don't have teeth.

Crossing to the bed, Bill placed a laptop and cases of disks on Stephen's tray. "I thought you might want these. The disks are copies. We had to keep the originals for evidence."

Stephen ran a hand over his laptop. "Thanks."

"And you," Bill said in a stern voice, "you're lucky Ron Mark had sent up a hue and cry when he discovered that those two little old ladies had slipped away from the winery. Otherwise you might not be sitting here now."

Stephen peered at me around Bill's large frame. "You must have been scared to death."

I sat back in the chair and crossed my legs. "It's funny, I really wasn't," I answered honestly. "I was desperate but not terrified . . . " I paused. "And I was ticked off that they were making me dig."

Stephen smiled. Bill frowned.

"When's Tink coming home?" Bill asked, changing the subject.

"Abby and I are picking her up later this afternoon."

"You'll be glad to have her home," he stated. Extending his hand, he shook Stephen's. "Glad you're going to make it, Larsen, and thanks for your cooperation."

"Not a problem, Sheriff, I only wish I would've been able to answer your questions sooner."

Bill turned and looked at me. "Do me a favor, Ophelia. Don't run into me for a while."

I clicked my tongue. "You got it, Bill."

He strode out of the room rubbing his head.

"He could've at least thanked you," Stephen grumbled when Bill was out of earshot.

I laughed. "I don't think gratitude is the emotion Bill associates with me."

"Hey, would you mind plugging this in for me?" Stephen asked as he handed me the electrical cord from his laptop.

I did as he requested while he opened it and booted it up.

"I have a question for you," I said, sitting back down in the chair. "Did you ever meet with Ben Jessup?"

"No," he replied, his eyes never leaving the computer screen. "We were going to meet Monday."

I leaned forward in the chair. "What about Karen? Do you think she's okay?"

Stephen's eyes stayed on his computer. "She's fine. I called her last night. She's staying at her sister's in Idaho."

"Good." I clasped my hands around my knees. "I was afraid something else had happened when I couldn't reach her."

"Left her cell phone in St. Louis," he murmured as he began to type on the keyboard. "She didn't want to risk being tracked. She'll be back to work next week."

I was shocked. "She's still working for you?"

"Yeah, we've always known something like this could happen." He typed faster. "She waited around too long to leave St. Louis. Next time we'll know better."

We sat not speaking, the only sound in the room Stephen's fingers flying across the keyboard.

"Well," I said slapping my legs. "I'd better go—it's my first day back at work."

"Hey, wait a minute," he said, finally looking at me. "I'd like to see you again. Our first meeting didn't go so well." He smiled ruefully. "But I promise the next one will be better."

As I returned his smile, I thought about Madeleine and Henrick. Although he'd loved her and avenged her death by sacrificing his own life, he was unwilling to make room in his life for her. She'd been "on the side." Watching Stephen, I knew he would be the same way. Anyone in his life would only be needed between books. They would never be let into the life that existed for him in the room that overlooked the river.

No, the wheel of fate had turned. Madeleine and Henrick's circle was closed. And I didn't want to be a part of whatever new challenges, new circles, Stephen faced in this lifetime. I had my own to face.

Standing, I stepped close to the bed and laid a hand on his arm. He stopped typing and looked up at me.

"Thank you, but I don't think there's room in your life for a small-town librarian like me."

His eyes widened in surprise. "But—"

"I'm glad you're going to be okay, Stephen." I gave his arm a little squeeze. "And you can bet I'll be anxiously waiting to read the next Stephen Larsen book, but for now, I want to get back to my own little world."

Before I left the room, I paused at the door and glanced over my shoulder. Stephen's face wrinkled in a frown as he read something on his laptop, and then his fingers once again flew across the keyboard.

With a smile, I turned and walked down the hall.

* * *

I skipped up the steps to the library. It felt good to be back where I belonged. It was a feeling tinged with a sense of sadness whenever I thought of the Gaspards, but tonight Tink would be home and all would be right with the world.

I stopped just inside the door and let my eyes travel the room. Darci stood hanging over the counter, gossiping with Georgia. An elderly woman, dressed in linen pants and a summer weight cardigan, browsed the history section. I didn't recognize her. *Hmm, she must be new to Summerset.*

My gaze landed on someone I did know. Evita stood looking over the latest young adult books.

Striding over to the counter, I scooped up a handful of candy and strolled up behind her.

Bending close, I whispered in her ear, "Finding any books about smiling dogs?"

With a squeal, she twirled around and clasped my waist. "Miss Jensen, you're back!" she exclaimed.

"So are you," I said, patting her head with my empty hand. "Here, hold out your hands."

When she did, I dropped the candy into them.

"So many," she whispered, wide-eyed.

"They're for all the books you *would have* returned over the past couple of weeks," I said, chuckling.

"Thank you."

I crouched down in front of her. "Are you doing okay?"

She nodded, her black curls bobbing up and down. "Papa had to talk to the police," she answered in a low voice.

"I know."

Before Bill arrived that night, I'd insisted that Antonio say nothing about why he had come to the church. He hadn't shot anyone, and in the end he helped save us by tackling Enrico. Why bring any more trouble to his house?

"Papa is sad about his sister," Evita continued, "but he said to give you a message from him."

"He did?" I asked, smiling at her.

Again she nodded and leaned close to whisper in my ear. "He said to tell you you're a pretty good *bruja*."

My laughter rang out. "Tell him thank you, okay?" I said, straightening.

"I will . . . Mama's waiting," she said, dancing around me and toward the door. When she was at the doorway she turned back and called out, "I'll see you tomorrow."

"Yes, you will," I replied in a confident voice.

I took a step toward the counter when the elderly woman wearing the sweater approached me.

"Yes? May I help you?" I asked.

"Oh, no," she replied in a heavily accented voice. "I'm just looking around while my son and daughter-in-law shop at the antiques store."

"Well, we're very proud of our library," I said with a grin. "Are you just passing through?"

"Yes, we're from St. Louis and on our way to Minnesota."

"To one of the lakes?"

"Yes, I hope it'll remind me of Sweden, where I spent most of my childhood with my parents," she said, her dark eyes watching me intently.

I shifted a bit uncomfortably under her close scrutiny.

She noticed and chuckled softly. "I'm sorry, I don't mean to stare, but you remind me of someone."

"That's okay—I've got one of those average faces. People always think they know me from somewhere," I replied with a nervous little laugh as I crossed to the reading table and picked up a pile of magazines.

"No, this is someone I knew long ago, but I think of her often. In fact, you really don't resemble her." She pointed back toward the young adult section. "I couldn't help eavesdropping on your conversation with that little girl, and the way you spoke to her reminded me of the woman I once knew."

"Oh, that was Evita." I grinned and fanned the magazines out on the table. "She's a real charmer."

"You gave her sweets. The woman I knew gave me candy, too. It was the best I've ever tasted," she said as her eyes took on a faraway look. "And the last time I saw her . . . I was so cold that night and she gave me her stocking c—"

She didn't finish. A woman came rushing in the door and over to her. "There you are—we were worried."

The woman's eyes refocused, and she looked at the younger woman with a frown. "I told Jack where I was going."

"Oh," the younger woman replied with a flap of her hand, "you know how he is—he never listens. Are you ready? He's waiting in the car."

"Yes." The elderly woman turned to me and took both of my hands in hers. "Thank you for listening to an old woman's reminiscing."

"My pleasure," I said, squeezing her hands. "Stop by again."

I watched as the two women headed for the door. The younger woman suddenly halted. "Rosey, aren't you hot in that sweater?"

With a roll of her dark eyes, she allowed her daughter-in-law to help her out of the cardigan. She turned and looked at me from across the room. "Thank you again," she called as her daughter-in-law took her arm and escorted her out the door.

My mouth went dry and I couldn't speak. My legs felt like lead. All I could do was lift a numb hand in good-bye as the door closed behind them.

My eyes filled with tears as I stood staring at the closed door.

When Rosey had turned, I saw the amulet that had been hidden by her sweater, hanging from her neck. It gleamed in the light with a fire all its own.

Four petals surrounded by a golden circle.

Investigate the Hottest New Mysteries!

**Sign up for the FREE HarperCollins monthly mystery newsletter,**

## The Scene of the Crime,

**and get to know your favorite authors, win free books, and be the first to learn about the best new mysteries going on sale.**

To register, simply go to www.HarperCollins.com, visit our mystery channel page, and at the bottom of the page, enter your email address where it states "Sign up for our mystery newsletter." Then you can tap into monthly Hot Reads, check out our award nominees, sneak a peek at upcoming titles, and discover the best whodunits each and every month.

*Get to know the magnificent mystery authors of HarperCollins and sign up today!*